FEAR NOT
THE DEAD

BRAD RICKS

UNVEILING NIGHTMARES LTD

Dedicated to my lovely wife Terri.

Thank you for putting up with me and being my first reader/editor.

CONTENTS

1. Part One   1
   Decisions

2. One   3

3. Two   11

4. Three   15

5. Four   19

6. Five   23

7. Six   27

8. Seven   29

9. Eight   33

10. Part Two   39
    Welcome to Cardinal Crest

11. One   41

12. Two   45

13. Three   49

14.	Four	57
15.	Five	67
16.	Six	73
17.	Seven	81
18.	Eight	89
19.	Nine	101
20.	Ten	105
21.	Eleven	111
22.	Part Three Shadows From The Past	121
23.	One	123
24.	Two	129
25.	Three	133
26.	Four	137
27.	Five	147
28.	Six	153
29.	Seven	159
30.	Eight	171
31.	Nine	179
32.	Ten	185

33.	Eleven	193
34.	Twelve	199
35.	Thirteen	203
36.	Fourteen	211
37.	Fifteen	221
38.	Sixteen	225
39.	Part Four Memories Unlocked	235
40.	One	237
41.	Two	243
42.	Three	247
43.	Four	257
44.	Five	265
45.	Six	267
46.	Seven	273
47.	Eight	279
48.	Nine	285
49.	Ten	291
50.	Part Five Symphony in Motion	297

51.	One	299
52.	Two	305
53.	Three	311
54.	Four	315
55.	Five	321
56.	Six	327
57.	Seven	331
58.	Eight	335
59.	Nine	341
60.	Ten	345
61.	Eleven	351
62.	Twelve	355
63.	Thirteen	357
64.	Fourteen	361
65.	Fifteen	363
66.	Sixteen	371
67.	Part Six	377
	New Residents of Cardinal Crest	
68.	One	379
69.	Two	383

70. Three   389

71. Four   395

72. Five   397

73. Part Seven   403
     Epilogue

74. One   405

75. Acknowledgements   411

76. About the author   413

77. Excerpt from The Night Crew   415

PART ONE

DECISIONS

being out of control, in danger, like I was being watched, stalked."

"Right," Dr. Stiller agreed. She made new notes on her yellow pad. "Being around people brought out this terrible anxiety. It impacted your life, your marriage to Jim, and worst of all, missing out on your children's lives. Standing outside of the car at Chandler's game is a big step forward."

"I stood there, but the feeling still stayed."

"You are taking the pills I prescribed, right?" Dr. Stiller asked.

"Yes, and I know they are supposed to help, but... But there's still so far to go," Ann blurted out.

Renee nodded. After a few seconds, she asked more of those probing questions that Ann hated. She told herself those questions were the ones that would eventually lead to the breakthrough that would leave her cured and back to normal, but that didn't stop her from hating them. And they didn't stop her from coming here every Tuesday.

"We've only just scratched the surface of what caused these panic attacks."

"My mother," Ann said before Dr. Stiller asked it.

"Yes, your mother. Your dad's passing reopened the wound from your mother's death. Ann, you saw your mother killed in front of you as a child. That would be traumatic for an adult to witness." Renee's tone dripped with therapist care. "But as a ten-year-old child? You had to repress those terrible images.

"I know you feel like some things are worse as we unpack those memories, but there will be an end."

Tears welled up in Ann's eyes. From the coffee table in front of her, she instinctively reached for a tissue.

"That was almost thirty years ago, though. Sure, I may not remember exactly what happened, but why would I want to? My dad took care of me. He would run into my room when the nightmares awoke me."

"But your nightmares were real, Ann. That's how your mind rationalized her death. It was a real-life nightmare that you pushed into being a dream. One that you pushed out of your mind as we often do with dreams."

Again, Ann had heard this before. They were a month into therapy when she finally started remembering the nightmares from her childhood. Flashes at first. Fragments as if from a dream. A struggle followed by the sharp crack of a pistol firing. Flashes of blood on the ground, on a couch. The more Dr. Stiller explored the dreams with Ann, the more they realized those weren't dreams.

After about a month of working through those memories, Ann realized that her dad's passing unlocked the wave of emotions that had culminated in her anxiety and sheer paranoia. The man who probably encouraged her to forget the trauma as much as she wanted to forget it. Since that light bulb went off, the two of them slowly pieced together what happened, hoping to eventually give Ann peace and closure. But for Ann, it seemed like the more that was revealed, the worse she became.

"Renee, I just wish... Is there another pill, or maybe some kind of shock treatment, that would make me better?" Ann asked, defeated. She was tired of the past few months of her life and wasn't sure how much longer she could keep fighting.

"So, Ann, I was thinking about just that the other day."

"About enrolling me in shock treatments?"

"Not exactly that," Renee chuckled. "Take a look at this." Dr. Stiller flipped up the pages of the yellow notepad and pulled out a brochure like what Ann usually saw in hotel lobbies. Renee handed it to Ann.

Ann looked at the picture on the cover. A large multi-story estate filled the pamphlet. The air in the room grew heavy, pressing its entire weight onto Ann's shoulder. It felt too thick to even breathe. The picture flooded her with anxiety, and all the feelings of nauseousness resurfaced.

"I..." Ann started but couldn't finish.

"I'd like for you to go back. I'll be there as well. For those few days, consider it a therapeutic retreat. Or maybe call it immersion therapy. I've already called and confirmed they have openings. You should talk to Jim about it."

"I don't know if I can," she finally forced out. She shook her head, reaching her arm out to hand the brochure back to Renee.

Renee waved it off. "You hold on to it. Talk to Jim. It's summer. Your kids are out of school. The house is a beautiful bed and breakfast. Being there will help you come face-to-face with the tragedy, but you won't be doing it alone. I'll be there. Your family will be there. All there to support you in your recovery."

With trembling hand, Ann pulled the brochure back to her and placed it in her lap.

Two

Ann drove her silver Toyota Prius home as if on autopilot. Cars passed her. Traffic slowed and sped up. Everything that typically happened on a typical drive home happened but without Ann's head present. Her mind collapsed into itself. Go there? Renee actually wanted her to go back there? It was literally her nightmare right now. Why would Dr. Stiller want her to willingly step back into the nightmare?

Before she knew it, muscle memory brought Ann back to her modest home in Norfolk, Virginia. She had the house to herself. Lauren and Chandler were almost done with sport camps for the day. Jim would be waiting patiently for them to finish up, knowing Ann couldn't stomach even waiting in the car with all the other parents around.

She opened the car door, quickly grabbed her purse, and bolted for the front door. She tossed her purse on the kitchen counter and went to the living room, mindlessly flopping down on the couch.

Ann waited for Jim and the kids to get home. She held the brochure for Cardinal Crest Estate in both hands not believing she might actually broach the subject with him. She barely remembered the house. Had forgotten about it until it came out one day during a therapy session. Cardinal Crest Estate. The location of her mother's death.

Ann Walker fumbled with the pamphlet, trying not to look at the picture on the front. With each glance, she felt as if a raw wound was being scraped. Healed-over scabs reopened and exposed. She flipped the brochure over, no longer looking at the picture but at the address on the back. Roxboro, North Carolina. Middle of nowhere upstate North Carolina. A short three-and-a-half-hour car ride from their home in Norfolk.

At the thought of it, a brief chuckle escaped her throat. A three-and-a-half-hour car ride with a sixteen-year-old girl and an eight-year-old boy in the back seat? She could already hear the fighting and bickering starting about thirty seconds into the drive and lasting the other three hours, twenty-nine minutes, and thirty seconds. Then what about when they got there? The brochure said Cardinal Crest Estate "is a relaxing country estate. Escape the distractions of your busy lives. Enjoy the peace and serenity of Cardinal Crest Estate." What would they have if not for their busy lives? Ann felt confident her kids were allergic to peace and serenity.

With the brochure in her hand, she stood up from the couch and marched into the kitchen. Ann crumpled it while heading toward the trashcan when she heard the front door open. Her shoulders tensed and her back tightened as the noise level increased one hundredfold. Stimuli bombarded her.

"Hey, Mom," Chandler hollered when he walked in.

"Hey, Mom," Lauren echoed. "Get out of my way, Fungus," she yelled to her brother who kicked off his shoes, still standing in the doorway. Her voice seemed to double in decibels.

"I'd go faster if you'd stop pushing me," he snapped back.

"Hey, Honey," Jim said from just outside the door. "Do you two have to fight the moment you walk in the door?"

She stood in the middle of the kitchen as she heard him push his way past the sparring siblings and join her. Her hand rested on the island, and the other clutched the crumpled pamphlet. Just hearing the children walk through the door solidified her thoughts about an extended weekend away.

"Hi, sweetie," she said to Jim as he walked over, slightly lowered his head, and kissed her. Since she stood five and a half feet tall, he only had half a foot on her. "Thanks for picking the kids up from their camps."

"Speaking of," he said. He directed his attention to the noise in the entryway. "You two. Showers. I'm going to have to Febreze the car to get your funk out of it."

"Whatever," came in unison before thundering stomps proceeded up the stairs.

Jim Walker turned back to his wife and wrapped his arms around her slender frame. "How was your day?"

"Good," she said. "Fairly uneventful."

"Therapy today?"

She squeezed the brochure in her hand out of reflex. "Every Tuesday."

"Any more breakthroughs? You seem in better spirits today."

"You've seen me for a whole two minutes. The majority of which consisted of a kiss and yelling at children. How do you know I'm in better spirits?"

"I can just tell," he said with a smile.

"James Walker, you're full of shit."

She pulled away from him with a smirk and walked the rest of the way to the trashcan. She tossed the brochure in. *So long, Cardinal Crest Estate.*

THREE

Jim mindlessly scrolled through Hulu looking for something to distract him until he felt tired enough to fall asleep. Lauren and Chandler had already said their goodnights after being ordered to go to bed. Bedtime was fungible during the summer, but he tried to keep them on somewhat of a schedule. Ann lay in bed, reading some book on her iPad if he had to guess.

Nothing caught his interest, so it was time for option two. He stood up from the recliner, stretched his arms out, and walked to the kitchen. Despite their best efforts to give the kids only healthy options for snacks, some form of chocolate was always hidden in the pantry somewhere. A nighttime snack should help. He opened the pantry door, stared at the dried fruit snacks, granola bars, and rice cakes, and closed the pantry. *Better stay good*, he thought.

An innocent banana sat on the counter. He grabbed it, tore the peel away, and scarfed it in a few bites. His mouth still full, he walked over to the trashcan. With his foot mashed on the pedal, the lid flew open. He let go of the peel into the nearly full trashcan, and it fell next to a wadded-up brochure. Jim saw part of a house, and the word "Estate" printed across the top.

What's this?

He scooped the ad off the top of the pile, placed it on the counter, and flattened it out. Cardinal Crest Estate. He looked at the house on the front. It reminded him of a large plantation home. Big windows all around it. A wrap-around front porch.

"Peace and serenity," he said aloud to the empty kitchen. Thinking of the daily fights their two upstairs have, that sounded like a beautiful idea.

"Hey, Babe," Jim said, speaking just loud enough for his voice to carry into their bedroom.

"Yes, Dear?"

"What's Cardinal Crest Estate?" He picked the flyer up and walked toward their room.

"Oh, that," Ann said.

Jim thought she had a slight tremor in her voice.

"That, um, that was something...I thought about...well, Dr. Stiller thought... Just ignore it."

He turned the corner and saw her lying on their bed. The iPad lay next to her with the reading app open. He unfolded the wrinkled brochure as he walked to the bed and sat down next to her.

"If this was something that Dr. Stiller thought we should do, then why throw it away?" As he brought it closer to her, she recoiled.

"Honey, what is it?"

"That's the place," she said, her voice shaking.

"The place?" He laid the ad for Cardinal Crest Estate on his nightstand, relaxed on the bed, and placed a comforting arm around his wife. She melted into his side.

"That's where my mother was shot," Ann said.

Jim bolted upright, bouncing Ann's head off his chest. "Where your mother was shot?" He had to have heard her wrong. "Why would she want you to go back to that place?"

"She said it's an immersion therapy thing. We'd go as a family, and she'd be there too. I can be at the house where it happened. Recover all those lost memories. I told her I'd talk to you about it, but the summer is just too busy. I'm not sure we could take a few days away."

Hearing Ann relay what her therapist said seemed to make some sense. He wasn't a therapist and didn't have the remotest expertise in that area. He sold computer software. With Dr. Stiller there and Jim and the kids to support Ann, maybe that wasn't such a far-fetched idea.

"What do you think?" Jim asked.

"I'm scared. Until a couple of weeks ago, I didn't even remember this place existed. Now, not only does it exist, but a traumatic event from my childhood so bad I only remember snippets of it happened there." She went quiet for a minute and trembled next to Jim's arm.

He placed his arm around her again, trying to steady her.

"If the doc thinks it'll help, then maybe we give it a try? The kids and I support you no matter your decision. We just want you well." He ran his hand up the side of her arm and shoulder, comforting her.

She leaned her head over and kissed his hand as it brushed her shoulder. "Love you," she said.

He kissed the top of her head. "Love you too. The brochure said they promise peace and serenity. A few days of that sound great."

"Chandler and Lauren will be with us. Peace and serenity are not in their vocabulary."

"Leave that up to me. Call Dr. Stiller tomorrow and get this booked." Jim curled down into his pillow. "Alexa, lights off. Goodnight."

Ann's hand rested on his shoulder. "Goodnight."

FOUR

A s the sharp ringing of the speakerphone echoed in the empty kitchen, Ann kept repeating in her head, *What the hell am I thinking? What the hell am I thinking?* She hoped that Dr. Stiller wouldn't answer. That she had more time to procrastinate. If she waited long enough, the summer break would be over. The kids would be back in school. The fall school schedule was a nightmare. How could two kids need to be in three places at once?

The ringing stopped. "Good morning. This is Dr. Stiller."

"Dr. Stiller. Renee. Ann Walker."

"Oh, Ann. I hoped you'd be calling me soon. Did you speak with Jim about what we discussed?"

What the hell am I thinking? What the hell am I thinking?

"Yes, we discussed it last night." She decided to skip the part where she threw the brochure away, and if not for Jim seeing it on accident in the trashcan, they wouldn't have discussed it at all. Damn fate. She can be such a bitch.

"We decided that, if you really think it'll help, then let's do it."

"Ann, that's great news. I know this will be a huge step forward to where you want to be. You will get back to the person you and your family deserve."

"Do I need to call Cardinal Crest to get it scheduled?" Ann asked. She didn't want to be the one to do it, but if she had to, she still had the procrastination way out. Oh dear, where did the summer go?

"No, not at all. I'll get everything arranged for you." *Damnit.* "If it helps, I'll even coordinate with Mr. Walker so there's as little stress and anxiety on your end." *Double damnit.*

"I appreciate that."

Ann and Renee said their goodbyes and hung up. She sat on the couch with the formally crumpled brochure on the coffee table in front of her. The large house seemed to stare back at her, beckoning her to come. For a moment, she thought she saw an image of a small girl in the attic window, but when Ann blinked, the window was just a window.

Stop projecting yourself into that house.

The anxiety medication that Dr. Stiller prescribed sat next to the brochure. She grabbed the bottle, popped out two pills, and dry-swallowed them.

FIVE

Gina stood in the small hallway, a dozen feet from Dr. Stiller's door. She'd been watching the doctor for a few days, ever since the first appointment was set. This wasn't part of her initial plan, but she could work with this.

Dr. Stiller walked out of her office and pulled her office door closed. She reached into her purse and began fumbling for the keys.

"Dr. Stiller?" Gina said.

"Yes?" Startled, Dr. Stiller, Renee according to the placard on the door, turned to Gina.

"Could I have a moment of your time?" Gina, with her purse in hand, walked closer to Renee. At five and a half feet tall, Gina towered a good six inches over the aging therapist. This would be easier than she anticipated. The actual muscle was in the car just in case, but Gina doubted that would be needed. She'd let them do the cleanup. She hated that part anyway.

"I'm just locking up for the evening," the soft-spoken therapist said.

"It's ok. Could you put me on your calendar?"

"You're not a current patient, and I'm not taking on anyone new at this time." Dr. Stiller pulled out her keys and turned to the door. "If you call me tomorrow, though, I can give you a referral to a good therapist."

Gina saw Dr. Stiller slide the key into the lock. She had hoped to get into the office first, but this would have to do. With Dr. Stiller facing the door to lock it, Gina grabbed the knife from her purse. With just a few quick steps, she stood at Renee's back. She drove the knife into the doctor's lower back and cupped her other hand around Renee's mouth, stifling the expected scream. Her skilled attack pierced the kidney. As Gina withdrew the knife, she twisted the blade for maximum effect.

Dr. Stiller tried to turn, but Gina, who had to grow up strong, easily overpowered the elderly doctor.

Gina buried the knife into Renee's upper chest. She left the knife sticking out of Renee's chest, pulled the keys from the lock, opened the office door, and pushed Dr. Stiller back inside.

As the door shut, Gina pulled the knife from Renee's chest and heard a sucking sound from the wound. *There goes the lung.* She tossed her on the leather sofa with ease.

Blood dotted the carpet and pooled on the couch from the massive kidney wound. Renee gasped for air. Her eyes gaped at Gina.

"You're going to bleed out in a few minutes so there's no time to argue." Gina reached into Renee's purse and pulled out her laptop. "I need your passwords."

Dr. Stiller tried to breathe in but with only one working lung, she struggled.

"Clock's ticking, Doc."

Renee pointed to the small filing cabinet against the wall.

Gina walked over and looked at the sticky notes plastered on the outside of it. Random phone numbers. A few reminder notes. She saw one sticky note that had gibberish. She pulled it off the filing cabinet and stepped back to the couch.

"Are these your passwords?"

Renee's head nodded.

"You wrote your passwords down on a sticky note? That's really bad security, Doc. And you just have one password for everything? Your laptop, email, calendar, therapy notes?"

Again, a head nod but noticeably slower.

"Makes it easy for me. Thanks, Doc. I'll give Annabelle Adams, I mean Walker, your best. I'll take good care of her, just like I did her father."

Gina sat down on the chair across from Dr. Stiller and placed the computer on her lap. With the screen open, she typed the password from the sticky note. The familiar Apple chime sounded.

"Close your eyes, Doc. It'll be over in another minute."

Gina reached into her own purse and pulled out her cell phone, clicking on the saved clean-up contact.

Six

Gina Delfina stretched across the leather couch in her new office. Playing doctor was exhausting. She didn't know how the late Dr. Stiller did it for so many years. Thankfully, Ann agreed to go back to that house. Just the thought of her endgame finally being in motion made the tension in her shoulders ease. The irony was going to be sweet.

After killing Ann's father, Gina had planned to torment her, and then kill her and her family in their quaint suburban home. Gina hadn't expected Ann to become paranoid. Such a weak bitch. It was a welcomed treat. Well, before it felt like work, at least. Gina was able to toy with Ann, but that grew old. She wanted this to be over with. Cardinal Crest would be a suitable place for it to end.

Not just for the Walkers, though. There were two families to blame. Maybe she could get both in the same spot. Kill two birds with one stone. Kill two birds...

A smile broke across Gina's face, and she let out a brief giggle while staring at the ceiling. If she convinced them all to go to Cardinal Crest, she wouldn't have to go through all of this again in Tennessee. Fingers crossed.

Gina rose from the couch and swiped up on her phone. This one would be a little harder, so she had to be convincing. Ann was a pushover. Kathryn would not be.

SEVEN

"Set the butt securely against your shoulder," Kat whispered into Carly's ear. "Do you have a good grip on it?"

"Yes, Mom. I got it. This isn't my first time," the nine-year-old Carly said.

Kathryn Miller, still standing just behind her daughter, pressed on the barrel of the twenty gauge. The shotgun wiggled a bit. "Last time, it kicked you in the gut. Left a bruise for a week." She pressed on the end again but with less wiggle this time. "You ready?"

Carly shifted her feet. Her cheek rested on the stock. Her scrawny arms stiffened into position. She was already anticipating the recoil. "Ready."

"Steady your breath. Focus. And this time, you call it."

Kat took a few steps back. She recalled when her father took her shooting. She loved it. Those were the great memories with her dad. She grew up such a daddy's girl. Whether it was hunting, fishing, or just sitting on the porch listening to him strum his guitar, she had enjoyed the time. Having these times with Carly and Jake left her feeling nostalgic for her younger years. Back before cancer got her dad.

"Pull!" the girl shouted as loud as she could, jolting Kat out of her head.

Kat stepped on the pedal for the trap, slinging the clay pigeon high in the air. Kat watched Carly's eyes and the barrel of the shotgun find the target. Carly traced the clay pigeon; then she pulled the trigger. The percussion echoed off the hills and the trees. The pigeon floated gently to the ground, untouched.

Damnit, she thought.

"Damnit," Carly said. She slid the shotgun from her shoulder, breaking it open and emptying it.

"Excuse me?" Kat said in return. She had to smile, though. Carly verbalized exactly what Kat thought. "Practice makes perfect. At least you held on tight this time. You aren't doubled over, unable to breathe." Kathryn slid off her ear defenders, walked over to Carly, and took hers off. Kat ruffled the top of Carly's long brown hair, then held out her hand for the rifle. "We'll shoot some more later. You don't have anything else to do this summer anyway."

Carly turned and ran toward their house. Kat glanced at the skeet thrower and decided to leave it where it was.

If it looked like rain, she'd have Carly or Jake load it up on the John Deere Gator. With the gun over her shoulder, she followed Carly, looking like a soldier marching off to war.

EIGHT

Doug and Kathryn Miller inherited the house and the two hundred acres when her father passed away two years ago. The kids didn't have to change schools, which was the only thing that Jake cared about; he was twelve when they moved into the house. Carly was seven and loved going from the small house to having the great outdoors to run around in. The girl was made for the outdoor life.

For Kat, it was the memories of growing up here. Whether it was fishing in the creek down the corner, hunting with her dad in the woods, or making out with Bill Preston in the shed on her dad's tractor. That memory she didn't relay to her kids. She didn't need to give Jake or Carly any ideas.

The modest farmhouse sat just past the field that Kat walked across. The front porch extended from end to end. Big enough to have a swing and a few rocking chairs. When her dad built it, he said he wanted to have plenty of room to smoke a cigarette, sip on his Jack Daniels, shoot some doves, and rock in his chair. There was plenty of room for that and more.

Doug sat in the swing mounted to the top of the patio, swaying back and forth. "How'd she do? She went running past me so fast, I didn't get a chance to ask."

"She's getting better. Kept it against her shoulder this time."

"That's good. Care to join me?" He tapped the empty seat next to him.

"Sure." She walked up the steps and leaned the shotgun against the house next to the front door. Just as she sat down, the phone rang.

"Mom. It's for you." Carly was always quick to answer. Cell signal was weak, and the Internet was non-existent so her only communication with her friends was the land-line.

Kat heard Carly's feet stomp on the hardwood floor, marching the cordless handset to her mother.

"Probably a sales guy," Doug said. "Our car doesn't need an extended warranty." He smiled at himself.

"And here I've been saying yes every time they call. I think I've extended us out about thirty years now."

"If I didn't know you were being sarcastic..." Doug shook his head with a smirk on his face.

Carly opened the screen door and handed the cordless phone to Kat before disappearing back into the house.

"This is Kathryn," she said.

"Kathryn Higgins?" a female voice asked.

"Not for the past eighteen years. Can I help you with something?" She started to pace the front porch.

"My apologies," the voice said. "We've never met. My name is Dr. Renee Stiller. I'm a therapist in Norfolk, Virginia."

A therapist from Norfolk? Confusion crossed over her face. She glanced at Doug who must have seen her look. He wore one of his own.

He mouthed, "Who is it?"

Kat shrugged.

"Before you hang up on me," the voice, Doctor something Kat didn't recall, said, "please hear me out. It's about something that happened almost thirty years ago. Do you remember Cardinal Crest Estate?"

Kat placed her hand on the receiver and leaned the phone away from her face. "Some doctor asking about something from when I was a kid." She returned to the phone conversation. "Whatever you're selling, we aren't interested."

"I'm not selling anything," the doctor said as fast as possible. She then slowed her speech, "I'm not trying to sell you on anything. This is to help a friend. Do you remember Cardinal Crest Estate? About thirty years ago?"

Kat hesitated for a moment. She thought back to when she was twelve, and her dad, mom, uncle, and she went to the large bed and breakfast for the weekend. It wasn't a trip they usually went on, but one of dad's customers had a broken heater. Dad didn't have the heart to charge the struggling family at the time. Later that spring, though, things got better for them, so the couple gifted him a weekend stay for four at this B&B they found. She smiled, remembering they thought her dad had two kids.

Mark Higgins, Kat's dad, didn't want to accept, but her mom, Judy, helped him reconsider. Uncle John graciously volunteered to take the unused ticket and join them.

"Kathryn?" the doctor said.

Kat realized she'd been standing there lost in her thoughts. "Sorry," she said. "Yes, I remember it, and I remember what happened."

"Great. I've been working with the other family that was there, the daughter specifically. She's about your age, and has her own family, too. We're organizing a reunion of sorts, remembrance of the event."

"Wait. What?" Kat's confusion stopped her pacing. "Isn't this some kind of HIPAA or therapist/client violation or something? And why would anyone want to stage a reunion over that?"

"I understand your concern. Nothing is being violated. They've given me permission to work on their behalf."

"Well, as great as a weekend away sounds, I don't think we can afford it right now." She looked up at Doug.

His expression of confusion stayed plastered on his face.

Kat placed her hand over the receiver again and leaned the phone away. "I'll fill you in in a sec."

"...a thing," Dr. Stiller said.

"I'm sorry. I missed what you said."

"I said, you and your husband wouldn't have to pay a thing. The costs are covered. For you and your family. I'm working on coordinating the weekend. We have one we are tentatively looking at. If you agree, you would be doing a lot of good."

Kat took a moment to think. "We need some time to discuss it. What's your number?"

Renee gave Kat her contact information before they said their goodbyes.

"So, what was that?" Doug asked.

Kat filled him in on the conversation.

"So, she's just giving us a free weekend getaway?" he asked. He leaned back in the swing and turned his eyes up to the top of the patio.

"It sounds like that, but don't start rationalizing this. I know that look." Kat paced the porch.

"Wasn't this the place that your mother said was bad? And how many people died that weekend?"

"My mother used to say that house had demons. She said it felt bad, and what happened only proved that. Four people died that weekend. Because of that, Dad taught me to shoot."

She kicked her foot up on the swing next to Doug. Her boots were scuffed and muddy. She reached inside the right one and pulled out the hidden knife. "He also made sure I always took this with me."

PART TWO

WELCOME TO CARDINAL CREST

ONE

A week later, Ann Walker's head pounded, so she canceled that week's appointment with Renee. She probably could've forced herself to go, but it was a great excuse to avoid talking about Cardinal Crest. Jim didn't bring it up either. She wondered if Dr. Stiller had reached out to him after all. Ann contemplated asking him, but she hoped the silence would lead to forgetting about it. The longer the summer went, the better the chance they'd have to cancel altogether.

Unfortunately, those hopes only lasted for so long. A few days after her missed appointment, Jim told her they'd scheduled the weekend. It was only two weeks away, at the end of June, long before any back-to-school events started. He told her it was going to be great, and that in preparation, her weekly appointments were on hold. Ann could tell he was excited. Whether it was the weekend away, the hope that this would help speed up her recovery, or a combination of reasons, she didn't know.

A trip away excited Chandler and Lauren as well, much to Ann's surprise. The day before they were set to leave, each had a bag packed, ready to go.

Ann slow walked her packing to the extent that Jim accused her of being a zombie. If only he knew how much she struggled. Trying to explain it to him didn't help. She fought this battle inside herself. Ann trusted Dr. Stiller knew what was best, but this immersion therapy could bring out all her demons. She was terrified of going back there. Each time she'd see the image of that house, fear gripped her. Her chest tightened, and she swore the air itself pressed on her shoulders.

When Friday morning arrived, Jim and the kids loaded the bags in the car. Ann sat quietly in the passenger seat and stared out the window, ignoring the trunk slamming shut and the chaos as Lauren and Chandler jumped in the backseat.

Jim climbed behind the steering wheel. "Ann, are you alright?" he asked. "Do you need anything? Snack or a drink before we hit the road?"

She closed her eyes with her head still turned to her window. With a deep breath, she opened them and turned to him with a fake smile. "Yes, I'm doing fine. This will be a great weekend." She didn't know which one of them she was lying to. "When we stop, I'll take a bottle of water, please."

"Sounds great. Need to gas up the car as we hit the road."

Two

The trees converged into a continuous blob of green as the drive took them further and further into the North Carolina backwoods.

Somewhere in the distance, Ann heard the kids bickering in the backseat. She tried to congratulate herself on her prophetic skills, but it didn't take Nostradamus to know when two siblings are in close proximity of each other, fighting would be inevitable. Instead, she stared into the green abyss.

The melodic drone of the road grabbed and hypnotized her. She was present in the car, but in body only. Her thoughts and spirit drifted elsewhere. They centered on a little girl in the backseat of a 1995 Land Rover Range Rover who made this same drive almost thirty years ago.

The little girl had a small pink suitcase on the seat next to her. She wore a brand-new yellow sun dress that flared around her when she spun.

"Annabelle," her mom said. "Can you please stop doing that?"

Annabelle had been rocking side-to-side on her leather seat. The dress allowed just enough of her skin to contact the warm leather. With each rock, a ripping sound echoed. "Shcriip." Another rock. "Shcriip".

"Annabelle," her mother said louder. "Your father and I are having a conversation."

"Sorry, Mother," Annabelle said. She sat still in the car and stared out the window.

"Thomas, are you sure the security detail is needed?" her mother said.

Annabelle tried not to eavesdrop on her parents' conversation. Most of the time it was about her dad's job, and that was boring. But since she was stuck in the car with them and couldn't make any noises, what else could she do?

"Liz, it's for the best right now. After the hearings are over, this won't be an issue anymore. Plus, Brian's a nice guy. And this place is big enough that we'll barely notice him."

"I hope you're right. Annabelle?"

Annabelle turned away from the window and looked at the front seat.

Her mother turned to the back to face her. There was a hole just above her mother's eyes, and a trail of blood ran down her mother's face. The back of her head blossomed out. Hair matted with blood covered the exploded pieces of skull.

Annabelle's eyes gaped wide.

"Annabelle?", her dead mother said again. "Annabelle!" she screamed.

"Ann!", her husband yelled at the same time her kids yelled, "Mom!"

Ann jerked her head up from the window, bouncing it off the glass. For a moment, she didn't know where she was.

"Mom, are you ok?" Lauren asked. "You were screaming your name."

"I was?" The fog of sleep slowly dissipated from her eyes. "I must have been having a bad dream."

"That was super creepy," Lauren said. "Didn't even sound like your voice."

Ann turned in her chair and looked back at Chandler and Lauren. Both were sitting wide-eyed. Chandler nodded his head in agreement. She looked at Jim who also nodded. When all three of them aligned, then something wasn't right.

"Sorry for scaring everyone. Just a nightmare."

"Good time to wake up anyway," Jim said. "We're here."

An iron archway spanned the gravel drive. Across the top of the arch, the words "CARDINAL CREST" were welded into the frame. The fence line continued in both directions as far as Ann could see. As Jim pulled up to the wrought iron gate, it automatically opened from the middle. Each half swung to its respective side, inviting the Walkers to drive in.

THREE

Ten-year-old Annabelle stared at the shiny iron archway. The way the sun shone off the words made Ann imagine it was on fire. The gate was already open, and her dad turned their Range Rover off the paved road. She heard the usually quiet sound of the road turn into a series of crunches as the SUV drove onto the gravel driveway.

All Annabelle saw were rolling hills of green grass. A tree line sat a half mile back of the road. Only when they topped the first big hill was the large estate house visible. Even then, it was at least a mile back from the main road. She kept staring at the picturesque landscape for the whole five minutes it took her dad to drive them to the front of the house. When she turned around to look, she could barely see the outline of the black sedan that followed them. Their car kicked up so much dirt she was glad they were in front. *Poor Brian,* she thought and chuckled. He was going to be mad about the dirt on his pristine car.

When the car finally reached the front of the house, the dust cloud subsided. Thomas Adams pulled their SUV to a stop, and Brian Hayes parked his car next to them. An elderly man stood on the front steps waiting. Annabelle hopped out of the backseat with her small suitcase in her hand as the man walked to the car.

"Hi," Annabelle said. "I'm Annabelle Adams. What's your name?"

The man, gray hair with a gray mustache, wore a button-down flannel shirt and jeans. "Hello, Annabelle Adams. I'm Bill."

"You sound like my grandpa," she said. She drug her suitcase through the gravel beside the SUV. "Do you work here?"

"I do work here. You could say I take care of this place." He started to the back of the SUV as Thomas opened the trunk. He held his hand out. "Bill Monroe. I'm guessing you are Senator Adams."

"Thomas, please," Ann's dad said, shaking Bill's hand. You've met Annabelle. That's my wife Elizabeth. Brian Hayes is in the other car."

"It's a Pleasure to meet you. Let me help you with those bags." Bill helped Thomas remove the two suitcases. "I'm not sure if they told you, but there's another family staying here. They're just here for the weekend. As you can tell by the look of it, there's plenty of room." Bill grabbed one of the two large suitcases. He turned to Annabelle, spinning in circles in her sundress. "I'll take your little suitcase, Princess."

Annabelle felt the crunch of the gravel beneath her shoes. Each step reminded her of eating Rice Krispies. Snap, crackle, pop. "Ok. I'll leave it here," she said, still spinning as she talked.

"How far back does the property go?" Thomas asked.

"Well, the whole thing is just over a thousand acres. Most of it is trees, though. There's a pond that sits just over the hill. Not much for fishing but feels great on a hot day."

Annabelle saw Brian get his suitcase out of the car and walk toward her dad and Bill.

"How big is the house?" Brian asked. All three men stopped and looked up at the large estate home.

Annabelle stopped spinning and turned her attention to the front of the house. Steps led up to the front porch which wrapped around it. The house was a deep red color with large windows on the first floor. Smaller windows were on the second floor, and above that, there was a little window. As she raised her head up, the house loomed over her. She almost lost her balance from the combination of spinning and now looking up.

"The bottom floor has a dining room, kitchen, living room, and a den. The master also sits on the bottom. The second floor has all the guest rooms—there are six of them. There are two bathrooms on the first floor and four upstairs. There's a large attic and a pretty sizable basement. The staff and I use those for storage."

Annabelle looked around and saw her mother standing by the SUV. She had her hand just over her eyes, blocking the sun as she stared up at the house. She wore a pair of white lounge pants and a blue blouse.

From the other direction, Annabelle heard someone laugh. She turned and saw a girl about her age in a long blue dress. The blonde-haired girl, also spinning in circles, stood in the open field across from them.

"Mom! Mom! Mom! Can I go play?" Annabelle ran to Elizabeth and collided, knocking the wind out of her.

"Don't go too far. You'll need to get unpacked and cleaned up."

Turning toward the other little girl, she screamed, "I won't!" as she ran. Annabelle sprinted across the gravel driveway into the freshly mowed grass. The elevation change didn't slow her down as she climbed to the top of a hill. She reached the top and breathed hard.

"Hi," she said through quick breaths. "I'm... Annabelle... What's...your...name?"

The little girl stopped spinning. Annabelle noticed how old her dress looked. It had a few tears at the bottom, and the sleeves kept slipping off her shoulder. The girl stared at Annabelle for a minute, almost like she looked through her instead of at her. After the silence, she finally said, "I'm Betsy."

"Betsy's an old name," Annabelle said and chuckled. "Do you live here?"

"Yes, I've lived here my whole life. The house is our home," Betsy said in a thick drawl.

"Daddy says that we're going to be staying here for a while. Something with his work. Maybe we can be friends. Are there any toys to play with?"

Betsy stared off into the sky as if she didn't hear Annabelle. Finally, she turned back to her. "I have a few dolls in the attic. I can't play with them often. Only when daddy isn't upset. You don't want to upset daddy. He has a temper." Betsy's eyes dropped down the hill to the house.

Annabelle followed her gaze and saw her dad, Brian, and Bill, the caretaker, standing outside. She guessed Brian was still getting the lay of the land for his security stuff. Bill seemed nice enough. She had a hard time picturing him with a temper. He reminded her of her pawpaw. They even dressed the same, too—blue jeans and a flannel shirt. If

Bill smelled like pipe tobacco, then they might as well be related.

"Wanna play by the pond?" Betsy asked. "It's over there." She pointed just beyond the hill at the edge of the tree line.

"Uh, I don't know," Annabelle said.

Her mom's words echoed in her head. She didn't want to go too far off, where she couldn't hear them if they yelled for her. She didn't know everything going on with her dad's work, but since Brian's been around, her parents, especially her mom, hadn't let her go too far away. They even told her teacher she couldn't play outside. She had to stay inside at recess, which sucked. She wouldn't have cared if it had been a month ago. At that time, the weather was so cold it hurt. But now, it felt great. Not cold. Not hot. Not humid yet. She wanted to play on the playground. Some days she didn't get to leave school until late. Mom had to sign her out. No more taking the bus home. She had to sit through the "Don't Get in the Car with a Stranger" Discussion more times than she could count. She knew that rule. Everybody knew that rule. She'd even known it since she was six.

"It's fun and far enough way not to upset daddy," Betsy said.

"My mom said not to go too far away," Annabelle said.

"You can almost see it from here. Follow me." Betsy took off down the hill. Her dress flowed out behind her as she ran. One sleeve kept slipping off her shoulder and she continuously adjusted it back.

"Ok. If it's not too far."

Annabelle started after Betsy.

"Annabelle!" her mother hollered. "Annabelle! Come back and start unpacking."

"I gotta go, Betsy," she said, turning back down the hill toward the house.

Four

J im threw the car in park in front of the large house. A cloud of dust billowed behind them from the dirt road. When he put the car in park, both back doors swung open, and a kid hopped out of each side.

The doors slamming shut jolted Ann out of her walk down memory lane.

From inside the car, Ann could hear Lauren and Chandler. "I swear. If I had to be in that car five more minutes with your farting..."

"I'm sorry," Chandler said, taking an AirPod out of each ear. "I had these set to annoyance cancellation. I guess your voice counts."

Jim opened his own door and stepped out of the car. "Kids, grab your bags," Jim said.

Ann opened her door and stepped out as the trunk hatch opened. She stared up at the colossal house. Now that memories of this place were coming back, she noticed it hadn't changed a bit. The same dark red brick covered

Cardinal Crest Estate. A dark wooden door and large bay windows sat just behind the white pillars accenting the front porch.

The house's front door opened, and a very large man stepped out. He was bald and stood well over six feet tall. He waved to them. "Hi there," he said. His deep voice billowed from the front porch as he walked toward them. "Welcome to Cardinal Crest. Here, let me help you with those." With his large stride, he made it to the Walker's car in a few steps. He held out his hand to Jim. "Name's Frank Malone."

Jim shook his hand. Frank's hand swallowed Jim's. "James Walker, but you can call me Jim. This is Lauren and Chandler, and my wife, Ann. I bet that road is a bear to drive up when it rains."

"Pleasure to meet everyone. We have your rooms ready for you." Frank grabbed the two smaller suitcases that Chandler and Lauren had in one hand, and the bigger suitcase for Jim and Ann in the other. "I'll show you where they are."

Frank led the family across the gravel driveway and up the steps to the wooden front porch. Jim walked just behind Mr. Malone, followed by Lauren and Chandler. Ann was the last up the steps.

She thought back to the caretaker from thirty years ago. Bill Monroe. She wondered what happened to him. He was her grandfather's age thirty years ago, so she doubted he was still around. That'd put him pushing ninety if not more. He would be retired, although he probably should have been retired back then.

The memory of the little girl in the blue dress that was just a bit too big for her was now fresh in her mind. Ann glanced to the hill's top where they had spun in circles. When had she last seen the little girl? She couldn't remember. Part of her hoped and part of her feared that it would all come back over the next few days. Immersion therapy.

Frank opened the solid wooden door. It groaned audibly on its hinges as he did.

The entryway opened to a large foyer. A giant, wide-mouthed wooden staircase with etched handrails ascended to the second floor. From the bottom, Ann saw the second-floor landing. The same railing spread in both directions across the second floor until it met hallways containing bedrooms.

"Wo," Chandler said as they stepped inside.

The expansive interior caught them off guard. But not Ann. It was smaller than what she remembered. Granted, she was remembering from the viewpoint of a much smaller ten-year-old.

She breathed in leather and cedar.

"Over here is the den and living space," Frank said and nodded his head to the left. With a head nod to the right, he said, "The dining room and kitchen are that way. Your bedrooms are all upstairs." He proceeded up the stairs, still carrying all three suitcases.

Jim, Lauren, and Chandler started up the stairs, but Ann paused. She saw the fancy leather sofa, the love seat, and the stone fireplace in the den. Somewhere deep in her head, she heard a gunshot. She closed her eyes. Her legs locked in place. She felt ten years old again.

She wore a pretty red dress. Her dad and Brian Hayes, his security detail, were there. Her mother wasn't next to her dad but on the floor. A pool of maroon blood spread across the hardwood floor, leading from the gaping hole in her mother's head. Gray chunks of bone and brain matter covered the fireplace. Even at ten, she knew it was her mom's. The mom who was strict but who loved her. The mom who made her a proper lady.

A few other people stood in the den. Another little girl about her age. Ann tried to remember her name but couldn't. It wasn't Betsy. Betsy wasn't there that night. She wasn't sure where Betsy had disappeared to. She said she lived in the house, but Ann only saw her around a few times.

"Ann?" Jim stood behind her. He placed his hand on the small of her back. "Ann, are you ok?"

The feel of his hand against her brought her back to the present. Ann opened her eyes, forcing each individual muscle that had tensed up to relax.

She peered into the den. No one was there. Just the furniture and the empty fireplace filled the room. A few decorative pictures and portraits lined the walls. Faces of people from decades ago stared at her, judging her.

"Yeah," she lied. "Just some Deja vu." She turned away from the den and started for the staircase. "Kids already go upstairs?"

"Yes, Frank walked them and their bags to their rooms. He said ours is up and to the left. You sure you're good?"

"I said yes. Come on."

Ann walked to the staircase. She let her hand drift across the railing, feeling the smooth, polished oak under her fingers. With each slow, deliberate footfall up, the stairs groaned beneath her. After counting the twenty steps, she reached the second-story landing. Ann turned and leaned against the rail overlooking the entryway. She stood almost eye level with the glass chandelier above the entryway. She saw herself reflected in hundreds of tiny crystals. Occasionally, she liked the person in the reflection. More often, she hated the scared little girl staring back at her.

Following close behind her up the staircase, Jim moved next to her on the landing. He again placed his hand on her lower back, his subtle way to get her attention.

She felt the slight nudge of his hand, so Ann turned to him. From just over his shoulder, she saw Frank standing next to a door with their large suitcase next to him.

"Guessing that's our room?" she said to Jim.

"Right this way, Mr. And Mrs. Walker," Frank said as if in response. "Ms. Lauren is in that one, and Mr. Chandler is in that one." He pointed to the two rooms across from theirs.

"Thanks, Mr. Malone," Jim said.

"Call me Frank."

"Thanks, Frank."

Jim led Ann into the large bedroom, grabbed the suitcase and pulled it with him, and then Frank walked back down the hall.

Like the other parts of the house, the room was an explosion of dark red oak. A king-size bed sat in the middle of the room, bookended by a gigantic headboard and baseboard. An armoire filled the wall across from the bed. A lounge chair sat next to the window. A doorway led to the connecting bathroom.

Jim grabbed the suitcase's top and side handles and threw them on the bed. He unzipped it and laid out clothes. She knew he hated living out of a suitcase. When he had the chance, he'd first unpack into the drawers or the closet. She couldn't count the number of hotels they'd stayed in over the years where he'd repeated this same process.

Walking to the lounge chair, Ann sat down and stared out of the window. Their room overlooked a large open meadow that eventually ended at the tree line. Vibrant green grass filled the area with the occasional yellows and reds spotted throughout. It was a calming view. *I bet the sunrise or sunset is beautiful.*

"Penny for your thoughts?" Jim asked, still putting clothes into the armoire.

"This all feels so familiar," Ann said, staring over the field. "That same feeling of Deja vu as when I walked past the den. I feel like things are coming back in chunks."

Before Ann could let herself drift back into another memory, she heard a commotion outside their room. She stood up from the comfortable lounge chair and walked to their bedroom door.

Jim stopped what he was doing and joined her. A handful of voices came from the entryway. Ann and Jim walked down the hallway and back to the second story landing. From the other side of the chandelier, they saw the front door standing open. A man and a woman stood just inside the doorway.

"You two, come on," the man said.

Ann stared down at the woman. She was of medium build and had shoulder-length straight brown hair. The woman's short-sleeve shirt was rolled up. Her arms weren't thin like Ann's but had definition. She wore blue jeans and boots. The feeling of Deja vu rushed back over Ann as she glanced at her husband.

"I assumed we had the place to ourselves," Jim said. "Big place, so I guess I should've confirmed first."

A sudden flashback hit Ann. The little girl standing in the den that night whose name wasn't Betsy. Her name was just on the tip of her tongue. Her head raced to find it. As it did, her heart kept pace. It pounded in her chest. Whether it was the stress of being there or the increased blood pressure, she didn't know, but Ann started to feel lightheaded. Her vision blurred, and she stumbled into Jim.

Out of nowhere, a locked-away memory popped into her head. "Like the animal?" a younger version of herself asked.

"Yes, but not spelled like that."

Jim held her close, catching her. He eased her down to the ground.

"Ann, are you ok? Ann?"

The feeling of Deja vu hit her like a tsunami. Snippets of memories stashed away for her own protection. The house, her parents, the other family, her mother dead on the floor. Quick flashes shot through her head. No one memory was complete.

She placed the palms of her hands on the hardwood floor and rested her back against a baluster.

"Ann?" Jim kept repeating her name.

Finally, she took a few deep breaths. Her vision started to clear. She blinked her eyes a few times, ensuring they stayed focused, and looked up at her husband.

"The woman's name is Kathryn," Ann said. Her tone was calmer than she expected as if she was introducing a business partner. "But she goes by Kat, like the animal but not spelled like that."

FIVE

"I need to have a conversation with Dr. Stiller," Ann said. "She never mentioned anything about this." She raised her hands, and Jim grabbed them to help her to her feet. Lightheaded, Ann steadied herself and leaned against the top railing.

From below, Mr. Malone stepped through the front door with another suitcase, followed by two children each carrying their own. The four stood in the entryway, gawking at the interior of the house. Frank delivered the same spiel he'd given the Walkers not long before. This time, his arms were empty as he started up the staircase.

"Over there is the den and living space," Frank said and pointed. "The dining room and kitchen are..."

"Hello, Kathryn," Ann said, interrupting Frank's tour of the house.

Kathryn and her husband raised their heads to the second floor.

"Ann?" Kat said. She squinted her eyes. Obviously, they needed to adjust to the darker, interior light.

"Why are you here, Kat?" Ann spoke in a very flat tone. She hoped her displeasure came through. This unexpected turn caught her off guard. Ann put a lot of trust in Renee to even entertain the idea of being here. She hated that she was even doing this to begin with; that she even needed to do this to get better. As much as she knew they wanted to help, it was embarrassing enough that her kids and Jim went through this with her. For Renee to have invited another family to watch her descend into madness? Heat rose in her cheeks.

"Ask your therapist," Kat snapped back. "She called me."

"Oh, I plan to. Where is she? Mr. Malone..." Ann said.

"Frank," he interjected.

Ann's immediate stern look at the interruption caused the hulking man to drop his head and stand still on the third step of the staircase.

"Frank, has Dr. Stiller arrived already? She would've arranged this trip."

Before he could answer, a car door slammed shut. Everyone turned to the door, anxious to see who the next arrival would be.

"Oh, that better not be someone else," Ann whispered to Jim. "Find the kids. I'm of the mindset we're about to drive back home."

"Agreed." Jim disappeared down the hall, leaving Ann alone at the second-floor railing, looking down on the new arrivals and at the front door.

Renee walked through the front door and stopped the trailing suitcase just behind her. Her eyes darted from Frank standing on the staircase to Kathryn, her husband, and kids in the entryway with their bags, then finally up to Ann looming over everyone. The silence screamed.

Finally, Renee Stiller said, "Well, I see everyone's had a chance to meet."

"Renee," Ann said. "We need to talk." Her voice echoed in the large entryway. She hoped she projected it with enough strength that her therapist knew how serious she was.

"Of course, Ann. Give me just a few minutes. The downstairs master bedroom has a sitting area that I'll be using as my office. We can discuss in there." Renee turned to Kathryn. "You must be the Millers. Pleasure to meet you in person." She walked to Kat and gave her cordial hug. "Thank you so much for doing this."

"I thought you said..." Kat started.

"We'll talk more in a bit," she interrupted. "Mr. Malone, please show the Millers to their rooms. Ann, if you'd like to come this way, we can speak."

Renee walked past the staircase, dragging her suitcase behind her. She disappeared beneath the second-floor landing.

As Ann walked to the top of the staircase and started down, Frank took Kathryn and her family up to the second floor. Ann turned at the bottom of the stairs and saw Frank lead them to the right side of the hallway. The opposite direction of her room. She turned under the large staircase and followed the hallway to an open doorway.

The master suite was decorated much like the others. Ann wondered how many oak trees were cut down between the house itself and all the furniture inside of it. Whoever built and furnished this house had a look and feel they were going for.

Renee stood by a large bay window with a seated nook. She had the same view that Ann had of the bright green landscape. "I know what you want to discuss," she said, staring out the window.

Ann walked past the bed and stood by the window as well. She crossed her arms and glared at Renee. "Why didn't you tell me?"

Renee didn't look at Ann, continuing to watch the outside. "Would you have been more or less likely to agree to this if you knew?"

"That's not fair," Ann snapped back. "I should've at least been given the choice. This has been hard enough to go through in front of my own family. Now, for you to bring a stranger into this?"

Renee finally turned to Ann. "She's not a stranger, though. Kathryn was here. She witnessed your trauma firsthand."

Ann's arms dropped to her side. A million thoughts ran through her head. "How did you know that? I didn't remember her until five seconds ago."

With a smile, Renee said, "I'm good at what I do, Ann. I did my research. Her family was here that weekend, as you now recall.

"Your sessions this weekend will still be private. My hope is that the general conversations throughout the next few days will help unlock your lost memories. With each recovered memory, you can process what happened, deal with the emotional fallout, and let go of the scared little girl trapped inside of you. Based on your reactions, I gather some of those memories have already started unlocking."

Ann sat down on the window seat and stared out over the field. "I've seen flashes. Fragments like from a dream.

I walked into this house and looked into the den. I saw images. Ghosts from the past. Until Jim touched my back, I'd have sworn they were right in front of me."

"It's very common in this type of situation." Renee placed a hand on Ann's shoulder. "You may see and hear things that aren't there as your mind makes sense of where they should go. That's what we're here to do—sort everything out and make it right."

"Thank you, Dr. Stiller." Ann placed her hand on top of Renee's.

"Please, this weekend stick with Renee. We're all here as one big family."

"Regardless, I wish you'd have told me in advance." Ann stood up from the seat. "I owe Kat and her family an apology."

SIX

There was a gentle tap on the door, and Ann walked over and opened it.

Still by the window, Renee saw Frank Malone on the other side of the door. "I can come back," he said.

"No, that's ok," Ann said. "I'm sure Jim has us and the kids already packed back up. I need to let him know that we're staying."

Ann stepped past Frank and disappeared up the staircase.

Frank turned to Renee, who motioned for him to come in. As he did, Frank closed the door behind him.

"Is Joseph here yet?" she asked.

"Yes, Ms. Delfina," he said. "He's been here since this morning, working in the kitchen." He walked over to her. His large frame eclipsed Gina Delfina.

Despite the size difference, she had no worries about him or Joseph Jacobs. Both men were loyal. She paid well, and like most people in their circle, they feared what would happen if they crossed her. Gina had proven herself over the years, feeding off her hunger for this moment. Every person she killed was just a substitute. Killing Thomas Adams, Ann's father, started to fill the void finally but also gave her a taste of closure that only made her thirst for more. Putting a knife through Brian Hayes's throat was exhilarating, but there was no sport in killing an old man in his sleep.

This, though. This was her masterpiece. This was *her* Fifth Symphony, *her* Mona Lisa. She had orchestrated everything and everything was to be perfect. Gina didn't panic when she heard Ann question Kathryn. She knew that would happen and already planned the response. Of course Ann would want to leave. Ann didn't want to be here in the first place, but Gina learned over the last few months of therapy exactly which strings to pull.

This would be talked about for ages. This weekend would become legendary. How Gina Delfina, the orphan tossed from foster home to foster home, abused, neglected, and tortured, finally got her revenge.

"Boss?" Frank asked.

She snapped out of her daze. "Keep playing nice. You're doing great. I'll let you know when it's time. Now, go grab Jacobs and make drinks for our guests. They need time to mingle."

"I will do that." Frank opened the door, stepped into the hallways, and closed it behind him.

Gina sat down on the window nook.

"Gina." The voice came as a whisper on the wind.

She spun away from the window, almost falling off the seat. The room was empty. A subtle chill walked up her right arm, leaving tiny goosebumps in its wake. With her left hand, she rubbed her right forearm. A slight tingle went down the back of her neck almost as if a lover had laid a soft kiss there and then exhaled. The hair on the back of her neck stood up straight.

Gina stood up and dropped her arms to her side. She shook her arms around and moved her head from side to side, stretching her neck. "Need to get some blood flowing after the drive," she said to the empty room. She walked to the private bathroom, stood in front of the sink, and turned on the hot water. Within a few seconds, steam rose, obscuring the mirror that hung in front of her with a cloudy film. She ran her hands and arms under the scalding water. She preferred the water this way. Capturing some of it in her hands, she dropped her head and splashed her face, feeling the heat flush her cheeks.

"Gina," the whisper came again, but this time it had a certain familiarity to it.

She shot her head up and quickly wiped the fog off the mirror. For an instance, she saw a man standing just behind her. But she didn't see the face or features so much; she just saw darkness. As if a shadow had come loose from its source. She blinked, and as quickly as it appeared, it was gone.

With her hands braced on the sink, she stood there momentarily, staring into the mirror. Gina Delfina looked not just at herself but beyond herself. She searched for random shadows that shouldn't be there. She listened for the whisper, but nothing came. Finally, she eased her hands off the sink, straightened herself up, turned off the hot water, and dried her face and hands.

Gina walked out of the bathroom and then out of the master suite. From the den on her right, she heard voices and conversation. Ann's voice she recognized quite easily. Just outside of their view, she paused and took a deep breath. The familiar whisper still sat perched in the back of her mind. It couldn't have come from the conversation in the den. They knew her as Renee Stiller, therapist. They'd not have said her real name.

Time to go back to Dr. Stiller, she thought.

"Sounds like everyone is getting along," Renee said, finally stepping around the corner into the spacious den.

Ann and Jim Walker sat on the couch. Ann held a wine glass with what looked to be rose' in it, and Jim had a smaller glass with bourbon. Across from them, Kathryn and Doug Miller curled next to each other snuggly on the love seat. Doug had his arm on the back of the chair, and Kat sat sideways laying her back into him. Both had a bottle of Pabst Blue Ribbon in their hand. In the far corner behind a built-in bar stood Frank.

Everyone turned Renee's direction.

"Yes, we are," Ann said. "We've been getting reacquainted."

"Great to hear," Renee said. She pointed to the drinks in everyone's hand. "Alcohol always helps."

Doug sipped on the beer bottle and wiped a few droplets from his thick black beard just over his lip. "As a therapist, do you prescribe alcohol often?"

Kat elbowed him, causing the others to chuckle.

"Well, that wasn't necessary," Doug said to Kat. "Almost spilled my beer. I was going to say, if alcohol is now a part of therapy, I may have a few issues I need to get worked out."

"Mr. Miller," Renee said with a smirk. She hated putting on the fake smile, but at least it wouldn't be for much longer. "Mr. Miller, unfortunately, no. Alcohol isn't something I prescribe in therapy, but it can help to alleviate potentially tense situations."

"Again, I'm really sorry about that, Kat," Ann said, turning back to the couple on the loveseat. "I was caught off guard, but things are better now."

"Water under the bridge," Kat said and drank a swig of her Pabst. "So, Ann, tell me this because Doug and I have no idea. How hard is it to raise a sixteen-year-old girl? Carly's only nine, but we're already pulling our hair out." She reached over and snatched Doug's hat off his head before he could stop her, revealing a defined forehead with a receding hairline. "See what I mean?"

"Give that back," Doug said.

Kat placed it sideways on his head, and he quickly readjusted it.

"Lauren hasn't been that much of a problem," Jim said. "She's a good kid and keeps up with her grades. Mainly, we just have to referee her and her brother. Those two are a pair."

"Carly and Jake are the same way," Doug said. "They're going to kill each other one day."

Renee heard the two families talk about their kids but wasn't really interested in listening. She didn't care to. When it came to Ann's kids, she'd heard so much about them already, she was sick of their names. Finally, she interjected. "Speaking of the other four, where are they now?"

Ann said, "Well, ours would be in their room on their phones."

"Same," Kat said.

This brought a genuine smile to Renee. This was also part of her orchestrated plan. Everyone walked around with a device in their pocket. Glued to their phones most of the day. She didn't need them calling for help, though. It's time to get rid of those devices.

"Oh, that reminds me," Renee said. She turned to Ann. "There's something we need to do so that you are more immersed in the experience with less distractions from the world beyond Cardinal Crest Estate. I'm going to need your devices."

"Our devices?!" three of the four said in unison.

"Yes. I'd like you to be here, present in the moment, you could say." With no way to call for help, she thought, "I'll set out a basket for you to deposit them in."

"I'm not sure about that," Jim said.

"Oh come on, Jim," Doug said, garnering a surprising look from the others in the room. "It's only a few days. I always love the chance to disconnect. Part of the reason I love to hunt and fish. Get away from technology and back to nature."

Doug's unexpected response delighted Renee. She prepared herself to combat any pushback regarding their separation from their phones, but Doug's challenge to Jim made all her preparation unnecessary.

"Few days, huh?" Jim asked. He leaned back on the sofa and finished off the bourbon in his glass. "Frank, I'm going to need a refill, especially before I tell those two upstairs. This should be fun." He stood up. "Ann, you're not out of this either. Come on." He held his hand out to her and helped her off the couch.

"I'll leave you be," Renee said. "I have a lot of work to catch up on before dinner in a few hours. The basket will be out here by then. Enjoy the happy hour."

Renee left the den and walked back to her master suite. Back in the bedroom, that soft whisper jumped back into her head. Her real name was whispered in her ear. Between that and the image of the shadow in the mirror, she felt the cold chill run down her spine again.

SEVEN

O ne by one the members of each family brought their cell phones and tablets down and dropped them into the large wicker basket Dr. Stiller placed at the foot of the stairs. Jake and Carly came down first. Since most of their days were spent without them anyway, they didn't put up much of an argument. On the other hand, Lauren and Chandler fought every step of the way. The pleading and begging lasted the entire way down.

"Mom, I have to have my phone. What if something important happens? What if Craig breaks up with Amy this weekend, and it's my only chance ever to message him before someone else does?"

Finally, Jim dropped his cell phone in, making him the last person to do so. He didn't argue but drug out the process.

With the last of the electronic devices deposited, Joseph Jacobs grabbed the basket and took it into Renee's bed-room. Chandler, sitting on the upstairs landing, watched his beloved iPad disappear underneath the staircase. At eight, his parents hadn't given him his own cell phone yet (Lauren didn't get hers until she was fourteen), but he at least could play Roblox with his friends. Now that the large guy with the black hair and goatee took them away, Chandler needed something else to keep him occupied.

He hopped off the ground and marched to Lauren's room. Without knocking, he opened the door.

"Out," she demanded.

"I'm bored and all you're doing is laying on the bed," he said, hopping off the floor and landing his butt on the foot of her bed.

"You don't think I'm bored, too? It was bad enough that we had to be stuck here for a weekend, but this has to violate the Geneva Convention." Lauren rolled from her back to her stomach and buried her face in her pillow.

"Want to go explore with me?"

"Hell no. Go ask one of those other kids."

"Lauren, please? And I'm telling that you said hell."

"No, and you just did too. Now go away."

"Fine." Chandler slid off the foot of her bed and left her room.

Standing in the hallway, he looked toward the Miller family's rooms. The end of the hallway was a dead end. Just a solid wall. No window to allow light to stream in. With so much wood everywhere, the hallway already came across as overly dark, but Chandler thought the whole thing was caked in a shadow at that moment. He glanced to his right and saw a portrait of a man. He eased his foot back and took a small step backwards. The eyes followed him. He'd heard scary stories about hallways of pictures where the eyes follow the passersby. He'd been to Disney World and braved the Haunted Mansion. Those eyes did follow him, but he knew they were perfectly designed by the Disney Imagineers.

On second thought, bored in his room sounded better than haunted in a hallway. He needed to move as he felt all their eyes train in his direction.

"Lauren?" he called out.

"Go away, Fungus," she said still lying on her bed.

He started down the hallway, keeping his eyes forward and ignoring his peripheral vision. The eyes may have been following him, but as long as he didn't look, there was no proof—plausible deniability.

He sped up when he reached the opening that led to the first-floor foyer. Sunlight flooded through the windows, and the chandelier sent darts of light all throughout. Once he reached the other side of the hallway, though, the light was behind him, and he was left with eyes that had adjusted to the brightness.

The hallway was even darker now.

A few steps further, he was at the first door. He knocked on the one in the same position as his room. After a few moments, the door opened. The girl about Chandler's age stood there with a puzzled look on her face.

As fast as he could, Chandler blurted out, "Hi, I'm Chandler. I'm really bored. What's your name?"

"I'm Carly, and I'm also bored." She stuck her hand out. "Pleasure to meet you, Chandler."

"They took my iPad away," Chandler said while shaking Carly's hand. "I got tired of just sitting in my room staring at the wall."

"Same. How'd you like to go exploring?" Carly asked. With her long brown hair pulled back into a ponytail, the excitement of an adventure filled her face.

"Exploring?" Chandler looked down the hallway where the pictures waited. The pictures that he knew stared at him.

"My mom said she and your mom did some exploring when they were here. It'll be fun. Don't tell me you're chicken."

Even at his young age, Chandler felt his manhood being questioned. "Exploring sounds fun," he finally forced himself to say.

Carly reached down next to her door and picked up her sneakers in one hand. Stepping into the hallway, she closed the door behind her and shot diagonally across the hall. She knocked twice and then opened the door.

Chandler stepped back into the light of the foyer while Carly darted around.

"Dad," Carly said. "Me and..." She looked back his direction.

"Chandler," he said.

"Chandler and I are going exploring."

"Don't go too far," her dad said from beyond the door. "I think dinner is in about an hour."

She turned and hollered, "We won't," as the door shut. Carly ran past Chandler, shoes still in her hand, and speed stepped down the stairs. At the bottom, she paused by the door to slip her shoes on her feet. In a flash, she opened the front door and raced outside.

Chandler took the stairs a little slower, glad not to be among pictures that stared at him. At the first floor, he sprinted outside and leaped off the porch onto the gravel road. A few paces more, he stood in an open field, relishing the setting sun on his face and the slight breeze keeping the temperature down. Apart from playing baseball, which for him meant standing in right field waiting for someone to hit it that far, he'd rarely seen this much open space.

As Chandler made it to the field, Carly reached the top of the first hill. She moved fast. He took a deep breath and tried to catch up to her, but she dropped behind the hill and out of sight before he was halfway up.

"Hurry up," she shouted. "I want to get all the way to the trees." Her voice had a rhythmic bounce to it.

"The...trees?" Chandler tried to shout through gasps of air.

He topped the hill and saw she was almost to the tree line. Knowing there was no way he would make it that far, he flopped on the ground, facing the house. From this vantage point, he had a great view of the property. A small pond sat on his right. If Carly had run a few hundred yards to her left, she'd have run into it. It looked to be a great place to go swimming tomorrow. He hadn't had a chance to get in a pool yet this year so at least there was that to look forward to.

Cardinal Crest Estate and the small barn that sat behind it were the only buildings he saw. Everything else was just shades of green apart from the white gravel driveway they drove up. Even the main road was out of sight thanks to the rolling hills. The trees extended back as far as he could see.

Leaning back on his hands and looking at the house, something in the upper left window caught his eye. Using the windows, Chandler counted the floors. The big ones were on the first floor. Just above those were the windows for bedrooms. This tiny window sat just above those. A third floor? Maybe a hidden attic?

"What are you doing?" Carly made it back and sat down beside him.

"Do you see something in that window?" He pointed to the house.

She squinted at the house. "Your pointing doesn't help. Which one?"

"The tiny one at the top. Got a round top on it and a square bottom. I think there's a third floor."

"Oh yeah." She placed her hands on her brow. "I don't see anything. Why? What did you see?"

"It looked like a girl our age wearing a blue dress."

Carly peered hard at the house. "Nothing. Sun must be playing tricks on you. That happened to me when my dad took Jake and me deer hunting. They didn't let me shoot, so I just sat there staring out of the stand. As the sun came up, I swore there was a deer, a huge one that was like a twenty-point buck. Dad said once you stare into the woods long enough, all the branches start looking like deer. The sun can do that."

"I guess so," he said, doubtfully.

"Maybe Frank is keeping someone tied up in the attic. Or it's like that movie where the people live in the walls. Want to go check the attic?"

"No," Chandler said. He didn't care how much of his budding manhood would be insulted; he wasn't going up there. "Let's go back. Dinner must be soon, and I'm starving."

EIGHT

The dining room table sat twelve. It was a massive table that reminded Kathryn of ones in the movies. The exaggeratively long ones where the wife sat on one end and the husband on the other, and a servant brought food back and forth between them.

The Walkers took four seats on one end, and the Millers took four on the other. Dr. Stiller sat in the middle.

Frank and Joseph served dinner. Conversation was non-existent apart from the occasional "Pass the salt" or "Mr. Jacobs, can I have a refill?"

As dessert came out, both Kat and Ann tossed their napkins on their plates and called it quits. Jim and Doug threw in the towel not long after. Lauren couldn't finish her dessert, and Jake and Carly tapped out after their plates were spotless. Kathryn saw Chandler debating another slice of cake after licking his plate clean, but following a stern look from Ann, he finally leaned back in his chair and rubbed his overly full stomach.

"That was delicious!" Doug Miller said. "I haven't eaten that well in ages."

"Oh really?" Kat said, turning to him. She patted his rotund belly. "I don't feed you enough?"

"I didn't say that, Dear. Obviously, I love your cooking."

Kat shook her head. She turned to the rest of the table, saw the smiles, and heard the giggles.

"The fireplace in the den is lit," Renee said. "There are plenty of chairs for everyone."

Ann glanced around at James, Lauren, and Chandler. "Sounds great."

"Can we turn the lights down and tell ghost stories?" Carly asked.

Hearing Carly ask that brought a smile to Kathryn's face. She remembered her dad taking her camping. They'd sit around the campfire at night. The tree cover obscured the stars or the moon.

Dad loved to go into the woods as far as it would take them. Nothing but the two of them in the deep dark forest. Sometimes her uncle John came along, but never her mother. Camping wasn't her thing.

When the flames died down to embers, her dad would sit across from her. The shadows would play tricks with her eyes. Shadow branches had extended like fingers reaching out to grab her. Occasionally a light breeze would brush fine strands of her hair across her neck. Her dad, blanketed in darkness, would tell her about the man with the hook hand or La Llorona who searched for her missing children and could still be heard moaning at night. "Mark Higgins," her mom would say, "why do you scare that girl?"

"Carly," Kat said. "We'll have to see if everyone else likes ghost stories first."

"Sounds like fun," Ann said from the far end of the table. She pushed her chair back and stood up.

Chandler was quick to follow, but Lauren gave a definite eye roll. Kat thought back to their conversation earlier about raising teenagers, especially teenage girls. Lauren gave the impression that she was going through the motions. A sixteen-year-old without her phone, isolated on a weekend trip with her family and strangers, and during the summer no less. Kat could only imagine what better options awaited her at home. If it was anything like her at sixteen, then she assumed it included the movies, driving around aimlessly, and of course, boys. Hopefully, Lauren didn't give her parents as many fits as she gave hers. That brought a smile to Kat's face. Oh, to be young again.

"Well, I'll leave you to your evening tales," Dr. Stiller said, sitting at the table. She turned to Ann who'd already made it into the den. "Ann, we will start your first session here in the house tomorrow morning. I'll see you shortly after breakfast."

Ann Walker walked back into the dining room and stood at the end of the table. She rested her arms on the back of a chair. "I had my reservations when you first brought this up. Then, when I saw that Kathryn and her family were here, I was ready to leave. But now..." Ann walked to the middle of the table where Renee still sat, leaned over, and wrapped her arms around her. "Thank you, Dr. Stiller. I can already tell this is going to help me."

"Those are the words every therapist wants to hear." She patted Ann on the back.

Ann raised up and wiped her wet eyes.

"After breakfast. My office."

"Yes, Ma'am," Ann said and joined the others in the den, leaving Dr. Stiller at the table while Mr. Malone and Mr. Jacobs cleared the dishes.

"What did I miss?" Ann asked, sitting down next to Jim on the leather couch. Lauren sat in a chair next to the couch, and Chandler sat on the floor at his parents' feet. The coffee table sat almost eye level in front of him.

Across from Chandler, Carly sat on the ground. Kathryn and Doug Miller took up the love seat again while Jake sat on the edge of the fireplace. Kat noticed him steal a few shy glances at Lauren. Of course, he would. He was fourteen, and she was a very pretty sixteen. No wonder he'd been so quiet lately. He usually talked a lot more. Not more than Carly, but not many people did. If that girl could get paid for talking, she'd be a billionaire.

The only light in the room was the fireplace.

"Mom's about to tell a scary story," Carly said. The excitement in her voice bled through.

"Sounds great," Ann said. "Give us a good scare."

Kat looked around. The flames from the fireplace cast dancing shadows on the wall. The faces in front of her were partly obscured. Each person had a dark half, the other half illuminated by the glow from the only light source in the room. What wasn't shadowed was blanketed in deep oranges and yellows. The off-white, almost smoke-colored walls absorbed the essence of the hue. The room emanated a dark sickness.

Kat felt a tingle crawl up her spine and goosebumps erupt across her arms. All eyes were on her. And not just the ones she could see. Sitting on the couch next to her husband, she would've sworn she was on a stage with a thousand pairs of eyes burrowing in to her.

Get a grip, Kat.

She took a deep breath, willing a story to pop into her head. She leaned forward stretching her neck out. Her head sat nearly over Carly. Her motion drew everyone else to lean in as well. She had their attention.

"I have a tale to tell, but it isn't your typical campfire story. This one happens in a large plantation style home. But not just any plantation style home. This one. Cardinal Crest Estate."

Chandler's eyes were glued to her. Lauren's face gave an expression like she knew this was bullshit. Of course, she'd say it was here. They weren't in the woods. If they were, the story would take place in the woods. Kat mainly watched the four children. Channeling her dad, she focused on entertaining them. If the adults enjoyed it, that was just bonus. She couldn't quite see Carly's expression since Kat hovered just above her, but Jake's interest was piqued.

"Right here?" Chandler asked with a slight quiver in his voice.

"Oh yes. Right here at Cardinal Crest Estate." She could tell the setting, the ambiance, the whole setup already gripped Chandler. Her dad would have had him up all night, scared of every sound the woods made. And they made a lot.

He turned his head and glanced at his parents behind him.

Jim leaned forward and rubbed the hair on Chandler's head. "It's just a story, Chandler. Nothing's going to jump out and grab you. Isn't that right?" He looked up at Kathryn and smiled.

With his face shadowed, she couldn't tell if he wanted her to continue or try to dial it back. She decided to continue.

"Well, this story was told to me by the old caretaker of Cardinal Crest Estate. His name was Bill Monroe. Very nice guy. Your typical grandpa with a knack for spinning a yarn. Do you remember him, Ann? Every time I saw him, he wore those flannel shirts."

Kat paused. She wasn't sure if Ann would respond or not but gave her the opportunity. The way Dr. Stiller talked about Ann's memory issue, this trip down memory lane might open some forgotten locked door.

Just as she was about to speak, Ann finally said, "Yeah, I remember seeing him around a few times. The flannel shirts. Smelled like pipe tobacco."

"That was him. So one day, I'm not sure where you were," Kat said and gestured to Ann. "Maybe out on the hill with your imaginary friend?"

"I didn't have..." Ann started then darted her eyes around. She had the attention now, and it was obvious she didn't appreciate the weight of the stares directed her way. She seemed to shrink back into her seat physically. "So what did Mr. Monroe tell you?"

"I was walking upstairs in the hallway. I'm sure you've seen the pictures lining the walls. Well, I paced back and forth in front of them. The eyes followed me. You gotta remember I was like twelve. Mr. Monroe saw what I was doing and sat me down on the top of the stairs.

"'The eyes following you?' he asked." Kat dropped the tone of her voice and added a gruff to it.

"I nodded my head. 'Why do they do that?' I asked him.

"'Well, you could say this house always has guests here.'" Each time Kat switched to imitating Bill, she imitated his voice.

"'Busy all year round?' I asked.

"He laughed a deep, barreling laugh that echoed off the foyer. 'No, I mean this house is haunted.'

"'You're just trying to scare me. My dad does the same thing when we go camping. Ghosts aren't real.' I started to get up from the stairs, but then he told me to be patient for a second.

"'I guarantee you they're real. I see them. All the time. I can even tell you about one if you want to hear it.'"

Kat paused her story, taking a breath. She reached to the coffee table in front of Carly and grabbed her glass. Taking a drink, she kept everyone's eyes trained on her. She held them captivated.

"Of course, I wanted to hear the ghost story," she continued. "So, I sat back down, and he started to talk." Kathryn stayed in her normal voice. "'Back in 1932, a family took care of this place. A man, Clarence, and his wife and their little girl. They were poor, but that was ok. They took care of this house, and so they had a roof over their head and enough food, which was a lot better than what other families had at that time. The Great Depression hit a lot of families hard.

"'Well, one day, their daughter played in the fields. She went a few hills over where there's a pond. Not much fish in it, but it's a fun swim on a summer day. Well, a few hours went by, and their daughter hadn't come back from playing. When supper time started and she still wasn't there, Clarence and... Dorothy...Dorothy was the wife's name... well, they started to panic. They didn't know which way she went. They looked through the house, then through the barn. It was already dark out, close to midnight, when they made it to the pond. They found her floating on the top as blue as her dress. Poor thing drowned. Supposedly she was a good swimmer too. Swam in that pond a hundred times. No one knows what happened.'"

"The little girl died?!" Chandler half-asked and half-exclaimed.

"No way," Lauren and Jake said almost simultaneously.

Kat was so enthralled by her own story that she didn't even notice she'd captured the teenagers' attention. Their siblings had been squirming for a while, but she took special pride that she won them over, too. She saw Ann shaking her head. Ann was bleach white, as if all the blood had left her body. Even with the orange embers of the fire on her face, the paleness showed through.

"Oh yes. In the pond just over the hill. Mr. Monroe told me that around midnight you can hear a wailing through the house. Clarence and Dorothy are calling out for her. Do you want to know what's even worse?"

Heads nodded from all four children. Ann's head shook back and forth. Kathryn could sense something was wrong, but she was too enticed by the kids' excitement. She pushed on.

"He told me they had her funeral a few days later. The funeral was here at the house. The casket stayed here in the den just against that back wall behind me. That's how they did things back then. No funeral homes. People came to pay their respects, but Clarence and Dorothy didn't seem worried. They said their little girl was still here with them. They talked to her. Even a few of the guests said they saw the little Jenkins girl spinning in circles on the hill. And you know why? Ghosts that die here are trapped here. This place has a curse on it, and the spirits can't leave.

"And the last thing he told me as I sat on the top of those stairs...

"'It didn't end with her death, you see. It's not natural that the daughter you bury still visits and talks to you. As you can imagine, something like that can play with your mind. One morning, about a month after the funeral, the owners invited some guests to stay for the weekend. When they opened the front door for the guests, both Clarence and Dorothy Jenkins were swinging from their necks in the foyer. Hung themselves right in the entryway.'"

"Nope," Lauren said. "No, thank you. Is it too late to get a hotel that people didn't kill themselves in?"

"I'm right there with you," Jake said.

"What was the little girl's name?" Chandler said. Something sat behind his eyes that Kat couldn't see. "Did Mr. Monroe tell you what she looked like?"

Ann finally leaned forward and stood up. "Chandler, it's all make-believe anyway. It doesn't matter. It's late, though. Been a long day. We need to get to bed."

Her face was still bleached white. She fidgeted with her fingers as if she had a nervous tick, and her arms looked tight as a drum.

Kat decided to press Ann a bit. "It's not make-believe. You don't remember, do you?"

"Remember what?" Ann snapped back.

"You saw the ghost when we were here. You told me that."

"I told you I saw a ghost?"

"No," Kat said. Her posture changed. She straightened her back and raised her head up. "You told me you met a little girl in an old timey blue dress. Little blonde hair girl."

"I remember her. We played out in the field a few times. She said her dad worked in the house."

"Ann, there wasn't another kid here that weekend. Bill was the only person who lived in the house. There wasn't anyone else. You and I, My Dear. We were the only kids here."

Ann shook her head furiously. Her hair flew to both sides, slapping her face with each movement. "You're wrong. She was real. Jim, I'm heading to bed. Goodnight, Everyone."

Ann turned and took one hard stomp toward the staircase when Kat raised her voice one last time. "Betsy," she said. "The girl who drowned. Her name was Betsy Jenkins."

Ann sprinted up the stairs. Within a few seconds, the door slammed shut, sending echoes throughout the house.

NINE

G ina Delfina crawled under the quilt of the king size bed in her master suite. She sunk into the pillow top mattress, feeling the smoothness of the bedsheet against her skin, before adjusting the pillow and pushing herself up. She gave a slight wince from the stinging chill of the headboard when her back rested against it. The quilt fell to her waist. She grabbed the book she'd placed on the nightstand. *The Art of Hypnosis.*

While researching, she heard raised voices from the den. Gina had heard Kathryn start the ghost story before coming into her room. She could only assume Ann didn't like something about it. Ann getting upset was good, though. Gina needed them to stay here this weekend, but she didn't really need them to get along. Just being cordial to each other was fine.

Loud footsteps echoed above her. The stomps landed hard enough to send reverberations cascading throughout. Someone was pissed. Probably Ann. Ann was so high maintenance that Gina almost felt sorry for Jim. Almost. She smiled, and then suddenly, the door slammed shut. She continued to listen for any more commotion in the den but didn't hear anything. Some murmurs was all.

If Ann stormed off, Jim was probably saying some niceties to smooth things over. He seemed like he preferred conflict avoidance and would want to ease tensions. He was a pushover. I guess he had to be to stay married to her.

From what Gina knew of Kathryn, though, she was more of a fighter. She'd have to keep her eye on the Miller family.

With the noise from outside her bedroom gone, she went back to her book. This shit was so boring. She couldn't wait to be done with the charades. Done with all of them. Only a few more days for the cat to play with the mice.

She rubbed her eyes as the words on the page blurred together. After reading the same sentence a dozen times, she figured it was time to go to sleep. It'd been a long day, and tomorrow she was going to be busy. New things needed to be put in motion. Schedules needed to be kept.

Gina placed the book back on the nightstand and pulled the chain on the lamp. Darkness drenched the room. She slid her back down the headboard and laid her head on the soft pillow. She closed her eyes and let her body relax.

As sleep began to take her, she drifted into thoughts from her childhood. They didn't have it easy, but her dad took care of them. He did what he needed to do to make sure they had food on the table.

"Gigi."

The whispering in her head made her smile. She knew she was dreaming. How else could she be hearing her dad's voice?

"Join us."

The dream wanted her to come with him. *I will, Daddy. Have an errand to finish.*

She rolled over in bed, facing the window. Rays of moonlight drifted into the room. For a moment, her eyes opened. Before they could focus, a shadow standing in the middle of the room dissolved into nothingness. Her eyes closed, and she drifted back off into the abyss of sleep.

"Love you, Daddy," she uttered in her sleep through deep dream-filled breaths.

TEN

Pacing the bedroom floor, Ann couldn't believe how insensitive and flat-out hurtful Kathryn had been. With everything else she was going through, the panic attacks, the anxiety, barely remembering her childhood, why would Kathryn say that one of the few things Ann did remember was Ann playing with a ghost? How ridiculous! Was Kathryn trying to make her feel crazier? Trying to push her over the edge?

"Oh Ann, you remember that friend you had, the one you were spinning out in the field with, yeah, she was a ghost. Or she was imaginary, and you were crazy even back then. Of course, you'd be crazy now. You were a nut case as a kid. Obviously."

By the time, Jim came in the room, she'd worked herself up into a slight rage. Her hands were balled together so tightly that her knuckles turned white. Her shoulders had tightened up so much she'd thought they'd snap.

"What took you so long?" she snapped at Jim.

"Just telling the kids goodnight." He walked to the dresser and started to undress.

"Did everyone get a good laugh at my expense?" Heat rose up the side of her head. She knew her ears were blazing red.

"No one was laughing. She didn't mean any harm. She was telling a scary story about the house." Jim finished taking his clothes off and pulled out a pair of basketball shorts to wear to bed. He quickly slid those on.

Ann tried to process what he was saying but everything in her brain that dealt with logic was on vacation. Captain Anger had taken over, and he drove full steam ahead. Meant no harm in it? Then why did Kat single her out? Why did she call out Betsy by name? What a bitch!

"Some ghost story," Ann finally said. "It won't surprise me if Chandler is up all night. You know he doesn't do well with scary things."

"He said he was ok, and he knows where our room is. Told him to come straight over if he needs to. I can get up with him."

"Yeah, I'm sure." The pacing continued. She kept trying to breathe through the anger, the hurt, the embarrassment.

Jim crawled into bed without commenting on her remark. She wished he would've, so she had more reason to snap. She needed the release.

"Ann, come to bed before you wear a hole in that rug."

"I doubt I'll be able to sleep. I just...I can't believe her." Ann sat down on the edge of the bed, almost in tears.

"Do you want to try one of those pills Dr. Stiller gave you to help relax?"

Ann thought about it for a moment. "I'm going to have to. I'll never be able to shut my head off if I don't."

She stood up and walked to her side of bed. Pill bottles spread across the nightstand, different ones for different symptoms. She was so tired of fighting symptoms. At least being here addressed the root cause. If she could rip the issue out at the root, then there would be no more symptoms.

Ann grabbed the bottle she was looking for and shook out two pills. She walked to the bathroom, popped them into her mouth, turned on the sink water, and used it to wash the pills down her dry throat.

As she picked her head up, she looked in the mirror. She barely recognized the person staring back at her. The past few months had been such a weight on all their shoulders. Her eyes looked sunken and worn out. At a certain angle, the light made gray hairs appear on her head almost by magic.

Who are you?

She flicked off the bathroom light and walked to the dresser. She pulled out a nightgown and quickly changed. Ready to let the pills take effect, she slid into bed and turned off the light on the nightstand next to her.

Jim said goodnight and gave her a kiss. She reciprocated and rolled over, staring at the closed hallway door. Feeling the soft, cold pillow against her head, she prayed sleep would find her soon and closed her eyes.

As Ann fell further and deeper into sleep thanks to the pills, dreamlike images sparked behind her eyes.

Sitting on the front porch in the rocking chair, young Annabelle watched Kat's dad, Kat's uncle, and her walk to the pond. They carried fishing poles, a tackle box, and a cooler. Annabelle hoped they weren't trying to catch lunch or dinner. She didn't like fish. It tasted too fishy. She smiled at the thought of fish tasting too fishy.

"Psshhh," came a sound from around the house.

Annabelle turned her head and saw Betsy trying to get her attention. She stood on the front porch in the same blue dress that was a little big on her. *I'll see if she wants one of my dresses,* she thought.

As soon as Betsy locked eyes with Annabelle, she took off around the house.

Annabelle jumped off the wooden rocking chair and ran after her. She turned the corner of the house, but Betsy wasn't there. Annabelle jogged a little further but didn't see her anywhere. Betsy must be playing hide-and-seek. That wouldn't be fair. She lived here, so she knew all the good places.

She almost stumbled into a door with her eyes darting back and forth, looking for the blue dress. It wasn't up high, though. The door was on the ground and led down. She walked around the front of it and peered down. The cellar. Betsy was down there hiding. She just knew it. Why else would it be open?

She bent down in her green dress, her knees on the ground, and placed her hands on the edge of the cellar. She leaned her head in, trying to see into the dark.

"Annabelle?" her mother called. "Get off the ground in your dress and stay out of there."

She looked up and saw her mother marching in her direction. Brushing off her knees, she met her mother on the porch. "I was playing with the little girl."

"I think she went fishing with her dad and uncle. Come inside and help me."

The two of them walked back around the house, and her mother opened the door. The dream image stuttered and skipped. Everyone stood in the den. Annabelle heard a gunshot, and her dad fell to the ground, cradling her mother's head. "Mommy!" she screamed. "Mom-"

Eleven

"**M**ommy," Ann sat bolt upright in bed.

She was drenched; her pillow was cold and soaking wet. She tried to reach for her phone to check the time but remembered that Dr. Stiller took their phones away. Immersed in being here and not the outside world, the doctor had said. Instead, her eyes scanned the room for a clock and finally found a digital one in the corner.

Her chin dropped to her chest in disappointment. "Two fucking thirty a.m." she said.

Flipping the pillow over, she placed her head back down. This side wasn't as bad. She stared up at the ceiling and listened to Jim snore next to her. That man could sleep through anything.

Aside from her husband's breathing and croaking, only silence filled the air. Hopefully Jim's rhythmic noises could lull her back to sleep. Probably would have, except there was another sound, barely audible. Ann was certain it wasn't coming from their room. It almost sounded like a whimper.

"Chandler," she whispered to herself.

The scary story must've gotten to him. She sat up and looked over at Jim. *You'll get up with him, huh?* She swung her feet off the bed and stood up.

Thankfully, her eyes had adjusted enough that she could avoid any obstacles. She continued to hear the light whimper as she maneuvered to the closet and grabbed a robe to throw on over her nightgown. After a few more steps, she reached the door.

As she opened it, the whimpering stopped. Ann stood in the hallway as still as possible. She hadn't made a noise so doubted she'd woken Chandler up. Maybe the bad dream ended.

Just in case, she decided to stand there a bit longer. Last thing she needed was to be almost back asleep and then get woken right back up again. Tomorrow was going to be rough enough. Her first session with Dr. Stiller in this house. She didn't want to include restless sleep along with it.

Suddenly, all the way down the hall to her right, she heard another sound. This one was different. This was the laugh of a little girl—a high-pitched giggle from the darkness at the end of the hall.

There wasn't enough light for even her dark-adjusted eyes to see that far. She heard it again. A girl's laugh.

"Hello?" she whispered down the hall.

Ann stepped further into the hallway and pulled the door closed behind her. She took a few steps in the direction of the sound.

"Hello?" she asked again softly.

The childish giggle happened again.

Ann walked past Chandler's room. Then Lauren's. She could almost see the end of the empty hallway. The sound had to be coming from somewhere. Someone had to be up and playing at this late hour.

"Who's there?"

At the end of the hallway, she heard the laugh move. It grew louder as if the sound ran straight at her, then quieted again, but now came from the other side of the hallway.

Where did they go?

The laughter had gone right past her, but no one was there. She knew about the Doppler Effect. She'd stood at enough train tracks to hear what it sounded like. This sounded the same.

She shot her eyes from one side to the other. Just her in the hallway. No one else.

Slowly, she walked back to her room. As she passed Lauren's room, she eased the door open. Lauren laid on her bed, dead asleep. She pulled the door shut and moved to Chandler's room. Easing it open as well, she saw him sprawled across the bed, snoring just like his father.

A noise echoed down the hallway again, this time from downstairs. Frantic footsteps scurried across the hardwood floor. *The culprit*, she thought.

Ann rushed to the edge of the stairs and stared over the edge of the railing, hoping to catch a glimpse of the secretive child racing through the house at almost three in the morning.

Peering over the banister, she waited. Nothing yet. Just the silence of the house.

The chandelier swayed a few feet in front of her. She could see the den and the dining room. No lights were on. Just a few rays of moonlight drifted in through the windows.

After a few minutes, Ann gave up. Hopefully, the kid went back to bed, wherever that was, and stopped running down the hallway. Using her arms, she tried to push herself away from the banister but couldn't move. She felt pressure against her back, forcing her the opposite way, pinning her chest into the railing. Ann felt panic swarm her. She pushed harder against the railing, but the harder she pressed the more she felt her chest being crushed.

The top rail started to bend beneath the pressure. Her head went into overdrive. She saw the top banister splintering, spilling her body onto the first floor. She doubted the impact would kill her, but she'd be in a lot of pain.

Ann tried to yell for help, but the air had been forced out of her lungs. She gave one final push with her arms, hoping the railing wouldn't give out, and she thrust her body away from the edge. The pressure was gone as quickly as it had started.

Her heart racing and gasping for air, she stood in shock and terror. Her head shot from one side to the other. Still, no one else was there.

"Go to bed," a voice whispered to her. "You're sleepwalking and still dreaming."

Ann spun in a circle, sending her head in a daze. She knew she heard a voice. She knew that voice.

"Annabelle, you're sleepwalking and still dreaming. Go back to bed."

"The pills," Ann said out loud. "The pills are making me hallucinate."

With her equilibrium off, she grasped for the door to her and Jim's room and opened it. She used the doorknob and the door frame to maintain her balance, stepped into the room, and closed the door behind her. She leaned her back against the door and slid down to the floor, hoping the feeling of something solid would help her regain her sense.

It had to be the pills, she reminded herself. She had two of them not that long ago. She'd probably woken up before they had a chance to wear off. Muscle relaxers. Sleep aides. Only God knew what kind of tricks her already fractured mind could play on her with those added to the mix.

The spinning sensation began to slow. Ann placed her hand on top of the nightstand and eased herself off the floor. Briefly, her head started back up again, but she grounded her feet. *Fuck those pills,* she thought.

She adjusted the sheet on the bed so she could easily slide in without disturbing Jim. She froze when he shuffled on his side of the bed, catching her breath in her throat. If she woke him up, he'd ask why *she* was up and that wasn't a conversation she wanted to have right then.

Jim, facing away from her on his side, stretched his head from one side to the other, working a kink out in his sleep. They'd slept in enough hotels that Ann knew the discomfort of unfamiliar pillows. Some hotels had great pillows and made her feel like her head rested on a cloud. With others, her head dropped down to the mattress as if the pillow didn't exist. The great hotel pillow crap shoot.

Ann slowly relaxed again as sleep Jim finished working out the crick in his next. Then, with a sudden movement, he flipped over in the bed, bouncing from one shoulder to the other, asleep but facing her now. Ann looked at him and shoved her fist in her mouth to stifle a scream. It wasn't Jim's face lying on the bed. Well, it was, but his face was gray and bloated. She saw tendrils of moss gripping his head. Water oozed from his mouth. His eyes shot open. The sockets were empty. A vacant stare pierced her. Dirty, putrid water flowed from the sockets like tears.

Biting hard on her fist, she closed her eyes so tightly, she thought they'd never open again. Every muscle in her body, every ounce of energy she had went to keeping her from screaming.

It's just the pills. It's just the pills. It's just the pills.

Over and over again she repeated that. After a millennium, she painstakingly forced her eyelids to open. She slowly saw the bed but was obscured by her own eyelashes. As she opened her eyes more, Jim, Actual Jim, lay sleeping peacefully in bed, still snoring in his rhythmic pattern that typically lulled her to sleep.

The bathroom sat just in front of her. Ann quickly walked to it, closing the door before turning on the light. The brightness burned her eyes. She winced at the sudden illumination, giving time for her pupils to dilate back down. Her hands found the sink, and she rested there. She let the coolness of the porcelain calm her, ground her out of her anxiety.

Able to see again, she saw a small trail of blood from her hand flowing into the drain. Bite marks potted her skin on both sides of her index finger knuckle, deep enough to break the skin.

Turning on the water, she rinsed off her hands with soap and dried them before seating herself on the toilet and grabbing toilet paper to press against the small mark. Ann rocked back and forth on the toilet, holding her hand.

It's just the pills. It's just the pills. It's just the pills.

The mantra continued as she rocked. This hadn't happened before. She'd never hallucinated before. This new environment was meant to unlock whatever was hiding in her brain. No way this could've been the solution. Phantom sounds and voices, the image of Jim's dead and bloated face, and what the fuck forced her against the railing? If this was the solution to her panic attacks, she feared the cure might kill her. She'd have plenty to talk with Dr. Stiller about in the morning. Hopefully, Renee didn't just ship her immediately off to the loony bin.

After a few dabs of the toilet paper, the bleeding stopped. She tossed it into the toilet and flushed, not worrying about it waking up Jim. The man could sleep through anything.

Ann turned off the light and hesitated a moment. Everything was now pitch black. She eased open the bathroom door. The moonlight coming in through the large window illuminated the foot of the bed.

Out of the corner of her eye, she saw her shadowed reflection in the bathroom mirror. Just briefly, she thought she saw another shadow moving behind her. She shook it off and walked to the head of the bed. Ann slid into her side, wrapped the blanket around her, and curled into her husband's sleeping form. Jim instinctively wrapped an arm around her as they drifted off to sleep.

PART THREE

SHADOWS FROM THE PAST

ONE

With a cup of coffee cradled between her hands, Ann stood in the living room of Cardinal Crest Estate and stared out the window. She heard everyone else either in the dining room or the den, but the living room sat empty. More importantly, it was quiet. The silence allowed her to churn away on the thoughts rambling around in her head. She watched the first rays of sunlight reflect off the morning dew that blanketed the ground. The barn sat across the gravel parking lot, and she noticed the main barn doors were shut, but a smaller door on the second floor swung back and forth in the wind. Ann guessed that was probably a loft, not a second floor.

A dense fog obscured the memory she had of the events from the previous night. Fragments of certain images snapped into her head, but the rest hid itself behind grayness. Laughter. She remembered laughter echoing down the hallway. Was there a child running through the house?

Also, something happened against the railing, but maybe that was a dream?

Ann cursed the pills that Renee gave her. She wanted less fog in her head, not more. The whole purpose of this trip, this experience, was to clear out the junk drawer. Uncover the memories of what happened to her mother so she could process the death of her father better. All of that so the flood of anxiety around others would stop. So that she stopped freaking out at Chandler's baseball games. So, she could get out of the car to watch Lauren play soccer.

She hated her brain right now. Hated the mess that lived there. She wished she could just crack her skull open, untangle the spaghetti of thoughts bouncing around, and magically put everything back together again in its rightful place.

If wishes were horses, beggars would ride. She shook her head. An old proverb she could remember. But the weekend that her mother was killed in front of her? That was a fragmented mess.

The left large barn door started to creak open. It edged further and further out, exposing the inside of the barn. Ann guessed the wind was traveling from the open door at the top and escaping the large one at the bottom. Probably wasn't latched right.

She sipped her coffee, enjoying the bitter aroma and hazelnut flavoring. Warmth emanated from the cup and felt good against her hands. The caffeine rush would help in a few minutes when she talked to Renee.

From the corner of her eye, she saw someone walk from Cardinal Crest Estate toward the barn. Looking, she couldn't tell if it was Joe, Frank, or someone else heading out to close the barn door. The person's gait had a certain familiarity to it, though.

When she saw the flannel shirt, it hit her. Instead of the smell of her hazelnut coffee, the smell of pipe tobacco wafted across her nose as if a memory floated on top of a breeze. It was Mr. Monroe. Bill. A smile lit her face as he marched his way to the barn.

"Holy shit," she said into her coffee. Ann couldn't believe he still worked here after all these years. She turned away from the window and looked over the living room. The furniture was a close match to the den. She guessed when the owners shopped for furniture, they just bought two of everything to decorate both rooms. She saw the coffee table in front of the couch and placed her mug, still half full of coffee, on it.

She glanced out the window once more and saw Bill walking toward the barn. Ann hurried to the den, keeping her eye trained on Bill as she did. When she moved into the den, for a brief second, she couldn't see him. The entry way between the two rooms blocked her view. She veered outward just slightly to angle for the front door.

After a few quick steps in the den, the barn and gravel drive became visible through the right window. Ann stopped in her tracks. She felt her heart grind to a halt and knew her eyes betrayed her. Bill wasn't alone as he walked to the barn. A skinny blonde girl in a blue dress that was just a little big on her skipped circles around him.

Ann couldn't breathe. Her chest felt like a constrictor crushed the air out of her. Her brain cried out for reasoning. Was she going mad? Were the memories of the past stacking on top of the present like a double exposure picture?

The logic center of her brain told her that what she was seeing wasn't possible. Betsy would be in her late thirties or early forties by now, just like her and Kathryn. Anxiety brain told her she was cracking. This was the end of it. Loony bin, room for one please.

Maybe Betsy had a daughter, and that daughter could be the spitting image of Betsy at that age. The thought exploded into her head, and she latched on to it like a drowning person with a life preserver. Her dad used to say that Lauren reminded him of Ann. That she looked just like her. Betsy's daughter looks like her mother.

The little girl (*Betsy's daughter*) turned her face to the house, staring through the window and straight at Ann. She smiled from ear to ear. Shivers ran down Ann's back. Every hair stood up on her neck as an energy charge coursed through her body.

Searching for some rationale to hold on to, Ann turned for the front door, took a few bounding steps, threw it open, and sprinted around the side of the house. As she made the turn, she saw the barn, heard the loft door banging against the front of the barn, and stared at the empty gravel area between the house and the barn.

No one was there.

No Bill Monroe.

No Betsy Jenkins or her daughter or whoever the fuck it was.

Both large barn doors were shut. The only sounds were the echoes from the loft door slamming into the barn and the wind whistling around the house.

Ann looked back and forth, searching for where they went. Her hands shot to the top of her head and clasped together behind her neck like a runner gasping for air. Tears welled up in her eyes. The logic and reasoning side of her head threw up its arms in defeat.

She was cracking, and she knew it.

I'm insane.

Two

"I know it's above my pay grade, but haven't we been doing this long enough?" Joe Jacobs asked. He stood just inside the door of Gina's room as she dabbed the final touches of makeup to her face in the bathroom.

She had known the question would eventually arise. She should've expected it from him. Joe had a little more brain than Frank. Although, that meant he also should be smart enough to know not to question her.

"Joe," she said as she applied the last stroke of her lipstick. She blotted her lips with a napkin, removing the excess red. "You're absolutely right. It is above your pay grade."

Gina walked out of the bathroom and straightened her blouse. As much as she hoped the conversation would end there, it didn't.

"I get it. Revenge is a dish best served cold and shit like that, but is this whole game necessary? Why not just slit their throats like the old guy?"

"Because I want them to know why it's happening." Frustration with his questions started to show in her voice. "I want to see the realization in her eyes, and since right now, she barely fucking remembers what happened, I can't do that."

She didn't worry about him not doing what she said. He'd kill for her without any question; done it multiple times. Joe enjoyed it. If he didn't work for her, she had no doubt he'd be a mercenary for some government. His square jaw and broad shoulders carrying a machine gun with a stack of dead bodies behind him would look great as a black and white photo on the cover of Time.

Gina started to heat up thinking about him but told herself to stop. Strong killers with guns. She shook the thought away. She was the boss.

"Any more questions above your pay grade? Because that crazy bitch should be in here any minute." Gina needed him to leave. She needed time to get the illicit thoughts out of her head before focusing on Mrs. Walker.

"No, Boss." He opened her door and started down the hallway.

She adjusted the covers on her bed and hid the hypnosis book. Best to not let Ann realize Gina must have just learned about it. Dr. Renee Stiller didn't need to learn about hypnosis. One of her degrees probably meant she could make someone cluck like a chicken at a county fair or think they were naked. Who the hell knows.

"Doctor?"

Joe called for her from the end of the hallway. He stood by the den, almost at the front door. She trained them well enough to know when to call her Boss, Gina, or Ms. Delfina, and when to call her Dr. Stiller. Frank and Joe. Loyal killers.

"Yes, Mr. Jacobs."

"You might want to come see this."

Gina placed her hands on her hips, closed her eyes, and took a deep breath before marching out of her master suite and down the hall. She glanced at the picture on the wall to her right. Some of them gave her the creeps. The eyes seemed to always watch her.

Joe pointed into the den when she made it next to him, but then realized he was actually pointing past the den, through the window, to the skinny blonde crying outside. Ann looked ridiculous with her hands behind her neck and elbows stretched out to the side of her head. She was bent over at the waist. Gina would have thought she was stretching out her hamstrings. Her trainer called these Good Mornings. Appropriate. Except she didn't think the goal was to cry like a baby while doing it.

Gina turned to Joe and motioned for him to bring his ear close. "Go get her. Be nice. Help her into my office. This should be fucking interesting."

THREE

"So, Ann," Renee said. "I had a few things I wanted to try today, but first, why don't you tell me what happened outside?"

Renee sat by her desk with a notepad in her lap and a pen in her right hand.

Ann sat on the windowsill, staring into the field behind the house. The sun bathed her in light. A box of tissues lay in front of her, along with a pile of them already soiled with snot and tears.

Renee thought Ann looked small and weak. It would be easy to grant Joe's request, come up behind her, and drive her pen into Ann's throat. She let her imagination take hold, feeling the pen as it pressed against Ann's scrawny neck. There would be a slight depression as the skin first bent beneath the pen's ball point. She'd add more pressure so the skin could no longer stretch and had no choice but to separate. The puncture would quickly expand around the shaft of the pen as it descended deeper into Ann's neck, ripping a tear into her jugular and gouging her windpipe. Renee would get to hear Ann suffocate, drown in her own blood. Ann would cough some of it out of her mouth causing a fine, red mist to fill the air. It'd look beautiful in the morning sunlight.

She realized Ann hadn't responded while she was busy fantasizing.

"Ann?" she repeated, a little more forcefully. "What happened this morning?"

Her gaze stayed on the green field and rolling hills. When she spoke, it was as if she talked to herself, completely unaware of Renee.

"I know I'm crazy. That's the only explanation. Only thing it could be. This was too much for my mind to handle. It took one day. One day and I snapped."

"Ann, look at me."

Ann pulled out another tissue, blew her nose again, and shook her head.

"Annabelle Walker!" Renee didn't think she'd ever used Ann's full first name like that before. It did the trick, though. No wonder moms used it.

Ann's head snapped around so fast, Renee was shocked it didn't spin off her neck. "I'm sorry, Dr. Stiller. You were saying something?"

"Start with last night. I heard there were some hurt feelings before you went to bed."

"That was just Kat telling a ghost story. I thought she was making fun of me, and so I reacted. In hindsight, I reacted poorly."

Renee remembered the yelling and the door slamming. Poorly was putting it mildly. More like Ann threw a temper tantrum.

"Before bed, I took a few of the sleeping pills you gave me to relax. In the middle of the night, I think I woke up, or I may have been dreaming. I heard a child's laughter, a little girl's laugh. She was running through the house. Then, I think it was my mother's voice, telling me to go back to bed. Is that crazy?"

Yes! You are fucking crazy!!!

"Not at all. How we think is a very complicated thing. You have old memories that are trying to find their place again amongst the reality that you know. Your dream could've been a memory figuring out where it goes. Maybe as a child, you were here playing and laughing. You could've been the little girl you heard before your mother told you to go to bed. This is the opposite of crazy. This is healing."

Renee impressed even herself. She didn't know where she came up with such bullshit, but there it was. A gift, really. She was Queen Bullshitter.

Ann fidgeted with her hands, processing what Renee said. Renee noticed a small mark on Ann's hand between two of her knuckles that had recently scabbed over. It looked almost like a bite mark.

"I wanted to try something new today, but first, I need to know that you can relax. Do you think you can do that, Ann?"

Ann dabbed her eyes, drying up the last of the tears that hung in them. She first nodded hesitantly, then quicker as if she convinced herself she could.

Renee stood up from the chair and reached a hand to Ann.

Ann took it and let Renee lead her to the bed. "Lie down. You're going to close your eyes and take deep, full breaths. I'm going to try hypnosis. With these memories fresh in your head, I'd like to see what else we can unlock. If at any point, it seems like things are too much, I'll pull you out. You trust me, don't you, Ann?"

Ann sat on the edge of the bed. "I wouldn't be here if I didn't."

She eased herself onto the pillow, rolled onto her back, closed her eyes, and began taking deep breaths.

FOUR

Annabelle, wearing pink shorts with her favorite rainbow T-shirt, one of the few articles of clothing her mother let her bring that she thought was comfortable, very carefully placed one foot down on the hardwood floor, followed by the next. Her bedroom in this huge vacation house sat one door down from her parents.

From her room, she heard raised voices, but couldn't make out what they said. Just that mother wasn't happy with something daddy had done. They didn't fight a lot, but when they did, it could get loud. The walls muffled most of the argument, but Annabelle was nosy and wanted to know what was going on.

The second-floor hallway liked to moan and groan as she walked on it, so she had to be careful how she stepped. Easy does it. Tip. Toe. Tip. Toe. Light as a feather.

When she reached the door of her parents' room, she leaned in, getting her ear as close as she could without making a sound. If they heard her, they'd shoo her away and make her go play. Annabelle didn't want to do that, though. She hadn't seen Betsy around, and Kat would rather go fishing with her dad and uncle. Fishing was gross and boring. The bait was slimy, and she was never allowed to talk.

She closed her eyes and listened.

"I'm not sure how long we have to be here," Thomas Adams said.

"It's that bad?" Elizabeth asked.

"This could be a huge shit storm. The press is going to have a field day. Once the investigation finds out, there'll be Senate committee hearings. From there, it all comes down to who says what to whom."

"And running away to this place is supposed to help that?"

Thomas hesitated. "According to my campaign chair, the less my name and the more Carlisi's name is in the paper, the better. So, yes, I think coming here to get as far away from D.C. and the press as possible is going to help."

Annabelle had heard the name Carlisi in the news a few times. Salvatore Carlisi was some kind of mob boss. The television called him "A Modern-Day Godfather". His name was always followed by words such as racketeering, money laundry, and organized crime.

"Why, Thomas? Why would you ever get involved with him?" Elizabeth's voice cracked as if on the verge of tears or ready to start screaming again. Or both.

"In hindsight, I probably didn't need to."

"In hindsight?!"

Elizabeth's voice rose to a higher pitch. Annabelle did everything in her power to avoid that kind of reaction from her mother. Her dad really was in trouble.

"Thomas, that man kills people who get in his way. What happens if he sees you as a liability? Do you think being a Senator puts you beyond his reach? I'd say you can't be that stupid, but yet you did business with Carlisi."

Annabelle's eyes went wide. He's killed people. And her dad worked for him?

She suddenly felt eyes watching her in the hallway. She looked up and down a few times but didn't see anyone. The end of the hallway was dark, but she thought she would be able to make out if someone stood there. Even still, the feeling persisted. The hairs on the back of her neck stood straight up. She leaned her head against the door, pressing her left ear hard against it. She closed her eyes tight so she could concentrate.

"We're safe here. Brian's with us. It's secluded enough that we'll know if anyone is coming. He did a sweep when we first arrived..."

Someone cleared their throat directly into Annabelle's right ear. Her head bounced off the door as she jumped. She felt her heart rate skyrocket, and her heart nearly pounded out of her chest. She lost her footing and slipped onto her butt. A slight scream escaped her before she clamped her hands over her mouth.

Brian Hayes, the family security detail, stood next to her laughing. He laughed so hard, he doubled over and let out a snort.

"That wasn't funny," Annabelle finally said after finding her breath again.

The door shot open from behind her. Her dad looked at Brian and then at Annabelle sitting on the floor. Elizabeth Adams leaned over his shoulder to peer into the hallway.

"Did we miss something?" Thomas asked.

"Just a little birdie in the hallway," Brian said, still laughing.

Annabelle felt her face turn hot red. Her butt hurt and her pulse stayed high.

"Annabelle Adams," her mother said. "What have you been doing?"

Brian continued to laugh, and her dad started to chuckle as well.

Disgusted with the situation, Annabelle said, "Nothing, Mother." She hopped off the ground, dusted off her butt, and fast-stepped down the staircase. She thought about going outside but saw Kat and her dad heading up the front steps. She turned the corner to the dining room and decided to go out the back door instead.

Just before they went out of view, she saw Brian talking to her parents upstairs in the hallway. Of course he'd be telling them how she listened to their conversation. Her dad would probably say he'd handle it and have a talk with her. He'd sit her down and talk to her like she was five instead of almost eleven. And at practically eleven, she understood so much more than she had then. She wished they'd talk to her like the teenager she almost was.

She stormed through the dining room, fuming at herself, at Brian, at her dad, at her mom, and at that Salvatore guy. She found herself not wanting to be in this stupid house anymore. She wanted to be back in her own house and able to play with her own friends.

From the dining room, she stepped into the kitchen. The sound of sizzling and steam filled the air. The delicious aroma of tonight's dinner slowed Annabelle. No reason to rush through here. Her mouth immediately started to water accompanied by a loud rumble from her stomach.

Two men worked in the kitchen. One stood over the stove, and the other against the counter chopping vegetables. Broccoli and carrots from what she saw. They both wore clean white aprons. She never understood why chefs would wear white aprons. They would show everything. Although, that may be the reason they did.

Sneaking behind the two cooks, Annabelle nodded, thinking she was probably right. *See. Not thinking like a five-year-old.*

The back door was shut and sat just beyond the pantry. She moved just passed the two men when she saw an open door to her left. At first, she thought it was another food closet, but when she looked closer, it descended under the house.

A cellar! She found somewhere new to explore. Her feet still in the kitchen, she stared down into the cellar.

A light bulb hung on the end of a long electrical cable. As a breeze blew over Annabelle's shoulder, the bulb rocked a foot or two back and forth, casting its light on one side, then shifting to the other. When the light wasn't directly pointed somewhere, the rest of the cellar lay in darkness. Boxes sat on shelves stacked against one earthen wall. A few other shelves contained jars and canned goods. The rest of the cellar extended beyond what she could see.

As she placed one small foot on the first step, the light bulb began to flash. An electrical hiss joined the flashes. Annabelle reached up on either side of her, hoping for a light switch. She found one and flicked it off and then on again. The light flickered a few times, then stayed on. She went down one more step when something scurried across the dirt floor and ran under a shelf loaded down with glass jars.

Seeing the rodent made her pause. It was a good thing, too. The light bulb gave one more flash before she heard a single pop. Everything went dark.

She debated continuing down. The light from the kitchen probably made its way to some of the cellar. It couldn't really be pitch black down there. Or could it? Maybe just a few more steps.

She brought her foot down one more step when she first heard a voice, floating up to reach her ears.

"Annabelle," the whisper said. "Come down here. Come play."

"Hello?" she asked. "Betsy, is that you?"

"It's fun in the dark. Come here and play. Don't be scared."

Annabelle peered hard into the dark cellar. She begged her eyes to adjust to the darkness. She couldn't see anyone down there. It was as if the shadows were the ones whispering to her. The sound had come from everywhere and nowhere.

"Where are you?" Annabelle asked. "I can't see you."

Her foot hesitated above the next step.

In the darkness, she thought she saw a face, then another, then another. She couldn't make out what the faces looked like. Barely an outline with two eyes, a nose, and a mouth. The faces floated off in the distance close to the boxes. Shadows obscured their bodies, assuming there were bodies.

Of course, there are bodies. Heads don't float by themselves.

A tingle ran up her spine. She had a sudden desire to step back into the light, run out the back door, and stand in the safety of the sunlight. Sunlight felt safe. Nothing bad could ever get her in the sunlight.

Her foot reached behind her and felt the step. She eased herself back up. She brought her other foot up and found the edge of the step. As she leaned herself back, her foot slipped, and she started to lose her balance. She knew she was going to fall and land face first onto the dirt floor. The floating faces would pounce on her, devour her. She didn't know why she knew that, but she did. Too many scary movies. That's what always happened. The unlucky person fell giving the monsters enough time to catch up and...

A hand grabbed her arm. She yelped in fright and instinctively tried to jerk away. Her head shot around, searching for whoever grabbed her.

One of the kitchen staff, the guy who'd been cutting vegetables, held her arm.

She couldn't breathe. Every breath seemed like it wasn't enough. She'd heard the term hyperventilate before and guessed this was what it felt like. Fear burned in her eyes. Every muscle in her body wanted to run as fast as possible. She'd also heard about fight or flight response. Nothing told her to fight. Everything screamed flight.

"That's nowhere for you to play," he said. "I've got a daughter your age. I know you'll just end up breaking something."

Annabelle barely heard him. The pulsing of her heart and a ringing in her ears drowned out everything else. Finally, her legs unlocked. She hit the kitchen floor with her feet and sprinted for the back door, leaving the cooks staring at her as she bolted into the saving sunlight.

FIVE

L auren finished her waffles and orange juice. Breakfast wasn't typically her thing, but her stomach demanded that she eat something. The sweet aroma of Frank's waffles filled the dining room. She felt like a cartoon character floating on the scent with only her nose leading the way.

Not even twenty-four hours at Cardinal Crest and she was ready to leave. Not having her phone made it practically unbearable. The ghost story was the only highlight. She had serious doubts anything remotely approaching excitement would happen on this little getaway.

As she polished off the last of the juice, she thought about her mother storming upstairs at the end of the story. So maybe the story wasn't the only highlight.

Lauren had begged her dad to let her stay home. This was mom's trip. She needed to get her head on straight. Why did the rest of them need to go? She even volunteered to watch Chandler over the weekend if that would make him more comfortable. She wasn't going to throw a party or get into trouble. She just didn't want to make the drive. Finding out she'd lose her phone ushered a whole new round of protests.

She was trying not to resent her mother, but it was getting more and more difficult. When she freaked out at Chandler's baseball game, Lauren did everything she could not to die of embarrassment. She was glad her mom stayed in the car for her soccer games. Lauren knew any more side-eyed looks from her friends or their parents and she would be the one losing it.

As Lauren made her way back upstairs, she saw her mother bolt out of the house through the front door; her eyes locked on the windows facing the barn. Lauren took a few steps down to look on the off chance that something of interest was happening. A small door on the top of the barn swayed in the wind. *Well, that's something to rush out and see.*

She saw her mother run around the house and stop in the gravel before doubling over. Lauren shook her head. Deep down she hated herself for how she treated her mother. One day she'd apologize when she grew up more, she assured herself. Lauren found comfort in the thought they'd all look back on this time of their life and laugh, assuming her mother recovered and didn't end up in the nut house.

Back up the stairs and in her room, Lauren flopped on the soft bed and stared at the ceiling. The bed, the pillow that felt like a cloud, and the super soft comforter. Those were the real highlights from this trip. She barely remembered falling asleep last night. Her head hit the pillow, she wrapped into a cocoon, and sleep came immediately.

Now, while lying on the bed, a brief feeling of Deja vu brushed over her. A small memory from last night, or maybe a dream, popped into her head.

Was someone laughing down the hall in the middle of the night?

Small goosebumps trickled down her arm, and Lauren felt a cold draft sweep through her room. A tingle ran down her spine. She gave a full body shake to make it go away.

Suddenly, her door burst open, and she shot upright on the bed.

"Oh good, Lauren, you're here," Chandler said. He ran to her and bounced on her bed.

"Out!" She pointed to the door and quickly stood up. "And don't you knock? I'm going to tell."

"Dad told me to come get you." Chandler sat on his knees on her bed and continued to bounce up and down.

"That's wonderful," she said. Sarcasm oozed from her words. "However, I'm sure he didn't say," she dropped her voice a little deeper, "'Chandler, go barge into your sister's room and bounce on her bed.'"

"Those were his words exactly," he smarted back.

She rolled her eyes. After a very long pause and a deep sigh, she marched past her bed with Chandler still oscillating up and down, went into the hallway, and banged on her parents' room.

She had no doubt that her dad sent Chandler to get her. He probably even gave Chandler the message, but she didn't want to hear it from him. Any message Chandler gave her usually had some slant in his favor. What should have been just "Dad wants you to do the dishes" would have Chandler add in "and sweep the kitchen floor and dry everything by hand." Little brothers were assholes.

James opened the door. "Oh good. Guessing Chandler delivered the message?"

"He came barging into my..."

"Yeah, I told him to. I talked with Doug a bit ago. Jake and Carly are going to the pond. Chandler wants to go, but I told him not without you."

"But dad..." Lauren began her objection. She couldn't think of anything she wanted to do less than hang out at the pond with her little brother and two country bumpkins. Plus, she'd already noticed Jake checking her out a few times. Sure, he had a boyish cuteness to him, but she had no desire to have anything to do with anyone here. The sooner she could forget this place, the better. Unfortunately, her objection didn't get any further.

"No buts. This is what you are doing. Grab your bathing suit. If you let yourself, you may be surprised how much fun you can have."

With an audible sign followed by a frustrated grunt, she turned away from his door and stomped back to her room. Chandler no longer bounced on her bed but sat on his knees bent over with his hands on her bed. A grin extended from ear to ear across his face.

"Well?" he asked.

"Get out of my room. I'll be downstairs in ten minutes ...under protest." She hollered the last of it, hopefully loud enough for her dad to hear her.

Six

S till dazed and feeling like she just woke up from a long sleep, Ann walked up the large oak stairs. Her head swam with the unlocked memories. She debated on what confused her more. The conversation between her mother and father or the faces in the cellar? Her father, a respected Virginia Senator, had mixed himself up with a notorious organized crime boss? They visited Cardinal Crest to escape the press.

None of that sounded like the parents she remembered. The press adored her father. She used to have a shoe box of newspaper clippings about all the good things he did. He passed bills to help fight crime and put people like Salvatore Carlisi in prison.

From above her, Ann heard the pounding of footsteps on the staircase. Her eyes rose, and she saw the four children quickly descending.

"Bye, mom," Chandler said. "Heading to the pond. Dad knows already."

"Have fun, and be careful," she responded instinctively.

Excitedly, Chandler led the way to the pond. With her shoulders slumped, Lauren took up the rear and walked as if her feet trudged through quicksand. The first three sped around Ann, threw open the front door, and hopped off the porch. Ann faced the top of the stairs and continued her own mindless march. The front door slammed shut behind her as Lauren finally stepped outside.

The faces, though. Ann wished she had made them out more. It had to be people down there in the dark. Other kids playing? Maybe Betsy had other siblings?

Ann reached the second floor and shook her head. She could feel herself heading straight towards crazy town. She was afraid to learn anything else. Everything she uncovered only added to her instability.

Was her mind cracking? Only a few months ago, she was a normal - assuming that's a thing - woman with two children and a loving husband. A soccer and baseball mom that brought the snacks when it was their turn. Could someone go from sane to insane in such a short time?

She opened the door to her room and found Jim dressed in khaki shorts and a polo, ready to play a round of golf. Instead, he laid on top of the blankets reading a book. Ann walked to the bed and lay next to him.

"How was your session?" he asked without taking his eyes off the page.

"It was..." she started then hesitated. She didn't know how to explain it. So many thoughts and memories made an unfinished puzzle inside her head. "I really don't know how to explain it. Learned some new things today, but now I have so many more questions."

Jim placed his bookmark between the pages and closed the book, setting it on the nightstand. "Progress is good, Honey. On the road to healing." He turned toward her, placed his arm on her side, and gave her a kiss on the forehead.

Ann curled closer into him, burying her face in his shirt. "I keep hoping so, but it doesn't feel that way. Feels like I'm falling deeper and deeper into a well." She stopped for a moment and took a deep breath. She refused to start crying and leave a mark on his shirt. A thought occurred to her. She sat up on her elbow. "Did you know my father had business dealings with Salvatore Carlisi?"

"The mob guy? That doesn't sound like him. Where'd you hear that?

"I recovered memory from the last time we were here. I heard my parents arguing about it."

Jim rolled onto his back. "Your dad was one of those tough-on-crime politicians. Maybe he donated some money to your dad's campaign or some PAC trying to get in his good graces."

Ann lowered herself onto the pillow. "Maybe you're right."

"On a different note, I got a chance to chat with Doug while we ate breakfast. Interesting guy."

As he talked, Ann pieced together the memory again. She thought about the argument her parents had before being spotted by Mr. Hayes. She tried to remember the conversation but could only recall snippets.

"They live in this farmhouse on the edge of the woods. It used to be owned by..."

The cellar and the faces resurfaced. The cellar with the boxes in the corner. Old boxes like that usually contained old pictures or documents. If those boxes did have pictures, would they have pictures of Bill or Betsy? If the boxes had pictures of Betsy from before, Ann would know that was at least one thing she hadn't imagined.

"...about five different rifles and a few..."

"I need to go," Ann interrupted.

"Go? Where?"

Excellent question. Hopefully not to the nut house.

"There's something I need to look at." She raised from the bed and swung her feet over the side.

"Want me to go with you?" Jim also raised up.

"No, that's ok. Go back to your book. Relax. The kids are down at the pond, so enjoy the quiet."

"You sure?" he said. He sat on the edge of the bed.

Ann stood up. "I'm sure. I'll be back in a little bit. I'm not going far."

She left the room as Jim grabbed his book and rested back against the headboard.

With a newfound sense of urgency, Ann stepped down the staircase, so quickly that the stairs barely had time to groan.

Ann grabbed the wooden railing when she reached the bottom and spun toward the dining room. As she made the turn, she almost collided with Kathryn.

"In a hurry?" Kat asked.

"Something like that," Ann said.

"Glad to see you're in good spirits at least. I'm sorry about that ghost story last night," Kat started.

"Actually, about that," Ann said interrupting her. "I have something I want to look for. A hunch maybe. Care to join me?"

SEVEN

Why the hell not? Kat thought as Ann grabbed her arm and led her through the dining room. Her initial plans could wait. She'd hoped to grab Doug and sit on the patio swing. Beautiful weather always enticed her outside. Not too much longer before the summer heat and humid days outnumbered the nice ones.

"What are we looking for again?" she asked Ann.

"This place has a cellar, and we are going into it."

Ann's voice told Kat there was no convincing her otherwise. Plus, if Ann was in as bad of shape as that doctor made out, Kat doubted arguing with a crazy person would be a good decision. She concentrated on the feel of the metallic grip of her knife in her boot. *Just in case.*

As soon as they entered the kitchen, Ann released Kat's arm and hurried to the cellar door. Ann pushed on it a few times.

"Here, let me try," Kat said.

Ann moved to her right but stayed close, hovering over Kat's shoulder.

Kathryn stepped up to the white wooden door. The chrome doorknob had splotches of white paint that must've dropped down when someone was in a hurry. Kat gripped the knob and tried to turn it. She placed her shoulder against the door and leaned into it as she turned, hoping to provide more leverage. The door stood steadfast.

"One second," Kat said. She lifted her leg and reached her hand into her boot. She pulled out the knife.

"Always keep a knife in your boot or only on vacations?" Ann asked.

"Something my dad taught me a number of years ago. Never know when a knife is going to come in handy."

With the hilt in her right hand, she flicked the blade out. The flash of silver caught the sunlight streaming through the kitchen windows. Kat loved the shine. She shoved the six-inch blade between the door jam and the door and jimmied it back and forth. She felt the latch bolt against the edge of the blade. As she twisted the doorknob, she kept downward pressure on the knife, working it further and further between the latch bolt and the door jam.

Finally, she felt the knife slip just enough and pushed on the door. An audible sound tore through the air as paint ripped from the door frame. Hinges, long unused, complained under the full weight of the door.

"Holy shit," Ann said. "Great job. Carry a knife all the time. I'll remember that."

Kathryn stopped herself from making a comment about being crazy and carrying a knife.

Ann leaned into the doorway, and both searched the dark abyss. Ann reached her hand along the wall, sliding it down and back up. Kat heard the click of a light switch, but nothing happened.

"What now?" Kathryn asked.

"You wouldn't happen to have a flashlight in your boot, would you?" Ann asked.

"I usually have my phone on me which can be used as a flashlight, but your therapist hijacked it." Kat was certain Ann picked up the displeasure in her tone.

"Wait. I think I saw a flashlight earlier."

Ann disappeared around the corner, leaving Kat standing on the edge of the cellar door. The kitchen was empty. Just her and whatever creepy crawlies lived in the darkness. By the pungent smell of ammonia, she was sure as shit that a creature or two lived down there. Or had lived down there.

After a few minutes without Ann's return, Kat decided to sit down on the floor and placed her legs on the rickety steps leading into the cellar. Stretching them out, her feet brushed against the third step. She bounced her legs up and down waiting for Ann's return. She fought her own curiosity about what was down there and decided to wait a few more minutes before abandoning Ann. She placed her hands on the planks of the floor and leaned back.

Chills went up her spine and her skin crawled as a slight cool breeze blew up her pants leg. It felt like hundreds of tiny feet marched up her legs. She shot upright as fast as she could and pulled up her jeans.

Spiders covered her legs. Black, furry spiders. Each one no bigger than a dime. She started swatting at her legs and shaking them furiously. She probably looked like she was seizing but she didn't care. Her only thought was to get the eight-legged freaks off of her as fast as possible.

"Found a flashlight," Ann said. "Kat, what's wrong?" Ann sprinted to Kat still sitting on the floor, slapping her legs.

"Spiders!" she screamed.

"Where?" Ann asked in a panic tone.

Kat kept hitting her legs. "They're right..." She stopped moving. Nothing was there. Her white, tan less calves had red handprints on them, but none of the dime-sized black spiders. She rolled the pants legs back down, placed her hands on the ground, and stood herself up, brushing off her butt as she did.

She knew she had seen spiders on her legs. She'd felt them.

Is crazy contagious?

Ann flicked on the flashlight, and a beam of light shot to the ceiling. The blinding light caused Kathryn's eyes to immediately dilate as Ann passed the beam across her face and down the open cellar door, illuminating the dirt floor. A few spots danced in Kat's vision, but after a few blinks, they disappeared. She really hoped that was normal light spots and not more spiders.

"Ready?" Ann asked.

"Lead the way." Kat motioned with her hand for Ann to go first.

With the light still trained on the cellar floor, Ann took in a deep breath, leaned forward, and took the first step down. She grabbed the small handrail with her right hand and kept the flashlight pointed forward with her left.

Kat trailed behind her. The steps moaned under her feet. The wooden handrail was thin and untreated.

Nothing like grabbing onto a handful of splinters to improve the day.

The banister shook as well. If either one of them started to fall, there was no way it would stop them, Kat was sure of it. It had to only be there to make whoever came down the cellar steps feel better.

Before she reached the bottom, the light moved. At the same time, Ann said, "Over here."

Despite her better judgement, Kat paused on the steps. She didn't want to take a misstep and end up face first in the rat-piss filled dirt. "Before you move that way," she calmly said, "can you shine the light back here?"

"Oh sorry," Ann said.

The light flew around the room and hit Kat in the face again. Any night vision she had developed vanished in an instance. Ann dropped the light to the last few steps, and, after a second, Kat followed them down. Finally, her foot hit the hard packed dirt floor. She was glad she didn't faceplant. The landing wouldn't have been pleasant.

"What'd you find?"

Ann pointed the flashlight to the corner of the room. A stack of old boxes sat on a shelf in the corner. "These," she said. "I remembered seeing this stack of boxes. I want to know what's inside."

"See if there's a history of Cardinal Crest?" The connection to the ghost story dawned on her. "Oh, you want to see if there are pictures of Betsy Jenkins. Are you thinking I was right, and you played with a ghost?"

"I want to see what's inside these boxes," she repeated.

Kat joined her at the shelf. "Well, let's take a look." She pushed her hand into the handhold on the front of the first box, slid it forward, and reached to the back. Kat picked up the box and sat it on the floor. Dust particles danced in the beam of the flashlight, and both ladies started to cough.

"Let's hope...that was...just dirt," Ann coughed out.

Kat grabbed the flashlight out of Ann's hand and shined it around the cellar, looking for something to sit on. The cellar extended under the back half of the house. A few of the support beams split the cellar, Other than that, it was empty. On the far side, a few trickles of light came through. Kat realized there was an exterior entrance to the cellar.

"I'm not sitting in this dirt," Kat said.

"Suit yourself," Ann responded and dropped down on her butt, sitting with her legs crossed in front of the aged box. She flicked the lid off and stirred up another cloud of dust and dirt into the air.

Old documents and photographs filled the box.

Kat dropped to one knee, keeping the flashlight held steady on the box's contents. She grabbed a few pages as Ann grabbed a picture. Kat glanced over the document in her hand. "These are the original plans for the house." She ruffled through a few more of the documents in the box. "These date back at least a hundred years. And look at all of these old pictures and newspaper clippings."

Her curiosity got the better of her, and Kat went from one knee down to her butt. She pulled out picture after picture. Without realizing, she aimed the flashlight on the documents in her hands.

"I'm losing light," Ann said, thumbing through the box.

"Oh, sorry," Kat said. "But come over here and look at this."

Ann slid around, and kat moved to meet her. The two sat shoulder to shoulder and started taking out yellow, age-stained papers and black-and-white photographs.

Most of the old photographs were of the front half of the den. They looked like family portraits of people sitting on the couch. "Who are all these people?" Ann asked.

Kathryn's eyes danced as they moved from paper to paper. She spread the pages out in a grid in front of her and read through them as fast as she could. In the upper right of her grid, she saw something that caught her attention. She grabbed the document and brought it close.

"Take a look at this. I don't think these are family port raits...well, not exactly. These are post-mortems.

"Cardinal Crest Estate was once used as a funeral home." She grabbed another page. "And not just that. During the Spanish flu, it was used as a hospital. Its isolation made it perfect for those who were sick to be quarantined. Unfortunately, it doesn't look like many survived."

Ann flipped through more of the photographs. Kat briefly looked over and saw a corpse in each one. Some showed just the deceased person. Others with the body propped between family members.

After looking at over two dozen photographs, Ann set them on the ground and started to pick up scraps of newspaper clippings. "The investigation continues into the death of..." she hesitated, "...Betsy Jenkins. Although she died from an apparent drowning, her body also showed signs of..." Ann took a deep breath. "...showed signs of physical abuse. Police are still questioning her parents, Clarence and Dorothy Jenkins. Clarence has a history of drunken conduct, and acquaintances say drinking brings out his meanness."

Kat looked over at Ann. Ann held the newspaper clipping in one hand and a photograph in the other. Both hands shook. Kat moved the flashlight closer and saw the photograph was a funeral photo of Betsy Jenkins. Her blonde hair rested perfectly on the pillow in her casket. Her striped, blue dress swallowed her.

Ann began to shake her head violently from side to side. "This can't be true. I saw her."

Ann looked at Kathryn, and Kathryn saw something unnatural behind her eyes. "Did you plant these here? Why would you do this?"

"Ann, I didn't put these here." Kathryn turned to face Ann and grasped her shoulders with both hands, trying to stop the trembling. The flashlight fell from Kat's hand and spun towards the back of the cellar. For a moment, Kat saw shadows move across the wall and then dissolve away. She dismissed her imagination and focused on Ann.

"That door hadn't been opened in ages. We were both there. I had to force it open."

"I saw her. I fucking saw her this morning." Ann started to rock.

Kat didn't know what to do. If this was a movie, she would probably slap Ann's sense back into her. However, this was the real world. She tried to hold her steady, but Ann's rocking moved them both.

"Ann, listen to me. Mr. Monroe told me that ghost story. Told me about Betsy. If you saw her today, then maybe this place really is haunted. Maybe her ghost is floating around here somewhere. You weren't crazy back then. Take that as you not being crazy now."

She hoped what she said got through to Ann. Kat would rather believe in ghosts than have Ann snap right in front of her. She could handle ghosts better. Ghosts seemed easier.

"I've lost it. I'm completely looney tunes..."

"Ann, knock it off." She snapped her fingers in front of Ann's face, but Ann stared into the darkness. The blankness of her eyes matched the hue of the cellar. "Ann..." she said once more before she was interrupted.

Kathryn heard the front door open so violently it hit the wall behind it, followed by Chandler's voice screaming out, "Mom! Help!"

Eight

"Carly! Hold up a second," Jake called out as they shot through the front door and hopped off the porch.

Both Carly and the other kid ran ahead of him. He couldn't remember the kid's name. The needed to wait a minute. They were getting ahead of Lauren. Her name he remembered. Since he had first seen her, he'd struggled with trying to look anywhere else. Jake had even noticed her smile, although she didn't seem to do that a lot. At least not here. He couldn't blame her, though. Jake enjoyed the outdoors, and he'd probably be fine here if he'd packed his bow, or a tent, or something that could occupy him in the middle of nowhere. He felt for anyone who didn't enjoy being in nature.

They'd flown past Lauren's mom as she walked up the staircase. She worried Jake for a couple of reasons. First, although he wasn't sure of the entire story, he knew she had something to do with why they were spending the weekend at Cardinal Crest Estate.

Second, she had seemed unhinged last night after his mom's ghost story. *It was just a story, Lady, calm down.*

Third, her eyes just looked lost and dazed. Like she barely knew where she was most of the time. She came with her own doctor and looked out of it. Surely, she wasn't on some release program from a mental hospital. Jake knew of no less than five horror movies that said why that was a bad idea.

"Chandler. Wait a second," Carly said. "My brother is waiting for your sister."

Carly and Chandler eased up their sprint, giving both Jake, and finally Lauren, time to catch up with them.

Jake, wearing his bathing suit, sandals, and no shirt, looked out across the field. From his vantage point, he couldn't see the pond. He cupped his hands over his eyes like a visor and squinted. "Which direction is the pond?"

Chandler responded, "Once we get to the top of the hill, you can see it." He started walking again next to Carly. "Not too much further."

Jake and Lauren slowly followed behind.

"It's Lauren, right?" Jake asked when a couple of dozen yards separated them from their younger siblings. He typically wasn't a bundle of nerves, but his voice wanted to crack. "I'm Jake."

Lauren glanced over at him, then turned her attention back to Chandler and Carly.

"So, do you think this pond is the one that girl drowned in?" Jake asked her.

"No clue," she said, completely uninterested.

Finally, they reached the summit. From here, Jake could see the pond, the extension of trees, the house behind them. A strong breeze blew their hair. Jake knew what a good storm smelled like. Although only a few clouds hung above, he felt they were in for rain later.

Chandler and Carly were halfway to the pond before Lauren and Jake started down the hill.

"Yeah, me neither," Jake said, not giving up yet. "I'm sure the story was all crap anyway. I doubt there even was a girl."

Lauren shrugged her shoulders.

Finally, they made it to the pond. Carly and Chandler stood on the edge, letting the water lap at their feet. Jake kicked his sandals off and moved next to them, but Lauren stayed further back.

"What's wrong, Sis?" Chandler asked. "Afraid of the cold?"

"Shut up, Pill," she responded. She took off her cover-up, laid her towel on the ground, and sat down. "You swim. I'm working on my tan."

Jake forced himself to look straight ahead. Although Lauren was only two years older, fourteen to sixteen was a huge difference. Jake told himself to keep it cool. They lived hours away from each other. No reason to start planning their lives together.

Carly started into the water, and Chandler followed close behind her. Matching grimaces adorned their faces as they inched their way into the pond.

Jake started to follow them. As the water washed over his feet, up to his ankles, he regretted his decision. However, since he'd already started in, he kept going. When the water touched his back, though, he arched back and quickly sucked in air.

"Hey, Chandler," Carly yelled. The two of them were both submerged up to their chins. "Jake thinks it's cold."

"Carly, I swear," Jake said, trying to sound intimidating.

"Oh, do you?" Carly threatened. With a sharp movement, she sent a spray of water washing over him. Chandler followed suit, whipping his arms back and forth.

The initial cold water sent shivers up Jake's body. But after the first plummets hit him, his body adapted. *Screw it,* he thought and dropped completely under water. He shot up and ran his hands across his face and hair, removing any excess from his eyes.

Carly swam across the pond, diving down and popping her head back up. Jake had always been jealous of her fish-like water affinity. He just knew in a few years she'd be the star on their swim team. She was a natural.

Lauren continued sunbathing at the edge of the pond. Chandler continued to annoy her, and she continued to threaten his life.

Carly, treading water, decided to strike up a conversation. "So...do you guys think this is where that girl died?"

Jake broke out with a laugh.

"What's so funny?" Carly asked.

"That story was crap," Jake said. He glanced over at Lauren who hadn't moved from her towel. Although it was funny that he'd asked Lauren almost that same thing.

"It's not crap," Chandler said. He had stayed closer to the shoreline. He sat on his knees, running his hands through the mud. His head and shoulders stayed above the water. Staring up at Jake, the tentatively added, "I saw her in the attic window at the house."

"Oh yeah," Carly said. She flipped to her back and floated back. "You did say you saw a little girl yesterday. Spooky."

"My sister doesn't believe in any of that stuff. She's too cool to believe in ghosts."

Lauren, still with her head down and eyes closed, said, "Ghosts aren't real, You Little Toad. Now, leave me alone and keep playing in the mud."

"Don't worry, Chandler," Carly said, still on her back. "My brother usually believes in ghosts, too, but since he wants to make out with your sister, he's trying to act cool."

Cheeks flushing, Jake shot a quick glance towards Lauren. When he had assured himself that she hadn't moved, he returned his gaze to Carly. "Liar, that's not true." Using his right arm, he sent a wave of water crashing on top of Carly.

She dove underwater to avoid the wave. Once it past, she went back to treading water. "Which part? That you usually believe in ghosts or that you want to make out with Lauren?"

Out of rage, and a desire to stop Carly from talking, Jake dropped his body into the water and swam as hard as he could towards her. A few strong strokes and he'd crossed into the middle of the pond, but when he picked his head up, he realized that Carly had dashed to the far side of the pond. She really could move like a fish. *Or more like a barracuda.*

Treading water, Jake stayed there pondering the best way to get to her before she could say anything else to embarrass him. Hopefully, Lauren wasn't paying attention. While treading in place, he felt the first sting on his leg.

"Hey!" he shouted out. "Ouch! I think something bit me."

Chandler lifted his head up, and Carly slowly swam back towards him, but made a wide arc assuming it was a ploy.

"Fish biting your ding-a-ling?" Carly laughed.

"No, it..." he started before suddenly feeling something wrap around his foot and drag him under the water.

NINE

"Jake!" Carly screamed. "Jake!"

She hoped he was joking. She suddenly wished this was an attempt to get close to her so he could dunk her underwater for the Lauren comment.

But he still hadn't popped back up.

"Jake!" she screamed again.

Chandler stood up in the mud, and Lauren jumped to her feet. She walked closer to the edge of the pond, staring at the spot where Jake had disappeared.

Suddenly, Jake's head shot out of the water, and his arms thrashed to the side. "Help me!" His head dropped back under the water before briefly emerging again. "Something's pulling..." Below he went again.

Holy shit! she thought. Out of nothing but primal instinct, Carly dove her head underwater and swam in Jake's direction. She didn't care that whatever may be pulling him under could grab her as well. She just knew she had to save him.

She felt vibrations from his thrashing and reached her arms out. Kicking with all her might, her shoulder finally collided with his stomach. She used her momentum to help propel the two of them upward. She didn't get very far before she was pulled backwards.

Something's pulling me down.

She looked down at Jake's leg, thinking maybe he was stuck on a branch. The murkiness of the pond obscured her vision too much to make out exactly what held him, but something was wrapped around his ankle. She thought she saw a hand. It looked green and moss-covered, but only extended about three inches lower than the wrist.

Carly felt another presence around her.

Squeezing her eyes shut, she hoped that her vision would clear enough to get a better look at Jake's leg. As she opened them, she felt another set of arms close around Jake's sternum. Carly turned her head and saw Lauren's face inches from her own. Both girls circled him and kicked with all their might.

All three heads broke the surface of the water, and in unison, they gasped for air. The two girls grabbed Jake under the arms and kicked their feet as hard as they could, pushing themselves to the edge of the pond. Jake still kicked with his foot as if trying to get free.

They drug him onto the shore as he continued to cough up water. Carly looked down at his leg. Scratch marks covered it, and trails of blood encircled his ankle. The blood dripped onto the muddy pond edge and washed into the water.

"We need to get him back to the house," Lauren said.

She grabbed her towel and wrapped it around Jake's leg. He winced when she tied the end in a knot and pulled it tight.

"Oh, come on, Jake," Carly said. She attempted to mask the fear in her voice. "You've had a lot worse than this."

"Let's go, Jake," Lauren said, standing up. She reached her hand out. "Time to stand up and hop back. Chandler, run ahead. Get dad."

Chandler sprinted over the hill.

Carly and Lauren both grabbed an arm and pulled Jake onto his good foot. He turned his head to both girls as they dropped beneath him, resting his arms across their necks.

The trio went slowly. Carly could tell Jake didn't want to put any weight on his foot. He leaned heavily to her side. Every time she glanced down at the towel wrapped around his leg, she imagined whatever that was still gripping it tightly. She tried to convince herself that it must've been the dirty water obscuring a large branch. That's what he was tangled in. No way a severed arm pulled him down. Carly's skin tingled. *So why had she felt another presence?*

They topped the first hill and started down the other side. At the bottom, Jake said, "Can we stop for a second? Set me down."

"You sure?" Lauren asked.

"Yes."

The girls stopped and eased Jake to the ground. He sat down on his butt and stretched his leg out. He extended it and brought it back to him a few times.

"Help me take the towel off," he said.

"Are you feeling any better?" Carly asked.

Lauren knelt and started to untie the knot she had made.

"It's sore and throbbing, but I want to stretch it out."

"What happened?" Lauren asked. She finished untying the knot and began to unwrap the towel from his leg.

"First, something jabbed into my leg. Then it felt like a hand grabbed my leg. Like someone was dragging me down. And as hard as I tried to fight my way back up, I kept getting pulled under. It wasn't until the two of you showed up that it suddenly let go."

Carly's mind shot back to the image of the hand. *Just a branch,* she reminded herself.

With the towel fully unwrapped, the three of them stared at Jake's ankle. The scratch marks dotted his ankle and went a few inches up his calf. Some were in pairs and other in sets of three. A large red whelp encircled his ankle.

Carly reached for Jake's foot. Behind her, she heard movement and yells from just over the hill. Chandler's trip to the house had sent both dads heading their way.

"Do you mind?" she asked.

Jake nodded at her to go ahead.

Carly picked Jake's foot up with one hand. He inhaled sharply but not as bad as before. With her other hand, Carly reached under his leg. She placed his Achilles tendon in the palm of her hand and closed her fingers around his ankle. The red whelp, although not an exact match, closely mirrored her four fingers on one side of his leg and her thumb on the other.

Carly looked up at Lauren who sat there silently, eyes wide. Jake just shook his head back and forth.

"It was a branch," he said. "I got stuck on a branch."

Carly heard herself in his voice. Heard him trying to convince himself.

"Jake. Jake! Are you ok? What happened?" Doug said, breathless from running down the hill.

Both girls stood up and backed away, giving Doug room to squat down next to Jake. A few seconds later, Jim jogged up and joined them.

"What happened?" Doug repeated.

Jake glanced at the two girls.

"I think he got stuck on a branch in the pond," Lauren said. Her tone mirrored Jake's.

TEN

Gina heard the commotion from inside of her office. Somehow, the Miller boy had gotten hurt at the pond. She hoped he didn't need critical medical care. Everyone leaving did not work out for her. She'd have to resort to just plain old murder at that point. No grand scheme. No Gina's Ninth Symphony masterpiece. She was so close. Ann was on the brink of collapsing, and once she did and the killings started, those left would only blame Crazy Ann Walker.

This was too early, though. All she needed was one person to try to start a vehicle. They'd realize something was wrong. St this point, they might figure out the truth. No. It was too soon.

She looked forward to the panic, though. Frank and Joe had already disabled both cars. Nothing around for miles. The mice were trapped in her mouse trap and didn't even know it. Dead mice walking.

Gina Delfina stepped away from the desk in her office where she'd been mindlessly scribbling. She let her mind wander and her hand become its own entity, writing down whatever came to mind. Random memories of her father popped into her head. Memories she hadn't had in many years. She tried not to think about him very often. Ever since his murder, she'd tried to focus on other things. Revenge, for instance. How to survive. What she'd need to do, would need to become, to finally get revenge.

She opened the door to the master suite and stepped into the hallway. At first, the pictures creeped her out. Their tracking eyes unnerved her. But that feeling grew less and less with each minute. Instead of a hundred eyes watching, she began to feel an overwhelming sensation of protection. Like a child wrapped in their father's arms, protecting them from the bad in the world.

As she walked closer to the front door, she glanced through the window and saw Doug Miller carrying his son. His foot was wrapped.

How am I going to keep them here?

She reached for the doorknob when she heard someone behind her.

"Dr. Stiller, I'm glad you're here."

Gina turned around and saw Kathryn coming from the dining room. Her hair was frazzled, and sweat streamed down her face.

"I need your help," Kat said.

"I heard," Gina said. "Something happened to your son."

"No. He's fine. Doug's got him. It's Ann."

Kathryn reached out and placed her hand on Gina's shoulder, redirecting her away from the front door and to the dining room.

"I think she's having some kind of an episode." Kat continued. "We were looking at old pictures in the cellar, and she saw something that disturbed her and...well, you'll just have to see for yourself."

Gina let Kathryn lead her through the dining room and into the kitchen. Kat headed straight for the open cellar door and started down the stairs, but Gina hesitated. She failed to see the bottom until a beam of light shot across the floor. The light spun in circles, but sporadically. It was as if a lighthouse was broken, and the light bounced around.

Easing her head into the door, Gina saw Ann with the flashlight. She followed Kathryn's lead and descended the stairs, cautious not to lose her footing. The railing looked flimsy so she avoided it. Gina kept her eyes trained on Ann and forced back a smile.

The bitch may have snapped.

Ann faced the wall, directing the beam of light. As Gina stepped closer, she heard her mumbling. "I saw you." She spun around and redirected the light. "There you are."

Gina moved towards Ann like she was a wounded, feral animal. The light continued to dance around the room. Ann appeared to be playing a game of Hide and Go Seek with an invisible friend.

"Ann," she said in her best, most calming, therapist tone. "Ann, it's Dr. Stiller."

"Oh, good," Ann said and spun the light directly into Gina's face. "Kat said she can't see them. It'd be great if you could help. They like to hide in the dark. You can almost see them on the edge of the flashlight."

"Who? Who is hiding?" Gina asked very, very soothingly, masking sheer delight.

Gina looked past Ann to Kat. She shrugged her shoulders and shook her head.

"We were looking at old pictures," Kat said. "And we came across some articles talking about a little girl who died here. Her name was Betsy Jenkins. Last night I told a ghost story about her, and Ann claimed she played with her as a kid and even saw her this morning. When she saw the girl's picture, she just flipped out."

"Shhh," Ann said. The light slowly moved across the dirt walls. "Betsy's down here. She wants to play, I can tell."

Gina brought out her cell phone and turned the flashlight on. The look in Ann's eyes was, surprisingly, even more than Gina could've dared to hope for at this point. There was a mixture of vacancy and sanity. Had she snapped? Or did she see something they hadn't?

"Ann," Gina repeated. "Ann, we need you to come back to us."

"I'm alright, Doc, but I'm trying to listen. You've got to stop talking so I can hear her. Betsy said she's nice, but her dad has a temper. She told me that when I was a kid."

Gina glanced over at Kat again. "I'm going to be right back. I have something that'll help. Stay with her."

She turned and ran up the steps of the cellar and back into the kitchen. Frank and Joe stepped into the back door as she emerged. She walked over to them with her finger at her mouth miming "Shhh".

Standing directly in front of the two of them, she said, "After dinner, start getting everything ready. This is starting to move. And fast. In the meantime, check on the Miller boy. Make sure they don't try to leave."

She hurried through the dining room and back into her bedroom. Gina threw open her bag full of medicine and rummaged around, finally finding the one she wanted. She took out a syringe, filled it with the sedative, and placed a cover over the needle. "Don't worry, Daddy. I'm almost done."

Quickly, she raced back through the dining room. Out of the corner of her eye, she saw Frank help Jake to the couch and passed Joe bringing the first aid kit. Gina flicked back on her cell phone flashlight as she went down the cellar steps.

Ann still talked to the shadows but no longer moved side to side as much, as if she'd grown content at just listening to whatever voices she heard.

"Ann," Gina said. "Ann, you're going to feel a little stick, but don't worry. It'll just help you sleep."

Gina turned to Kathryn, still standing guard by Ann to make sure she was safe. "Hold her, please. I'm giving her a sedative so we can get her out of here."

Kathryn moved closer.

Gina rolled up Ann's shirt sleeve, but Ann gave no indication that she noticed. Gina placed the syringe cover between her teeth and clamped down. She pulled the needle free and jabbed it into Ann's upper arm. She depressed the plunger as fast as she could, then pulled the needle out of her arm. She replaced the cover and placed the syringe in her back pocket.

Within moments, Ann started to falter on her feet. She stumbled and would've lost it if not for Kathryn's help. The flashlight dropped and began to spin around on the ground again, moving the shadows ominously across the walls.

"Let's go, Girl," Kat said. She placed Ann's arm around her neck, and they started walking up and out.

Gina walked behind them, unable to contain her glee any longer. Ann's sanity was collapsing like a house of cards.

Eleven

After the excitement of Jake's foot coupled with Ann breaking down, everyone spent the remainder of the day in their own spaces. Jim and Chandler hung out in Lauren's room playing card games. He thought it best to let Ann sleep peacefully in their bed. No one even pondered going downstairs until the dinner bell rang.

The relative silence continued throughout dinner. Occasionally, the four kids glanced at each other. Three of them held on to their secret. Lauren hadn't told Chandler about the mark resembling a hand around Jake's ankle. She didn't trust that he'd keep quiet. When Lauren, Carly, and Jake looked at each other, it was as if they'd committed a crime and were all in on it together. An unspoken gallows' promise between them.

Once dinner ended, Lauren, Jake, Chandler, and Carly sat out on the front porch. Jim assumed they needed fresh air after the day's isolation. He would've loved some as well, but decided to relax in the den. He debated having a glass of wine but strolled over to the bar instead. A bottle of Woodford Reserve sat on the counter, so he grabbed a glass, dropped in a cube of ice from the ice bucket sitting on top of the bar, and poured two fingers worth. After a quick look at the glass, he added a third for good measure.

"Mind pouring me some as well?" Doug asked from behind.

Jim grabbed another glass. "Neat or on the rocks?"

"I'll take mine neat."

Jim poured the bourbon into the glass, turned around, and handed it to him.

"To better days and better nights," Doug said.

"I'll drink to that."

The glasses made an audible clink as they connected.

Jim and Doug walked back to the seats and found chairs to relax in.

"Jake looks like he's getting around better."

Doug took a sip of the Woodford and shot a glance outside. "Yeah. He must've gotten tangled up pretty good in the branches. Shook him up good, too. All the panicking he did caused some nice scratches, but after the hydrogen peroxide and bandages, he'll be fine."

Jim heard footsteps from the stairs and looked up. To his surprise, he saw Ann slowly making her way down with her hand on the wooden railing. Kathryn followed close behind her, helping her down. When the two women made it to the first floor, they turned and joined the gentlemen.

"I forced her to come down," Kat said. "Figured if she kept sleeping, she wouldn't sleep a wink tonight."

"I'm really sorry about earlier," Ann said as she sat down next to Jim. He lifted his arm, and she curled next to him. He gently ran his fingers through her hair, knowing it calmed and relaxed her.

Kathryn interrupted her. "Ann, don't even think about it. There's probably mold or something down there that caused us to see things. I wasn't down there as long as you were, and I saw the shadows move, too. We're just glad to see you up and moving around."

"For sure," Jim said, his fingers coursing their way through her hair.

After a few minutes of silence, Doug took another sip from his glass and asked, "So, Ann, do you remember any more about what happened that night?"

Kat popped him on the shoulder. "Doug, don't be an ass. It's been a rough day."

"I know. I didn't mean to. We're here to help her remember that night, unlock those memories, so she can get better. I haven't minded the free vacation, but I would like to be helpful."

Ann raised her head. "It's ok. I don't mind talking about it. The parts that are fuzzy, Kat can shed some light on."

Jim looked at his wife. He knew her to be headstrong, someone who wouldn't take no for an answer. Since all of this had started, he'd missed that version of her. Seeing her rise and decide to talk gave him hope that they were moving through this. "You sure, honey?" He still felt the need to ask.

She looked at him. Her eyes held a softness that made him melt in his seat. "I'm sure."

Kathryn stood up, walked over to the bar, and grabbed a bottle of water for Ann.

Ann thanked her as she opened the water bottle and took a large drink.

"From what I recall, we were all in this room. My parents sat where we are sitting. I was over by the fireplace. I had on a fancy dress that my mother had made me wear to dinner that night. She always wanted me to dress up. God, I hated wearing those dresses. Brian stood just inside the den against the wall over there." Ann pointed to the wall next to the den's opening. "I think he was talking with your uncle. Right?"

Kathryn nodded.

"You and your parents were over near the bar. I remember they were getting drinks before it started. Then, two guys rushed in with guns. Robbers, I think. There was a fight. Your dad, uncle, Brian, and the two guys. Somewhere in the struggle, a gun went off. I remember hearing the sound and thinking it wasn't anything like the movies. The next thing I know, my mother was on the ground bleeding. Dad was on his knees next to her. Brian and your family, they wrestled down the two robbers."

Ann paused and took another drink. "That's all I remember."

Kathryn started to speak. Jim saw her mouth open, but nothing came out. Her face kept repositioning as if words wanted to come out but the right ones just weren't there. Finally, though, she found them.

"That's not quite right," she finally added.

"What did I miss?"

Kathryn glanced around the room. Jim and Doug both stopped leaning back in their chairs and had shifted their bodies forward, attentively listening to the conversation.

"Well... those two guys weren't robbers. They were hit men. For some big mafia guy. I didn't know it at the time. But a few days after everything happened, I remember seeing pictures of all four that died that night on the television. The reporter talked about them being paid by a mob guy."

"All four? What do you mean? I just remember my mother." Ann's face dropped.

Jim saw the glimmer of that strong woman start to retreat again. She must've been so confident on what she knew that hearing something different put cracks into her foundation.

"Your mom, the two hit men, and Bill Monroe," she added, confused. "The caretaker."

Jim watched the light leave Ann's eyes. Inside, he begged for her to hold on, but he watched it fade. He didn't know what was going on inside of her head, but something seemed to have extinguished whatever flame she had held on to.

From the corner of his eye and through the window, he saw flashes of light. Lightning danced in the distance. With each bright brilliance of light, the storm clouds raced to Cardinal Crest Estate.

TWELVE

All thoughts within Ann's head vacated.

She didn't hear Jim asking if she was alright. She saw his mouth move, but her brain stopped processing words. Nothing but a ringing sound permeated the recesses of her mind.

As the ringing dissipated, it left a roaring silence in its wake. She had no inclination of time or space. She felt crowded but alone, surrounded but isolated in a void all at the same time. Had she been trapped for a minute or an hour?

When her cracked mind finally started to process information, it came in stutters.

No.

That's not right.

That didn't happen.

No.

She's wrong.

No.

This isn't real. That wasn't what happened. I know what happened. I think I know what happened. Do I know what happened?

My mother died. That's it. That's what Dad said. Mom died that night. He wouldn't told me about the others. Why didn't he tell me about the others? Why didn't he tell me the people responsible died that night? Why did he not tell me about that?

Bill Monroe didn't die that night. Not him. I saw him with her. I saw Betsy Jenkins, a girl that died over seventy years ago, drowned, probably as a suicide to escape her abusive father. She danced circles in her blue dress that was a little big on her around Bill Monroe this morning.

Maybe I am losing it or maybe this house keeps its victims. Maybe when you die at Cardinal Crest, you stay at Cardinal Crest. How did that line from Hotel California go? You can check out, but you can never leave. Is this Hotel California? Betsy died here and she's still here. Bill Monroe died here and he's still here. Are Betsy's mom and abusive dad here? What kind of ghosts would they be? What about all those that died here during the Spanish Flu? Are there sick and withered spirits living in the shadows?

Is my mother here?

With that last thought, Ann burst into tears, burying her face into her hands. If her mother was here, would her mother want to see her like this? Would she want her daughter to be this shell? She fought the urge to cycle into anger at herself.

She felt Jim's warm embrace around her, and as if the house could hear her thoughts, another set of arms wrapped kindly around her. A draft from nowhere settled right in front of her.

Ann took in a deep breath, and for an instant, she caught her mother's perfume. Her mother was there, holding her. Her mother was with her.

With a few more sobs and deep breaths, her crying slowed.

"I'm ok," she said. "I'm ok."

In the window outside, she watched the lightning dance across the sky.

THIRTEEN

Lauren, sitting on the porch swing, glanced over her shoulder. She saw her mother walk down the stairs with Kathryn close behind. She watched as her mother joined everyone in the den.

"Are we going to talk about earlier?" Jake asked. He leaned against the porch railing in front of her.

"What's there to talk about?" Lauren said. The tone of her voice sat flat.

Jake looked down at his leg. It was wrapped, covering up the scratch marks, but both knew they were there. He picked up his head, staring directly at Lauren. "The hand print around my ankle."

"Your foot was stuck in a branch. You panicked. That's all."

"I panicked?!" Jake half asked and half yelled. He then lowered his tone. "I didn't panic from being caught in a branch. Something grabbed my leg and jerked me under. You can deny it all you want, Ms. Too-Cool-For-Ghouls, but it happened. That little girl died in the pond, probably from the same...thing that grabbed me. If you and Carly hadn't been there..." his voice trailed off.

Lauren shook her head. She didn't believe what he was saying. She couldn't believe what he was saying. Ghosts weren't real. That was reality. Yes, she had a moment of doubt when Carly wrapped her hand around Jake's ankle. The redness could've passed for a hand print, but in all honesty, none of them had seen what the branch looked like. Maybe it was shaped like a hand. There had to be a more rational explanation than a pond monster drowning unsuspecting victims.

"I think you're being a little dramatic. The branch let go."

"No. *Something* let go," Jake corrected.

The sound of something sliding across gravel broke the silence. Jake turned around, and Lauren looked up. Carly and Chandler ran back and forth in front of the house and around the side of it playing tag.

"You two be careful," Lauren called out. As soon as she did, she recognized her tone. "Damnit. That sounded like my mother."

"Ah, to be young," Jake joked.

"We aren't that much older. Well, you aren't, at least." Lauren wasn't in the mood for humor. She was ready to be done with this entire experience.

"Ouch, that hurt. I didn't realize there was such an age difference between fourteen and sixteen. *Years* of development in the next..." Jake bobbed his finger in the air in front of him, miming counting. "In the next fourteen months. So, tell me, how soon in advance do I need to schedule the appointment to have that stick shoved up my ass that you have?"

Lauren rolled her eyes and shook her head. He was such an immature asshole. "Go play with the kids."

"I have a better idea," he said. He went to the edge of the porch and hopped off. "You coming?"

"Coming where?" After being an ass, he wanted her to follow him in the dark? She didn't think so.

"To the pond."

"I'm not going swimming. It's dark, and the way the wind is blowing, there's a storm coming."

"Yeah, I figured you'd be scared. That's ok. I don't want to go swimming, either. I'd get my bandages all wet.

"You left your cover-up thing on the edge of the pond. It's going to rain. I can already smell it. Let's go get it."

Lauren sat on the swing for a minute thinking. No, she didn't want to go for a walk with him, but yes, she completely forgot about her cover-up after jumping in the water and dragging his ass up and down the hills, and that was her favorite one. Finally, she stood up. "We're grabbing it and coming right back. If you try anything, make a joke, or some random sound to try and scare me, I'm going to kick you in the balls and leave you to your pond monster."

"Duly noted."

Lauren, still internally debating, walked to the edge of the porch and down the steps. Chandler ran towards her, trying to evade Carly's touch.

"Chandler," Lauren said, grabbing his shoulder as he passed. "I forgot my cover-up from earlier. Jake and I are heading to grab it, and we'll be right back. You two hang out here."

"Oooh," Chandler said playfully. "A walk under the full moon. How romantic."

"Ugh, Fungus," Lauren said. She watched as Carly came up behind him with her hand stretched out. "One more thing." she said while holding him in place.

"You're it!" Carly shouted as Lauren released him and both took off running.

Lauren turned back to Jake, and they started moving.

The full moon gave off enough light for them to see their way to the pond. When they topped the first hill, Lauren turned around. The wind had picked up, and within the fast moving clouds, she saw lightning streak across the sky. She tried to ease them along faster, but although Jake was putting up a good front, he still favored his injured foot.

As they started up the next hill, Lauren heard a sound drift through the air. At first she thought it came from the house. She turned, looking for the source, but the next moment, she realized the sound came from the other direction. From the other side of the hill. From the pond.

"Did you hear that?" Jake whispered to her.

"Oh, thank God. You heard it, too." For a moment, Lauren had thought she was imagining it.

"It sounds like someone splashing in the water," Jake said.

"And laughing," Lauren added. "Like...a little girl laughing."

Jake dropped low to the ground, and Lauren followed suit. The sounds of splashing and laughter drove away any concerns about Jake trying to scare her.

The two of them slowly crawled their way up the hill. Lauren felt her bare knees scrape the ground, sure that she'd have a few cuts and grass stains from this venture, but raising up never entered into her mind. Her heart raced listening to the sound of the girl playing in the pond.

It couldn't be Carly and Chandler. They'd left them at the house playing and, after earlier, Lauren was certain

Carly wouldn't be down here by herself. Chandler leaned more on the cautious side of things anyway.

Finally, they reached the top of the hill. Lauren felt herself drawn lower to the ground, her stomach dragging across the dirt. As they reached the little summit, the pond came into view. Although the full moon cast a fair bit of light in the open field, the pond was obscured. A thick, gray fog floated on top of the water, making it impossible to see. The fog didn't stop the splashing and laughing, though. It continued. As Lauren stared through the dense covering, she saw a plume of water shoot up as if someone jumped in. She saw a foot extend above the fog before dropping back inside of it.

Jake, his chest firmly against the ground, scooted slightly closer to Lauren before incredulously whispering, "She's playing where she died?"

Lauren wanted to believe that it was a kid from a neighboring house. A farmhouse close by they hadn't seen yet. That would make sense. A ghost girl swimming in the pond she drowned in? Nope. But there she was.

Lightning flashed across the moonlit sky. Something moved just beyond the pond, but the light faded too fast for Lauren to focus on it. Silence struck her. The lack of splashing sounds and laughter was somehow worse. Now her heart was trying to beat out of her chest, and the only competing sound was their too loud breathing.

Other sounds took their place. Tree limbs cracked and tall grass rubbed against pant legs.

Another flash of lightning. This time Lauren stared across the pond to the tree line some thirty yards back and saw it before the light faded again. When something hit her back, she nearly jumped off the ground and had to stifle a scream.

Jake's hand tapped her shoulder repeatedly while he still looked straight ahead.

"We need to go," Jake said.

"You saw them too?" Lauren asked.

"Fuck yes. How bad do you want that cover-up?"

"They can have it."

The wind picked up again, and the snapping of tree limbs and rustling of grass increased. Another lightning strike across the sky solidified what Lauren had thought she'd seen. Shadows in the trees. Shadows that moved. Moving shadows shaped like people. Silhouettes, dozens of them, underneath the trees. As Lauren's eyes adjusted, the silhouettes didn't fade away. She saw them moving, advancing out of the trees. A single step at a time, the shadow herd drew closer to them.

"Fuck this," Jake said.

He jumped onto his feet in a single bound. Jake gave a slight wince, but stayed up. He reached a hand toward Lauren. Without a glance behind them, they jogged back to the house together. Lauren's entire being screamed at her to full out sprint, but couldn't leave Jake behind, limping on one foot.

As she saw the house, Lauren felt the first drops of rain. A few moments later, she saw her dad on the front porch yelling for them to come in.

Fourteen

C arly tagged Chandler, then ran away, keeping one eye on her brother and Lauren heading towards the pond. She hoped the two of them stayed safe. What happened earlier had shaken Carly to her core. She knew she'd almost lost her brother to the ghost in the pond. Although she had threatened to kill him herself plenty of times, when it came to the reality of almost losing him, she didn't want that to happen. Going back to that place in the dark screamed bad decision.

But Jake was older than her, and she knew that no matter the reason, he was going to do what he wanted. Especially if he was still trying to impress Lauren. Why waste energy trying to stop him?

Chandler reached his arm out to touch her and almost did. While lost in her own thoughts, her legs didn't move quite as fast. She sped up just in time and bolted down the side of the house and to the barn.

"You missed me," she shouted.

Chandler stood by the porch. He rested his hand on the railing, gasping for air. "You sure?" he said between large inhales. "I thought I felt your shirt."

"You felt wind and my dust." She danced from side to side, taunting his lack of speed and endurance.

"Can we play a different game?" Chandler asked. He stood upright and rested his hands above his head, fully opening his lungs to take in as much air as possible.

Carly contemplated the request. They could run around all night, and Chandler would never be able to catch her unless she let him. That would get boring after awhile. As Carly looked around, one eye on Chandler making sure he wasn't faking, she thought about what else they could do. Except for the moonlight and the occasional lightning, it was dark. There was the barn not far behind her and plenty of hills with tall grass. Only one game popped into her mind, and since the only place that scared her was the pond, as long as she stayed away from there, the outside didn't bother her.

"Sure, we can switch. How does hide and go seek sound?"

Even in the low lighting, she saw the expression on Chandler's face. Where she wasn't scared, that same bravery didn't extend to him. She'd grown up watching scary movies. She'd been hunting and camping with her parents.

Nothing truly went bump in the night. All of that was just the imagination running wild. Except that one time when Carly was in a tent and a bear came sniffing around. That time, she didn't need her imagination to run wild. The wild stood a few feet from her, separated only by a very thin fabric.

She took Chandler's hesitation and threw it back in his face. "Oh, come on, Chandler, don't be a chicken. I thought your sister had a brother, not another sister."

Chandler's face garnered the reaction she hoped. "I'm not scared. That sounds like fun. What's home base?"

"Home base is the porch. The pond is off limits. Everything else is fair game."

"The pond is off limits? Now who's a chicken?" Chandler said.

She feared it would come off like that. Her mind raced for a comeback. "I'm not a chicken. I don't want to run into my brother making out with your sister. That's what really scares me."

"Ooh, gross. Agreed then."

"And you're 'it' first," she added.

"Why am I 'it' first?" he asked.

"Because you're 'it' now from tag, and you want to change. So, you're still 'it'. You have to count first. Get on the porch and count to one hundred. Loudly."

At home, Jake bossed her around. It felt good to be on the other side. In a few days, they'd be back home, and she'd be back to being the youngest. For right now, she'd take advantage of it while she could. Why not?

With his shoulders slumped, not a fan of the outcome, Chandler marched over to the stairs. He took each step as if he'd forgotten how and had to figure it out each time. Oh, the drama. When he reached the top, he drug his feet to the porch swing and flopped down. He raised his hands to his head and planted his palms firmly against his eye sockets. "One, two, three..." he shouted.

As loud as Chandler thought he yelled, the wind muffled his count. Carly spun around in circles, seeking out the best place to hide. The barn stood barely twenty feet behind her. Almost as tall as the house, it loomed in the dark. With the wind increasing, loose boards slapped against the side of it. Although it was a an obvious hiding place, she doubted Chandler would dare to venture inside. Even she hesitated to go near it. Yeah, no. The barn was out.

"Twenty-one, twenty-two."

She put her legs in motion and jogged closer to the house, examining the outside for a good place to become invisible. The house needed some bushes or shrubs, she thought. Nothing but gravel and dirt from the barn to the house. This was going to be harder than she thought.

Always the barn, she thought and dismissed the idea again. Probably ghosts and tetanus in there, and she wasn't sure which one was worse. As she thought about, she didn't know which one she'd heard more horror stories about. Her friend told her that their friend stepped on a rusty nail once, and the doctor gave them close to twenty shots. Or maybe it was fifty. She couldn't remember, but it was a bunch.

"Thirty-four, thirty-five. Can I stop counting now? One hundred will take forever."

Carly ran to the front of the house as fast as she could. "No, keep counting. And don't you dare speed up your counting. I haven't found a spot yet."

She could hear his eyes roll in his head. Chandler said, "Ok, but you'd better hurry. Thirty-six, thirty-seven..."

She sprinted back to the side of the house and realized how noisy the gravel was. She slowed down and moved towards the side of the road, trying to be as quiet as a mouse. The gravel wasn't as thick there. The back of the house had to have something.

A gust of wind blew and a lightning strike lit up the sky. A large crack of thunder followed a few seconds behind. She knew the storm grew closer.

She saw something white rise and fall towards the back half of the house. It looked as if it rose from the ground.

After taking a few steps away from the house, she moved forward until she saw it flip up again. She recognized it as a door that just flew open on its hinge. As she got closer, she realized it was a door to a cellar under the house.

"Fifty-three, fifty-four..."

For a moment, she thought the cellar would be a great place to hide. The cellar had two doors that opened in either direction. The wind caught the one side at just the right angle to lift it up and toss it open. Carly stretched her neck out as her legs mindlessly took her closer to the dark opening. Curiosity overrode any common sense at that point.

All that she saw was a square black abyss leading under the house.

When she finally made it to the cellar, she placed her right hand on the door frame of the open door and her left hand on the closed side. She peered into the void, half curious and half fearful at what would jump out at her. All she saw was nothingness. The black emptiness went far beyond what she was willing to investigate. To see further in, she'd have to lean in further, and she wasn't about to do that. What if the darkness swallowed her? What if it was a portal to an alternate realm of nothing where monsters wanted to eat the souls of children?

Her mind flipped through dozens of options, each fueled by some stupid B movie that she'd seen at some point. Or the cover art of a comic book. The imagination could be a wonderful thing, or it could cause someone to become lost in themselves and freeze at the potential possibilities.

Her eyes slowly adjusted to the darkness, and the wooden stairs materialized in front of her. The dirt floor made itself known. Although still dark and filled with shadows, at least the immediate opening was visible. That in and of itself helped her to reign in her wild fantasies. Unfortunately, as her eyes continued to adjust, sharp movements from below caught her attention. Shadows moved, but she knew that had to be her eyes still adjusting. Shadows didn't just move unless their light source changed, and the moon didn't move that fast.

From further back in the cellar, further back than where her eyes could see, where it was still hidden by the darkness, she heard a deep voice say, "You should come down."

It wasn't a whisper. It wasn't a mistake. She heard it as clear as she would hear her mother call her name for dinner. Something in the cellar's abyss wanted her to come down.

Her eyes grew large, and her breath came fast. Every fiber and nerve ending told her to run, but somewhere between her muscles and her brain, something wasn't firing.

From another planet, she heard a different, familiar voice. "Ready or not, here I come."

"Come down here. He'll never find you. You'll never be found down here." The cellar beckoned her again. The deep timbre of the voice rattled every bone in her body. She debated if the voice even made a true sound or just propelled vibrations that her ears only interpreted as sound.

She processed the words that echoed through her head. Never be found down there. Never be found down there. That phrase kept surfacing over and over. Did the voice mean that Chandler would never find her down there? Or did it mean that no one would ever find her? She wanted to believe the former but the latter felt more plausible.

The memory of her mother's ghost story came to mind. The little girl's parents had hung themselves in the house. If she went down in the cellar, would her parents find her hanging from a rafter?

A board creaked just a few feet below her. Someone (*something*) had stepped on the wooden stairs. Was someone (*or something*) coming up to get her?

Carly wanted to move. She needed her brain to unlock. She needed the fear to let go. She needed whatever vibrations that were sent through her body to stop. She needed...

A hand touched her shoulder.

Everything that was pent up inside of her released, and she screamed, falling backwards onto her butt in the gravel. Her eyes stared up at Chandler standing over her. Her heart was about to beat out of her chest if she didn't hyperventilate first.

"Found you," he said. "You were a lot easier than I'd thought you'd be. I figured you were going to make me search the whole barn for you."

Carly laid on the ground and looked up at the absent stars. The cloud cover had completely blocked them, and the moon's fullness grew dimmer. The first drops of rain fell onto her face.

Chandler reached a hand out, and she grabbed it. He helped her onto her feet as she dusted off her shorts.

"Kids, come inside," she heard Mr. Walker holler.

"Stupid rain," Chandler said. "Was supposed to be my turn to hide next."

He led the way around the house. Carly wasn't far behind. If the lighting had been better, she was sure they'd have seen how pale she was.

FIFTEEN

"You guys have fun playing?" Kathryn asked as she tucked Carly into bed.

The kids looked exhausted. The families had separated into their own rooms, and the parents had sent kids through the showers to get cleaned up for bed.

"This house has a cellar," Carly said.

Kathryn paused. That statement felt very random. The memory of being down there earlier in the day came back. Ann spinning in circles and talking to the shadows. While down there, even she started to see things and questioned her own grasp of reality. It wasn't a place for adults, so it definitely wasn't a place for kids.

"Yes, I know, but don't go down there." Kathryn was about to leave it at that, but then thought to ask, "How do you know about the cellar?"

"Chandler and I were playing hide and go seek."

"Did you hide down there?" Goosebumps ran up her arm, and she tried to stifle an involuntary shudder.

"No. Not at all. I was looking for a place to hide, and the wind blew one of the doors open. I looked inside, but it was too dark."

"The wind blew it open? It wasn't locked with a chain?"

That didn't sound right. She thought back to when she and Ann stood in the cellar. She remembered seeing the door that led outside. That was the only exit beside the door from the kitchen. It had to be the one that Carly was talking about, but when she saw the door, it was chained shut. The wind couldn't have been so strong it broke the chain. Maybe Frank or Joe forget to chain it back?

"Yeah, it was blowing in the wind. But, Mom, there was something else."

As her mother, Kathryn could always tell when the kids were worried about something. When Carly had a test that she hadn't studied for or that time when Jake was being bullied, Kathryn knew. The kids telegraphed everything on their faces.

"What's wrong, Sweetie?"

"There was a voice in the cellar. It sounds crazy, but I heard someone tell me to go down there."

Kathryn placed a hand on Carly's cheek and softly rubbed down to her chin. She felt the clamminess and cold sweat that developed there. Whatever Carly thought she heard really bothered her. If she didn't ease her worries, Carly wouldn't be able to sleep tonight.

"Now, Carly. You know how I've told you not to watch those scary movies, despite your dad letting you stay up with him?"

"Yes, but..."

"No, buts. It's just us here. No one is hiding in the cellar. The wind was blowing strong and bringing the storm in. I bet the wind made a noise, and your imagination got the better of you. It's a strange house, and it's a dark and scary cellar. It happens."

"I swear I heard it, though."

"I'm sure you did." Kathryn tapped the front of her forehead. "But you heard it up here instead of in your ears." She leaned forward and kissed Carly's forehead where she'd been tapping. "Go to sleep. I think tomorrow, we're heading home. Goodnight, Sweetheart."

"Goodnight."

Sixteen

L ying in bed, Ann tossed and turned. Whether from the long nap during the day or the thoughts racing through her mind, sleep alluded her. she felt trapped in a tug-of-war. When pulled one direction, sanity slipped away. When thrust the other direction, she felt more in control, more lucid than she had in years. She knew Kathryn thought she'd lost her mind in the cellar, but Ann knew she hadn't.

Before Dr. Stiller gave her the shot, the world had cleared itself up. She saw the basement clearly. The voices spoke with a clarity that she understood with ease. Although maybe that meant she had lost her grip on reality? And the tug-of-war continued.

Laying on one side, she felt Jim at her back. The feeling of human touch helped ground her to the here and now. Ann hoped his contact kept her firmly connected to the real world, that maybe he'd be her anchor to win the battle inside of her. Yet, as she stared at the shadows in the corner of the room, they seemed to change form, change shape, with every flicker of lightning. The shadow of an empty chair suddenly filled with in black as if someone set there then vanished. A black square grew arms before losing them again. The shape of a person lasted just longer than it should have. Like the lasting silhouette of a flash from a camera.

She flipped over to her other side. She watched Jim's chest rise and fall as he slept soundly. Fortunately, her constant rotating hadn't woken him up. As much as she'd love to have him awake and talking to her, she knew he needed sleep. There was no reason to wake him just to keep her company. All the friends in her head would be company enough. She smiled at the thought and hoped having a sense of humor about things was a good sign.

After watching him for a few minutes, she laid back and looked up. Occasionally, the room lit up from the outside storm. The slow sprinkle of raindrops picked up pace and became a steady flow of rain. Usually, the sound of rain soothed her to sleep, and she begged for the same to happen now. Instead, she stared at the off white hue of the ceiling. The turning fan sent a cool breeze across her face as long shadow arms from the blades circled the room. Sleep had no intention of taking her any time soon.

Screw it, Ann thought and tossed the sheet off her. She sat up in bed, spun her feet to the floor, and stood up. Hopefully, a change of venue would help. Or at least standing up for a bit would reset her head and get her into a more sleep friendly mindset. She quietly stepped over to the window and slid back the translucent curtain silently across the rod.

Ann watched the rain hit the ground. Puddles formed in the depressions within the gravel and dirt. She knew the more the rain fell, the worse the long road back to the highway would get. Hopefully, the weather would clear up, and the sun would dry everything before then. Jim wasn't a fan of driving in the mud. That would make a great ending to this trip, hearing him frustrated while the tires kicked up mud and rocks across the side of the car.

The lightning flashed, and something in the open field caught Ann's eye. Not just one something but multiple somethings. It looked like figures standing in the rain staring up at the house. Her imagination made her think of zombie movies where hordes of the walking dead stood outside while the helpless victims waited inside for their turn to be devoured. She only saw shadows, but her mind filled in the rotting corpses with teeth protruding from their jaws begging for brains.

With the next flash of lightning, the images were gone. As far as Ann could see with what little moonlight shone through, the fields stood empty. No zombie horde staring at the house waiting to consume the victims inside. No walking dead slowly dragging their feet to the house. Just rain-drenched, rolling hills that she knew would be a stark green during the daylight hours thanks to nature giving them a drink.

She convinced herself she was tired. That was why she saw things that weren't there. Her mind dreamed on its own while she was still awake. That made sense. At least she hoped it did. Sanity or insanity. The tug-of-war continued.

Not wanting to see what else her head would throw her way, she pulled the curtain back in front of the window. The solid images of hills and trees turned back into vague shapes distorted by the thin cloth. The steady sound of rain continued, filling the empty void of the room.

Ann turned around, determined to fall asleep this time. Instead, she stood motionless by the window, driving her fist into her mouth. She felt the pressure of her knuckles against her teeth and tasted the salty iron of blood. Her breath escaped her body so quick that even without her fist in her mouth stifling sound, there was no air to vibrate her vocal chords. Inside her head, though, screams of terror reverberated.

Standing next to the bed, leaning over Jim, stood a dark figure. It wasn't her shadow cast by the window behind her as she tried to first tell herself.

The figure stood as real and solid as she was. Not the ghost of a little girl. Not the ghost of an old man who once smelled like tobacco. The figure stood six feet tall. The skin had a green murkiness to it as if covered with moss and filth. It resembled a man but the features were so distorted it was hard to tell. Saying the figure wore clothes was true in the loosest of sense. The garments draped across it as if that's where the wind had blown them. The more she looked, the more she realized she'd seen that face before. Or something close to it. The figure had a touch of similarity to Clarence Jenkins, Betsy's father who hung himself in the house.

The figure stared at Jim lying in bed. Every muscle in Ann's body froze with terror. Movie clip after movie clip of the dead seeking revenge on the living flew threw her head. A montage of the worst possible outcomes, and with her locked in place, there was nothing she could do. It stared at Jim with a look of amusement and confusion. Its eyes looked down, and its head cocked to the side. When the head shifted from one side to the other, it did so in quick stutters of movement like an old still-frame movie. Each movement created an audible click that made Ann think the neck holding the head was broken. No neck that made that noise was held together correctly.

I'm asleep.

That was the first thought Ann had that made sense to her. She must've actually fallen asleep, and this whole thing, the figure standing over Jim, the zombie horde outside the window? All part of a nightmare. Two nights in a row filled with nightmares. That was all. What was it Dr. Stiller had said? Her mind was making sense of the memories, combining things together.

Last night's nightmare when she heard the child laugh, felt the pressure against the railing, before her mother's voice told her to go to sleep? Misplaced memories from her youth obviously. Tonight's nightmare must be some latent horror movie that Cardinal Crest was reminding her of. She was asleep, and this was a nightmare.

As if in answer to her thoughts, the figure moved its head. Each movement accompanied by that horrible clicking noise. The head slowly turned to look at her. She had thought it had eyes, but as the face turned to her, she realized she was wrong. Empty eye sockets glared at her. They stared at her as if a dark nothingness stared into her soul, burning a hole directly through her. The nothing stare burrowed into her mind, griping her. With sharp, sudden movements, the figure turned its whole body. The shoulders moved and snapped into place. The arms followed suit. The hips shifted and locked. Then a leg. The figure moved as if trying to discover which joint moved which limb. The grotesque sound of cracking echoed with each stuttered movement. The figure advanced toward Ann.

As tightly as she could, she squeezed her eyes shut. She whispered, "I'm dreaming. I'm dreaming." She stood like that until the cracking stopped. Once it did, she slowly counted to ten. With each number, she tried to control her breathing. Through one, two, and three, her breathing reminded her of quick breaths she took while learning Lamaze. By the time she reached eight, she filled her lungs with air, hoping the increase in oxygen helped to lower her heart rate. At ten, she opened her eyes.

The nothing stare filled her vision. The figure stood inches from her. Its vacant eye sockets transfixed on hers. She smelled the rot and decay of decades. Dirt, grime, filth, moss, and pungent death rippled off it. The smell cascaded in waves.

Ann's body shook from fear. Her breathing turned into quick, short gasps of hyperventilating air flow. She bit down harder on her fist, sending fresh tastes of salt and iron across her tongue. All she could do was stand there.

Her brain was misfiring. Through her fist still clenched in her mouth, she tried to eek out, "I'm dreaming. I'm dreaming."

The figure's head clicked to the side again with those sharp movements. The image of Michael Myers admiring his work after stabbing a teenager to the wall in the first Halloween movie popped into her head.

She couldn't keep staring at the nothing stare. She didn't care what happened to her. Continuing to gaze into the darkness of the eye sockets pulled that tug-of-war battle firmly into insanity's camp. Whatever this figure was going to do, she couldn't look at it anymore.

Through the last bit of willpower she felt she had, she shut her eyes tight once more. She heard a series of quick cracks like boards breaking apart before the only sounds in the room were the rain and Jim's snoring. Her body still shook, but after another slow count to ten, she eased her eyes back open.

She and Jim were alone.

Slowly, Ann removed her fist from her mouth and tried to relax the muscles in her body. She focused on her neck, down to her shoulders and back, then down her arms. Each muscle forcibly relaxed as she focused her attention on it. She breathed deeply, filling her lungs to capacity. When her legs finally unlocked, she shuffled to the bed as quickly as possible before her inevitable collapse. She made it just in time, right before her legs turned to Jell-O.

Ann fell onto the bed next to Jim, causing him to roll over and slightly stir before drifting back off to sleep. She stared at the ceiling before closing her eyes and repeating silently in her head, *I'm dreaming, I'm dreaming.*

PART FOUR

MEMORIES UNLOCKED

ONE

A nn sat straight up with a gasp. She reached next to her but only felt the cool mattress. No Jim. Disoriented, she'd have sworn she overslept, but no sunlight filled the room. It was still dark outside. But if it was the middle of the night, where was Jim?

The image of the nothing stare hung fresh in her mind. Those deep vacant eye sockets of the corpse of Clarence Jenkins had burned themselves into her psyche. Each time she closed her eyes, the darkness flashed before her. As the vision dissolved behind her eyelids like the phantom image of a light, it morphed into a skull, lingering in the air in front of her. She told herself over and over that it was a dream but failed in being convincing.

Her pulse increased, and her breathing became labored. She needed to clear her head, to get rid of the memory, but her mind was hijacked. And where the FUCK was Jim?!?

The pressure of the sheets that still lay across her legs confined her. The air felt heavy in her lungs. After feeling as if she made progress last night, she was mad that a panic attack gripped her.

She twisted her body towards the nightstand. Her wrist-watch should've been underneath the lamp, and she let out a sigh of relief when it was. Grabbing it, she checked the time. More relief washed over her, helping to bury the phantom image deeper into her memory. She found it ironic that they were there for her to unbury memories and now she actively tried to forget them.

It was nine in the morning.

Jim must've already woken and gone downstairs. Most mornings when he found her in deep sleep, he got ready for work before waking her. Those times, she was so out of it that he could've been as loud as he wanted without disturbing her. She half wished he had shaken her awake. Anything to have avoided the panic attack that she'd crawled herself out of.

But the darkness?

Ann eased her feet off the edge of the bed. She placed them on the floor and stood up straight. Her legs ached as if she'd done a hundred squats last night. One foot slowly in front of the other, she made her way to the window and pulled back the sheer curtain. Dark rain clouds covered the sky and drenched everything with their payload. Pools of standing water dotted the fields. It must've been raining all night long.

As she reached up to pull the curtain back, her hand hesitated in the air, visibly shaking. A strong sense of Deja vu washed over her. Last night, she'd fixed the curtain and when she turned around...

She didn't want to turn around. The figure would be there. She knew it would. She'd turn around, and Clarence would be standing inches from her face, staring at her with that dead stare. That nothing stare. No eyes, just the vacant sockets burning into her.

Her hand curled around the curtain, and she pulled it to the ground. Some of the hooks gave its own rip as they tore away. The pole crashed to the ground. She turned around practically daring the ghost of Clarence to be there, but the room remained empty. At that moment, she knew she couldn't take it anymore. She needed to find Dr. Stiller and finish this. Another round of hypnosis maybe. She couldn't sleep. She was seeing things. Sanity pulled as hard as it could in the tug-of-war, but insanity held its ground firmly.

Ann stepped to the dresser, took off her nightgown, and quickly dressed for the day. She didn't care what she looked like. She needed to find Dr. Stiller.

Bolting out of her room, she rushed down the stairs.

"Renee!" she said. "Renee, I need to see you now."

Her words came out with more force than she intended, but once they did, she liked the tone. That tone reminded her of the old Ann. If Lauren or Chandler heard that tone, she knew they'd recognize it. The "oh shit mom's mad and we're in trouble" tone.

By the time she reached the bottom step, Renee waited outside of the dining room. "Ann, good morning."

"I need you to do it again."

"Do what again?" Renee asked. She had a napkin in her hand, obviously dabbing away the last of her breakfast from her fingers.

"The hypnosis or whatever it was. I want to remember the rest. I can't take this anymore. All these memories are slowly breaking through, but there's so much confusion along with them. I'm going mad trying to keep everything straight. I'm seeing things that aren't...or can't be real."

As she spoke, Kat walked out of the dining room. Jim sat on the couch in the den to her right. He remained sitting while Ann spoke with Renee, watching her.

When Ann saw Kat, she had a revelation. Something that she thought might help even more. After what Kat relayed last night, she knew that Kat might have a better perspective. She needed Kat's eyes to unlock what she couldn't remember and probably didn't even see.

"Kat," Ann said. "I'm glad you're here. Can you follow me to Renee's office? I need a favor."

With a little hesitation, Kat cautiously stepped closer to the other two women. "I guess. What for, though?"

Ann turned to Dr. Stiller. She caught a glimpse of herself in the hallway mirror. Her hair was frazzled, her shirt wasn't buttoned correctly, and her eyes were fully dilated. Ann could understand Kat's hesitation. If there was a picture of a crazy lady, it was her.

After a deep inhale and exhale, hoping to bring her energy level down - and possibly help sanity out - she said, "I think you saw more than I did the night my mother was killed. You might remember the highlights of what happened, but I need the details. Would you agree to Dr. Stiller putting you under hypnosis?"

"Hypnosis?" both Kat and Renee said simultaneously.

"Yes. Renee, you put me under yesterday, and that's how I remembered the cellar."

"And we saw how that had ended up," Renee said.

Ann caught a tinge of something under her tone, but she couldn't quite put her finger on it. Her words weren't wrong. Dr. Stiller sedated her, and she slept most of the day away.

But beyond her words, something else lurked. An image of a snake hiding amongst tall grass came to mind. In just that short phrase, for the first time Ann picked up something hiding just beneath the surface of her therapist. A mask maybe.

Instead of pursuing that line of thought, Ann dismissed it. She had other things to worry with than the demons Dr. Renee Stiller had in her closest. She had her own sanity to tend to. Her sanity that fought a losing battle in her mind.

"I'll do it," Kat said. "I want you to get better, and if this is what it takes, then that's fine. But, Doc, I better not come out of it clucking like a chicken anytime someone rings a bell. I live on a farm next to the woods. No one will find you."

"Are you two sure?" Renee asked.

Both nodded in agreement.

"Then follow me back to my office. Let's crack open Mrs. Miller's head, shall we?"

Two

Gina pondered this interesting turn of events. Could she work this in her favor? Her initial plan had Ann slowly uncovering the truth about that night, creating her own torture along the way. That part had gone perfectly. Just looking at Ann, she saw her teetering on the verge of a complete mental breakdown. Gina's symphony was crescendoing to its conclusion.

With the current request, Ann wouldn't discover the truth through her own remembrance. Instead, she'd hear it recited to her while still fully awake and aware. The impact of that, hearing it come from someone else, could be the straw that Gina needed to break the proverbial camel's back.

"Gentlemen," Gina said as Ann and Kathryn started for the master suite, "enjoy the sound of rain while I steal your wives for a bit."

With a quick spin on her heels, she caught up to Kathryn and Ann. The portraits on the wall maintained their stares, but Gina paid no attention. If all went to plan, this place would soon be behind her. She'd drive back a conqueror.

A few times, she even thought of writing a book about what she'd accomplished. Of course, it would be deemed fiction. No reason to document the exploits and incriminate oneself after all. A blueprint on how to drive someone crazy, then frame them for the murder of their whole family. They'd have to kill themselves at the end, though. Gina doubted that would be an issue. Ann looked on the edge of that now.

She just needed one more push.

Ann helped Kathryn get comfortable on the bed. A repeat of what she did yesterday. Once Kathryn was situated and relaxed, Ann moved to the window seat. Her legs bounced in nervous anticipation, and while her arms dangled between her knees, she fidgeted with her hands. A nervous energy that Gina had seen time and time again during their sessions in Dr. Stiller's office. Ann stared straight at Kathryn, waiting.

Gina rolled the chair next to the bed. She glanced at Kathryn lying comfortable, then looked just past her at the mirror. An out of place shadow stood in the corner of the room then dissolved away. At this point, she'd grown used to shadows vanishing.

"Remember, Doc," Kat started.

"I remember. No clucking like a chicken. Now take a deep breath."

THREE

K at preferred to be in the outdoors by herself. She hated when all the adults gathered and she had to "act more ladylike", as her mother would say. Her dad and her uncle John never cared. For the most part, they let her do whatever she wanted. She usually wore shorts and a T-shirt with one of her knees having a healed-over scab or the faint memory of one.

Standing in the den of the huge house surrounded by adults, though, she found herself fortunate. Her mother already told her to mind her manners, be nice, be a lady, blah, blah, blah. She'd heard the lecture before. With all of that, at least she didn't have to be dressed up in that fancy dress the other girl was wearing. If her mother made her do that, Kat knew she'd have to suffer whatever punishment came with getting it messy or destroyed. On her, there was no way the dress would make it through the night.

Uncle John sat on the love seat in conversation with the other family. Her mom waited at the little bar while her dad made something for the two of them to drink. He also made one for Kat. He called it a Shirley Temple and told her it made her look fancy. Kat didn't care how it made her look. She just knew it tasted great.

With her drink in her hand, she rushed over to her uncle and flopped down next to him. Kat was careful not to spill her drink. She didn't want to lose any of it.

The little girl, Annabelle, sat on the stone in front of the fireplace. To Kat, she looked bored. Although she'd be bored also if all she could do was sit in that dress and try not to ruin it. If it was a smaller dress, Annabelle probably could have fit on the couch next to her parents.

"So, Senator," John started. "Do you think we should have kept moving straight into Iraq?"

Annabelle was the daughter of an important politician. That probably meant Annabelle had to go to fancy balls and dinners. She probably had to wear those terrible dresses all the time.

"We drove them out of Kuwait which was the objective. I doubt Saddam Hussein will be an issue again. Typically, once you make a dictator show weakness, they lose some of their control. I give him another two years before one of his generals thinks he can do the job better."

"How many CIA types do we have over there making sure that happens?" John asked. The corner of his mouth turned up in a sly smile.

"As far as I know, we are not doing anything like that. Granted, if we were, I couldn't divulge any of that information." The Senator met John's smile with his own.

"Ah. Plausible deniability. I get it." He nodded his head as he spoke then took a drink.

Listening to politics bored Kat. No wonder Annabelle was bored. She probably had to listen to that kind of stuff all the time.

While sitting there, she saw two of the house workers step into the opening of the den. Kat had seen them before in the kitchen, but hadn't talked to them. Both seemed tall to Kat, but one was skinny, and the other was kind of fat.

"Senator Adams," one of the guys said. "Do you have a minute?"

Annabelle's dad looked over at them. At the same time, the security guy who'd been standing against the wall turned to face them. His eyes looked the two men over.

"Is there something I can help you with?" the security guy asked.

"It has to do with the little one over there." The skinnier one pointed a finger at Annabelle.

Kat couldn't help but smile. Little Ms. Princess in the fancy dress did something that now she was in trouble for. Kat had been on the receiving end of those conversations enough to know the look from the kitchen guy.

"It's ok, Brian." Senator Adams stood up. "Please excuse me for a moment while I go see what kind of trouble Annabelle got herself into."

He walked with the two men as they backed out of the den and into the dining room away from everyone.

Kat's curiosity took hold of her. She wanted to know what Annabelle did to get the attention of the staff.

"Uncle John." Kat motioned with her finger for him to lean closer which he did. "Hold my drink," she whispered into his ear. "I need to go pee."

He twisted her head and whispered into her ear. "Too much information. Just say you need to go to the ladies' room."

Kat nodded her head and leaned back into his ear, but this time she didn't whisper but spoke in a louder than normal voice. "I need to go pee."

He recoiled from her yell into his ear and laughed. "You little turd. Give me your drink and go pee. And I'm not going to promise I won't drink it all by the time you get back."

Kat handed him her drink and hopped off the chair. As she started out of the den, she said, "You better not drink my drink." She turned the corner as if heading for the downstairs bathroom, but then stopped just beyond the stairs. On her tippy toes, she slipped back a few feet. Just enough to be in ear shot but also hidden by the large wooden staircase.

"I'm not going to play ball anymore," Mr. Adams said. "You can tell Salvatore that."

"He was afraid you'd say that," one of the staff said. It sounded like the tall guy. "We were sent to convince you."

"Convince me? Are you going to assault me in front of everyone? I'm sure Brian will have something to say about that. All I need to do is raise my voice."

Kat heard a familiar sound that sent a chill down her spine. She heard the hammer of a revolver click back. Her dad had one that he'd taken camping with them before. The only time he ever used it was on a snake.

The other person spoke up. His voice rang deeper. "Marco, that's not necessary. Thomas is going to pack up his family in the morning and head back to Virginia. He's needed in Washington to pass the bills Mr. Carlisi tells him to pass."

She lowered herself to the ground, trying to be as small as possible. Things were bad. She thought about running into the den, but they'd see her. If everyone came out to help, the shooting would start. Someone would get caught in the crossfire.

"Your boss can kiss my ass."

Marco spoke again. Kat couldn't see him, but she imagined the gun brandished in the air. "Tony, did you hear what he said? I have a new plan. You are going to take your ass to Washington. You are going to keep being the senator we pay you to be. Your kid and wife can stay here, though. If you are a good little senator, I'll promise not to fuck your wife too hard. If you're a bad senator, I'll mail you pieces of your kid, one at a time."

Kat clasped her hands over her mouth. If not, she'd have screamed. Her heart raced. She felt the beat throughout her whole body. Her mind raced. What to do? She needed to tell her dad, her uncle, the security guy, everyone. With her back pressed against the wall, she forced her legs to stand up.

"Thomas," a voice said while drawing closer. It was Annabelle's mother. "Is everything..." Her question trailed off.

She stood in the doorway. Kat saw her standing with her hand clasped over her mouth. Apparently, Mrs. Adams had full view of the three men in the dining room.

Kat took the opportunity to run past her and into the den. She glimpsed Marco and Tony pointing the gun at Mrs. Adams, marching her back into the den. She briefly heard one of them say, "Fuck!"

"Liz, go sit back down. I'm handling this."

"Too late now, Senator," Marco said. "Everyone against the wall. Now! Fuck!"

Marco held the gun at eye level. Sweat poured down his face.

Tony pushed Thomas Adams forward so that he was in the den with everyone else.

Kat's dad and mom, Mark and Judy Higgins, stood close to the fireplace by Annabelle. When Kat ran in, she bolted straight for them. Tears streamed down her face. She looked around. Annabelle sat on the fireplace as her mom backed her direction. John Higgins, Kat's uncle, sat on the love seat with the Shirley Temple in his hand. He didn't get up when they ordered.

Marco, with the gun in his right hand, pointed it at John. "Didn't you hear me?"

"I'm tending to the little girl's drink," he said.

"Why the fuck do I care?" he yelled. He stared at John and with his left hand, wiped swept from his eyes. "I said get the fuck over..."

Before he could finish, Brian leaped from behind the door and grabbed Marco's right arm. A look of shock crossed the gunman's face. Brian pushed the gun aside with one arm then drove his fist into Marco's temple with the other.

His eye immediately swelled shut. In a blind rage, his finger gripped the trigger of the gun. The report echoed through the den. Kathryn had been around plenty of guns but typically wore ear protection when they were fired. The few exceptions, she'd been outside, giving somewhere for the concussive sound to go. Inside the house, it left her ears ringing.

As Brian fought Marco, John tossed Kat's Shirley Temple to the side and jumped off the couch. Mark Higgins also rushed in as the gun fell out of Marco's hand.

In the few seconds that Brian and Marco fought for control of the gun, Tony realized what happened. He pushed Thomas out of the way and joined the melee.

Marco heard the gun hit the floor and slide forward. He thrust Brian off him and dove for the floor. As he did, Brian backed a few steps, reached into his side holster, and removed his own handgun. He trained his weapon on Marco, but before he pulled the trigger, Tony also dove for the gun.

Brian fired, and Tony hit the floor. The front of his shirt darkened with a deep red. He didn't move again.

Marco searched for the dark revolver on the dark hardware floor. Kat assumed Brian's fierce blows to Marco's head blurred his vision, leaving the gun invisible. He scrambled on his hands and knees across the floor as John and Mark struggled with him.

Kat watched as he clawed across the floor, dragging himself closer and closer to Annabelle. The gun lay inches from her feet. Kat had a perfect view of it, and if her mom didn't have a death grip on her, Kat could've grabbed it. Instead, she watched the kitchen staff-turned-gunman reach closer and closer to his goal.

Mark looked up, his arms wrapped around Marco's back, and his eyes widened. He later told the police he saw the gun and knew Marco would eventually find it. He planted his feet into the ground, and with his arms still wrapped around Marco's waist, he thrust forward as hard as he could. As he came off the ground, he twisted his body to the side.

The force propelled Marco forward. His whole frame left the ground. As Mark twisted his body, Marco also spun. His face, which was facing the ground, turned to the ceiling. The back of his skull collided with the stone fireplace directly in front of Annabelle. Kathryn heard a crunch that she could only assume was his skull caving into his brain.

Marco's body fell to the ground with a lifeless stare. Those dead eyes fixed onto Annabelle as his body convulsed. After the final pulses from the brain stopped, the body lay still.

"Mother," Kat heard Annabelle say. "Mother? Mommy?!" The words increased in volume and intensity.

Liz Adams lay next to the couch. At first, Kat thought she hid there, but then she saw the ever increasing pool of blood.

Thomas ran across the floor and shoved the couch out of the way. It slid almost to the front door. He dropped to his knees at his wife's body. His hand went to her head and brushed her hair. When he pulled it back, red smeared across his fingers and palm. With shaking arms, he pulled her body close to him and wept.

Annabelle set on the fireplace without moving. Marco lay dead in front of her, and her mother lay dead a few feet away.

Kat didn't understand why she just sat there. Maybe that was what shock looked like.

FOUR

"I don't understand," Ann said.

She paced in front of the window, wringing her hands together as she did. As Kat spoke in the hypnotic trance, fragments of memories came together. Like a puzzle being assembled, an image started to reveal itself. But what Kat said didn't make sense to her. She remembered her father's career in politics. Her mother died during his second term as senator. He served out his term, and despite people begging him to run for a third, he stepped away to focus on her. The state loved him.

Ann stopped pacing long enough to grab the bottle of water that Dr. Stiller gave her when the session began. Her throat had completely dried up while listening to Kathryn speak. She tilted the bottle back and finished it off.

"You don't understand?" Dr. Stiller asked.

The tone conveyed a cross between anger and confusion. The sense of something lurking underneath hit Ann again. The snake hiding in the tall grass. Renee sat next to the bed, bombarding Kat with questions, prying deeper and deeper into the memory. She wanted each detail uncovered. Even though it was from the perspective of a kid, she pulled out every element.

Dr. Stiller's eyes burned red, and dried remnants of tears painted her cheeks. Why did Kathryn's retelling cause Renee to cry? That look, her tone, and those tears caught Ann off-guard. In the short time she'd known the doctor, she never saw her like this. Never saw her get emotionally invested.

Kathryn's monotone speech stopped.

Ann stuttered, not sure how to address her therapist. "I don't... That's not how I... Daddy would never... He never..." Tears flowed from her eyes.

"Are you so sure about that?" Renee snapped back. She turned to Kathryn. "In a moment, I will count to three, and you will be fully awake and remember what you said. One, two, three."

Kathryn moved her head from side to side, then stretched her arms above her head and slowly opened her eyes. She looked at Dr. Stiller and then at Ann. "Ann, I'm sorry. I know that was hard to hear."

Kathryn's own bottle of water sat on the nightstand. She opened it and took a few quenching gulps before setting it back down.

Renee turned to Kathryn. "Don't apologize. She needed to hear it. She needed to know the kind of man her father really was."

"What kind of man her father was?" Kathryn asked confused. "I thought the point was for her to remember what happened to her mother, recover her memories, so that the panic attacks went away."

Ann sat down on the window seat. Her hands twisted together, tying her fingers into knots. Her head spun in circles. What was Renee saying? Kathryn had asked the question that she couldn't vocalize.

"Her father's corruption is at the root of everything." Renee stood up from her chair and walked over to the desk. She opened the drawer, grabbed a handful of news clippings, and threw them on the bed.

Ann stood up from the window seat and moved to the bed. She sat down at the end while Kat scooted closer to the clippings. Ann's head still felt cloudy. She fought bouts of dizziness but pushed through. Her hand hovered over the pages spread across the foot of the bed. She couldn't bring herself to grab them. Titles of articles jumped out at her. "Virginia's Corruption Continues". "Does the Mob Own The Senate?". "Is Senator Adams A Paid Stooge?". "Salvatore Carlisi, the Actual Virginia Senator."

"You're lying," Ann snapped at Dr. Stiller. "I don't know what kind of therapy this is, but you're lying. My father wasn't corrupt. He never took money from people like this."

Renee's face changed visibly at Ann's accusation. A fire erupted behind her eyes. She stopped being the helpful, caring therapist trying to cure Ann Walker of her panic attacks. Instead, hatred spewed from her.

"People like this?! Your father *was* this kind of person. Just look at the articles. His corruption caused your mother's death, and the death of..." She paused and took a deep breath. "The death of those men that Carlisi sent."

Kathryn turned her attention from the articles to Renee standing tall over the bed. "Doc, aren't you being a little harsh? I don't know if you are trying to push her into acceptance or whatever, but this doesn't feel right."

The idea of her dad's involvement with organized crime hurt. It went against everything she knew about her father. But even as she sat on the bed in disbelief, her head spinning as if she'd spent the morning drinking, the puzzle continued to build. A memory that she had recently uncovered from her time at Cardinal Crest fell into place. The memory of her mother and father arguing while she spied on them. Just before Brian startled her and she found the cellar, her parents argued about Carlisi, about why they had to be there in the first place.

Ann started to fervently shake her head. The news clippings spoke about campaign contributions from shell companies linked to Salvatore Carlisi. Her family escaped to Cardinal Crest Estate to get away from the press. Her mother died by the hand of two known gunmen with mob ties. Wave after wave of memories flooded her brain. They crashed into the image of her father that she clung on to with all her might.

Grieving husband and loving father who left the political scene to focus on his daughter. The man who stepped away from the public eye despite talks of cabinet positions or maybe more. A rising star that only grew in popularity by announcing his intention to take care of his little girl.

"Ann," Kathryn said. "Ann, are you OK?"

Ann could only shake her head. She struggled to hold on to the memory of her father as she knew him. Not what she saw before her.

Renee stood at the foot of the bed, glaring at the two women. Her mouth bent into a smile. When Ann looked at her, the vision of the snake in the grass blazed in her mind.

Kathryn kept talking to Ann. "You never suspected or looked up your dad?"

Finally, she turned to Kathryn and forced her vocal cords to work. Her words came slow and slurred. "Why would I? He was my father. I trusted him. He told me two robbers... With the shock, the memory of it just faded away."

Renee leaned into Ann's face. Venom oozed from her words. "All the death around you and it just faded away? It must be nice to be so privileged that the effects can just fade away."

Ann's head hurt. Her vision blurred, and the world spun. She couldn't think straight. She felt an uncontrollable urge to get out of there, to get fresh air. She needed to get out.

In a fit of frustration, she grabbed a handful of clippings from the bed. Instead of addressing Renee's statement, she threw the clippings at her face and leaped off the bed. When her feet collided with the floor, she felt the world do a somersault. It took every ounce of her control not to fall over.

She looked at the door and watched it twist to one side. Everything in her view contorted. Each step felt heavy. She reached for the door and nearly stumbled into the doorknob. Tossing it open, she stared down the hallway and set her sights on the front door. She didn't care about the rain still falling outside. The outside wasn't inside, and that was what was important.

With a hand against the wall to steady herself, she placed one foot in front of the other. Her pace quickened with each step. Something wasn't right in her head. Something was breaking in her mind. The pictures hanging in the hallway followed her with their eyes, and as she made her way to the front door, she heard them laughing. They laughed at her confusion. They laughed at how broken she was.

Her hand reached for the front door, and she fell into it with a loud thud that echoed through the downstairs. She found the knob, turned it, and threw the door open. In the corner of her eye, she saw Jim sitting on the couch. Although a different couch, in her head, she saw the old couch. The couch where her mother and father had sat. The couch that her father had thrown out of the way to get to her mother. Her mother whose brains had been scattered across the fireplace facade and the wall. Whose blood had pooled on the floor while all she did was stare into the dead eyes of her killer.

Ann ran down the steps and into the pouring rain.

FIVE

Kathryn reached for Ann as she jumped off the bed. Ann wasn't right. A glassy tint covered her eyes. Ann wasn't in the right head space, and Kathryn understood some of the reason. What she'd just found out about her father, a man Ann had idolized, had to be hard to hear. But something else was wrong.

She watched Ann run down the hall.

When Kathryn moved off the bed, she felt sluggish. She dismissed it as a lasting effect from the hypnosis, that her limbs needed more time to wake up.

Finally standing up, she saw Dr. Stiller collecting her clippings as if they were a prized possession. She paid no attention to Kathryn as she went through the door and down the hallway beyond.

By the time Kathryn stood in the middle of the hallway, her own head spun. She watched Ann throw open the door and race into the rain. Kathryn needed to help her. She needed to go after her. Although not responsible for the actions, she felt she owed Ann that much. It was her memories that pushed her to this point. Her memories and the brutal harshness of Renee. Kathryn couldn't fathom to what purpose unless she wanted to drive Ann mad. If that was her goal, it sure as hell looked like she was succeeding.

The hallway ended. Kathryn saw Jim head to the front door, most likely to go after Ann, but she needed to be the one. Despite her sluggishness and her feet growing heavier, it needed to be her.

"I got her," Kathryn said. Her own words sounded as if she had a pillow in her mouth. Her tongue felt in the way. "You guys make sure the kids are fine," she slurred.

Ann had left the door open, and Kathryn walked through it, pulling it closed behind her. The cold rain pelted her and immediately drenched her clothes. It added to the heaviness she already felt enveloping her. She followed Ann's path up the hill through the soaking rain.

SIX

"What was that all about?" James Walker asked Doug.

Jim just witnessed his wife run into the pouring rain. The top half of her body seemed to drag the bottom half along. Then, as he rose up to chase after her, Kathryn followed shortly behind and waved him off.

Both husbands stood in the den with equally shocked expressions across their faces. Of all the outcomes that Jim expected, those events didn't make the list. Over the past few months, their lives had turned upside down. The old normal vanished, so he and the kids had adapted to a new normal. Plenty of crazy things had happened since Ann's dad passed away. Her paranoia, the panic attacks, the isolation. With each thing, they modified their routine. Adapted.

But this was new.

With Doug leading the way, both men quickly went to the door. Doug opened it as Kathryn reached the top of the first hill and dropped out of view on the other side.

"Has Ann done anything like that before?" Doug asked.

"No. Kathryn?"

"No. Where's the doc?"

Jim heard footsteps behind him and turned. Renee approached the two men, seeming in no rush or worry about the two women who'd left her office and sprinted into the rain. Jim noticed a change in her mannerisms. She always came across as being well put together and sophisticated. The way she strutted down the hall reminded him of a snake slithering across the pavement.

"Just what the hell was that?" Doug snapped at Renee.

"Progress, Mr. Miller." To Jim, even the cadence of her voice changed. "You two relax. I'm giving them some time to work through the progress we made before I head that way. This is all part of the process."

With that, she turned around and slithered down the hallway and into her room. She shut the door behind her. Jim heard the faint sound of a click as the lock engaged.

He turned to Doug. "I'm going to sit on the porch and wait for them. Mind hanging out inside in case one of the kids comes downstairs? I'll yell when I see them coming back."

"You sure?" Doug asked. "I don't mind waiting out there."

Jim shook his head. "No, with everything, I could use the cool breeze and smell of rain. Have a lot going on in my own head right now and could use the peace."

Doug put a large hand on Jim's shoulder and gave it a pat. "I hear ya. I don't envy what you guys are going through. Holler when you see them."

Doug dropped his hand back to his side.

"Thanks," Jim said and walked onto the porch. He closed the door behind him, took the few steps to the swing, and sat down.

He took a large breath of cool air. The fresh smell of rain and ozone filled his senses. His eyes drifted to the hill that Ann and Kathryn had topped. A few times, he had to stop himself from going after them. His desire to help struggled against what Dr. Stiller said. Ann needed him. He didn't know what he could do, exactly, but he felt she needed him.

As he rocked back and forth on the swing, the occasional mist left a cold kiss on his face. The wind drove the temperature down, and Jim felt a chill run down his back. With the sun blocked by the dark cloud cover, only his watch told him it was almost eleven. The sound of rain ricocheting off the roof and the gravel driveway drowned out even the creek of the swing's chains.

Jim let his mind drift to happier times with Ann. He recalled their first meeting at Virginia Tech. They were at the Hokies Sports Bar, and both sat with their respective friend groups. Unfortunately, Virginia Tech was getting its ass handed to it by Virginia.

Jim finished off the pitcher which meant it was his turn to buy. He went to the bar, empty pitcher in hand, still yelling at the stupid call the ref made. "That ref wouldn't know pass interference if it bit him in the ass."

He was overly vocal about his displeasure. As he waited for the bartender to refill the pitcher, Ann Adams came to the bar to order a drink. She equally believed the ref had no idea what the definition of pass interference was. As they discussed the poor eye sight of the officiating crew, Jim offered to buy her drink. Their conversation continued through the game and after.

His Ann fought. His Ann didn't shy away from confrontation or hide in her car during soccer games. She didn't care what other people said about her, that other people looked at her. She wanted them to look at her. She was strong.

Pondering everything that'd happened over the past few months, from the changes he saw in his wife, the shell of who she was, to the fact that he was powerless to help her, caused him to bury his face in his hands and weep. He was supposed to protect her, but he couldn't do anything for her but be there for the kids.

He raised his head, his eyes bloodshot and red, and stood up from the swing. He walked to the porch railing and rested his hands on it. His attention stayed on the hill. Although not typically religious, he found himself saying a prayer for protection and strength over the two women in the rain. As he stared at the hillside, the saying about a watched pot never boiling came to mind. It didn't dissuade him from staring, but it did bring a smile to his face.

Out of the corner of his left eye, he saw movement and heard steps on the decking. Before Jim could turn his head, the side of his face erupted in pain. His cheekbone collapsed, and his mouth filled with the metallic taste of blood.

In a daze, he tried to twist when a second blow landed on the other side of his face, just above his jaw line. More blood filled his mouth and what he assumed was a piece of a tooth. Jim's vision doubled, blurred. He felt the railing next to him and waved his hands reaching for it. Disoriented and confused, he frantically tried to recover, hoping to brace onto something to help his legs regain control. But his legs buckled as his feet scurried to find balance. The railing offered the only support he could find.

He had almost recovered when a final blow met his chin from underneath. Whoever attacked him delivered a crushing uppercut. His jaw snapped closed, and he heard teeth crack inside of his mouth. The sound reverberated in his head, and with that, Jim lost all chance of recovery. He fell backwards and slammed onto the porch. He struggled to open his eyes as darkness moved in. Jim felt weightlessness as his attacker grabbed his body and hoisted him onto their shoulder.

As hard as he fought to hold onto consciousness, he lost the battle and the darkness of sleep overtook him.

SEVEN

D oug left the downstairs bathroom, intending to head upstairs and check on the kids. Carly and Jake's silence told him how disconnected they were. They wanted to leave Cardinal Crest Estate and go back home. Doug, although enjoying getting to know the Walkers, found himself ready as well. Enough strange occurrences had happened that he felt uneasy, and he wasn't the type that typically felt that way. He could find his place in any crowd or situation. And Kat was the same way, which made them perfect for each other.

When Kat and Ann ran out of the house and into the rain, he was surprised, but he also knew Kat would make everything good. She had a gift. Whatever ailed Ann, whatever memory sent her running from the house, Kat would keep her safe. That girl knew how to protect herself. And others.

He worried about James, though. The amount of stress that man was under showed through in his face. Doug had only known him for a few days, but the tension oozed out of his pores.

Thud!

The sound grabbed Doug's attention. He'd just stepped on the stairs when he heard noise come from the front porch.

"Jim?" Doug said.

He gazed through the front windows, expecting to see Jim pacing along the front porch. He cycled through each window, but Jim was nowhere to be found. Suddenly, Doug was hit with concern. What if the thud was the stress finally becoming too much for Jim, and the man's heart gave out? *Shit!*

Bolting for the door, Doug opened it and ran onto the porch. His head swiveled from left to right. He feared Jim would be passed out, and he'd have to administer CPR. In his head, Doug prepped by trying to remember the count ratio. Was it fifteen compressions or thirty compressions to two breaths? His mind prepared for the inevitable.

Yet, even after walking to the left side of the house and all the way back, past the front door and past the swing, Jim wasn't there. The porch was empty. What caused the thud? And where the hell did Jim disappear to? Doug hoped he hadn't run into the rain chasing after Kat and Ann.

He kept looking for the cause of the thud. Doug walked back to the left side of the porch, checking the grounds, and straining his neck out beyond the roof line. The rain pelted his face, but he wanted to make sure nothing had fallen on the house. The angle sucked, so he walked passed the porch swing and looked over the railing onto the roof. Still limited in visibility but better, he didn't see anything there.

Stepping back, his foot felt something just under his shoe. Doug knelt and clasped the small white stone between his thumb and pointer finger. He examined it while still kneeling. He rocked it back and forth a few times when he realized it wasn't a stone but a tooth. Why was a tooth on the front porch? Between all the baby teeth that Carly and Jake had lost, he'd handled enough teeth to realize this was no baby tooth.

Doug stood up and raised his head. At the door, Joe Jacobs stood watching him. The look on his face gave Doug an odd feeling.

"What you have there?" Joe asked.

"Nothing," Doug lied. "Needed to pick out a rock from my boot. All the gravel around."

"It happens," Joe said.

"Did you happen to see James Walker around? I thought I saw him go out this way."

Joe stepped onto the porch and stood next to the swing. "I think I saw him head that direction."

He walked off the porch and turned right at the corner of the house.

Doug followed him. He'd hoped to avoid getting out in the rain, but there went that idea. Immediately, his shirt became drenched. He still felt an uneasiness that he couldn't shake. His instincts told him something was off. Just over halfway down the side of the house, Doug saw two white doors hanging open. Kat told him yesterday about the cellar, and he figured that was the exterior access.

"Well, shit," Joe exclaimed. "I don't know why these are open. Could you give me a hand getting these doors closed?"

"Sure," Doug responded.

Joe stopped at the first door, and Doug walked past the opening, heading for the far door.

In the darkness of the cellar, something caught Doug's eye. He hesitated and leaned his head down, giving his eyes a chance to adapt to the low lighting. After a few blinks, he saw what looked to be a shoe and a pair of blue jeans. The shoe and jeans shifted.

"What the hell?!" Doug said, shocked.

As he went to raise up, something hard cracked across the back of his head. Doug collapsed into the opening of the cellar, his head and torso dangling against the steps while his waist and legs still clung to ground. He felt Joe grab his legs, and with a toss, Doug tumbled over the handful of steps, hitting them as he descended. He fell to the mud-filled cellar floor with his own thud. His face splashed against puddles of water pooling on the ground.

The water jolted his eyes open, and he reached his hand to the back of his throbbing head. Barely touching it, pain shot through his scalp and radiated down his neck. He pulled his hand back and saw blood on his fingers.

Slowly, Doug tried to lift himself onto his hands and knees. The pulsating pain drove him back to the ground twice. On the third attempt, he finally found his balance. With his head tilted forward, he gripped the ground in front of him and crawled a few feet.

Through blurry vision, he found the shoe and pants. James was unconscious; his face bruised and misshapen. Doug guessed at least one cheekbone was fractured. That explained the tooth.

He tried to speak and say Jim's name, but the surge of pain dropped him to the ground once more, falling on his stomach next to Jim. He heard Jim's labored breathing and felt relief knowing the man wasn't dead.

Doug heard movement in the cellar. He sat up on his hands and knees again. The ache and blurred vision drove his body the verge of puking, but he forced himself not to. He couldn't imagine what fresh hell the strain of puking would be for his head. He lifted his eyes in hopes to see the noise.

Briefly, he saw Frank Malone's silhouette before a fist connected with his jaw. His head twisted and his body followed suit, landing him on his back. At that point, the pain overwhelmed him, and he blacked out.

EIGHT

L auren laid on her bed listening to the rainfall. Since breakfast, Lauren decided this was where she would stay until her dad said it was time to leave. She had things to do back home. The rest of her summer to get to. She'd been without a phone for over forty-eight hours, which she figured had to be a new record. Well, outside of that time she was grounded for sneaking out of the house with her friends. Her mom was so worried about her. "Were there boys with you girls?" What the hell did that matter? She was smart enough not to get herself knocked up.

The rain kept the sky dark, and the sound soothed her soul. With the breeze from the fan blowing across her face, she felt comfortable and relaxed in the bed. After last night's events, she deserved a little relaxation. Even falling asleep the previous night was a challenge. Each time she closed her eyes, she heard the laughter.

Once, in the middle of the night, she walked to the window and looked out across the hills. She swore she saw figures standing in the grass, staring up at the house. People, dozens and dozens of them, all in various forms of decay with shades of green and gray, stood throughout the field, circling the house as if drawn to it. *They followed me from the woods and the pond.* After a flash of lightning, no one was there. She realized it must've been a dream. After that, she made her way to bed and fell fast asleep.

In the darkness of the room, relaxed under the quilt of the soft bed, she heard the front door slam shut. If she'd been less comfortable, she would've got up to investigate, but unless her dad came to get her, she had no intention of moving.

Minutes melted away as she dozed in the bed. Minutes stacked up to over an hour and passed in the blink of an eye.

Lauren shifted to her side and opened her eyes. She saw a humanoid shape in the corner, startling her. She bolted to her elbow. It stood within the shadow, as if part of the shadow itself. She wiped sleep from her eyes and focused on the corner, focused on the darkness. Nothing. She shook her head.

"Lauren, you're literally jumping at shadows now," she chastised herself.

She dropped the elbow holding her up and flopped dejectedly back into the soft mattress. Still on her side, she closed her eyes and began drifting back to sleep.

As her mind slipped off into dreamland, she heard a soft whisper in the room. "They need you."

Just part of a dream, she told herself, ignoring the words. She took a deep breath and exhaled.

"They need you."

Lauren stirred in the bed. Suddenly, she felt a hand brush against her cheek. She sat straight up, her eyes darting across the room, looking for who had touched her. She expected to see Chandler. Maybe he dropped down beside the bed after messing with her. She quickly went from one side to the other before sitting back in the middle of the bed. Was she going crazy, too? She couldn't get out of this house and back home quick enough. She rubbed the palm of her hands into her eyes, wiping away the last of the sleep.

As her hands fell back to the bed, she saw a lady sitting on the bed in front of her. Her throat wanted to scream, but her brain wouldn't allow it. Something about the lady had a calming affect. It was as if Lauren knew her. The bridge of her nose and the way her eyes sat in her head felt familiar. Lauren leaned her head over and noticed how translucent the lady was. A spirit!

Finally, her brain released enough of the grip on her throat for her to barely speak. "Holy shit," she creaked out. "You're a ghost."

The spirit gave a nod and a smile.

When it did, a flash went off in Lauren's head. Sixteen years of seeing her mother smile and laugh at her flooded her mind. Lauren's eyes filled with tears, and the first few made their way down her cheek. She mouthed the word "Grandma" but no sound could come out.

The ghost of Elizabeth Adams nodded her head, then said again in a whisper, "They need you."

Lauren swallowed hard and forced her throat to do its job. "Who? Mom? Dad?"

Elizabeth nodded.

"Both?" she asked.

The ghost nodded again.

"Where are they? What do they need?"

The figure of Elizabeth started to fade.

Lauren could tell she was losing whatever energy, power, strength allowed her to show herself and speak.

Putting forth one last effort, Lauren heard the ghost whisper, "Get others," before disappearing from the foot of Lauren's bed.

With her marching orders in hand, she threw off the covers of the bed, hopped out, and put on clothes as fast as possible. She sprinted around her bed, opened the door, and ran into the hallway.

NINE

"Chandler! Jake! Carly!" Lauren screamed from the hallway.

To Carly, her voice sounded frantic, rushed.

Carly sat down the handful of cards she held in her hand and hopped off her bed. She heard the other two doors open just moments before she opened her own.

At the mouth of the stairs, Lauren stood in the hallway in a pair of blue jean shorts and a gray T-Shirt. Her hair looked a mess as if she'd just woken up. Over the past few days, Carly couldn't think of a time when she'd seen Lauren not put together with her hair done and make-up on.

Jake and Chandler hurried out of their rooms. Carly noticed the same look of worry and confusion on their faces. Why would Lauren be hollering for them to come out? She never expected Lauren would want to gather the group together. Did she get her phone back already and want to take a group photo? Lauren would probably want to forget about this weekend as fast as possible.

Carly joined Jake as Chandler playfully hopped over to his sister.

"What's up?" Chandler asked.

"Something's wrong with mom and dad," Lauren said.

The look in Lauren's eyes alarmed Carly.

"What makes you think there's something wrong?" Jake asked.

"I..." she started, then paused. "Ok. This is going to sound nuts, but..." She took a deep breath. "My grandmother told me."

The look on Chandler's face mirrored what Carly imagined her face looked like.

"Lauren, Gramma's still in Norfolk. She didn't come here with us," Chandler said.

Lauren took a deep breath. Frustration poured out with her exhale. "Not Gramma Walker. Grandma...Mom 's mom."

"Isn't she the one who died?" Jake asked. Just as he said it, the whites in his eyes grew. "Holy shit! She's stuck here as a ghost, too! And she spoke to you?"

"Yes," Lauren said. Finally her shoulders relaxed as if a weight had been removed. "She told me they need help. When I asked if it was mom or dad, she said both. She told me to get the others." She looked straight at Carly, "Can you get your parents?"

Carly nudged Jake. When Lauren asked her, she suddenly found it odd they hadn't ran out when Lauren yelled. A sinking feeling dropped in Carly's stomach. Lauren called their names loud enough for the whole house to have heard, but only the four kids responded. No parents.

Both Jake and Carly ran to their parents' door, tripping over each other. They pounded on it, hollering for them, before throwing the door wide open. Empty. The room was completely empty. An overwhelming sensation of dread joined to the sinking feeling in Carly's stomach. Something's not right. The hairs on the back of her neck stood up.

The two left the empty room and walked back to Lauren and Chandler. Chandler held onto Lauren's side, and she had her arm around him. He was visibly upset and concerned.

"They aren't there, are they?" Lauren asked.

Jake shook his head.

"What about the doctor lady?" Carly asked. "Or the two guys who work here?"

Lauren shrugged.

Carly was at a loss. By the look on the others' faces, so were they. The four of them stood alone in what she knew was a haunted house. Lauren had expressed her doubts, but she admitted talking to her dead grandmother. Carly assumed that probably changed her mind.

"Let's go downstairs," Jake said. "It's at least less creepy than here. Do you think maybe they went outside?"

"It's still pouring rain," Lauren said. "We can check the porch, but why would my grandmother say they needed help if they're just rocking on the front porch? Nothing feels right. I do agree on downstairs, though. Jake, lead the way?"

"Why do I have to go first?"

"Because you're the oldest guy, and it was your idea."

Jake took a hesitant step forward. Carly stayed close to his back. Lauren walked just behind Carly with Chandler glued to Lauren's side. In formation, the four made their way down the stairs. Each step landed with such a delicate touch that the steps barely creaked. When they did, the group inhaled audibly.

As soon as they landed at the bottom of the stairs, Jake went for the front door, separating himself from Carly and the others. He opened the door and stepped outside. "Mom? Dad?"

Carly watched him run to the left side of the porch then back to the right. He kept calling out every few steps.

"You guys!" he finally said to the other three. "Come out here!"

Carly led the way onto the porch and found her brother standing by the swing.

"That looks like blood," he said and pointed to the ground. "Like a lot of blood."

A puddle with a crimson hue lay pooled on the front porch.

"Back inside. We need to find the doctor." Lauren shouted over the rain.

TEN

Lauren led the way back into the house, leaving the front door open. She hoped Dr. Stiller was in her bedroom. Maybe the doc knew where their parents went.

Jake took up the rear.

As she walked down the hallway, Lauren's shoulders tensed and a tingle ran down her spine as she passed the pictures. She'd been the center of attention before and knew what it felt like to have everyone's eyes on her. That same feeling invaded her now. Reflections in the picture frames caught her eye. But in those reflections, she saw more than just the four of them. Shadows that shouldn't be there stood watch. Shadows shaped as people. She forced her eyes to look straight ahead, but her peripheral vision betrayed her. With each picture, there were more. Some stood still. Others moved.

When they reached the door, she rapped on the outside and turned the knob at the same time. "Dr. Stiller?"

No answer.

"I don't like this," Chandler said. His voice quivered with fear. "They are all gone. No adults. Just us."

"Don't worry, we'll find them," Carly reassured. Her attempt at sounding brave failed. The shake in her voice gave her away.

"Dr. Stiller?" Lauren said again, leading the other three into the room.

Lauren realized she'd never been in this room before. The large window with the seat would've had a beautiful view of the landscape, except the rain blurred the ability to see clearly. The water rushing down the window made the outside look more like a Van Gogh painting. News clippings lay stacked on the desk. Lauren thumbed through them as the others walked past her.

The articles talked about the night her grandmother was shot. She quickly scanned them, building a summary of what occurred. Two men who worked for the accused mob boss Salvatore Carlisi were hired to strong arm Senator Thomas Adams into passing legislation favorable to Carlisi and his businesses. The attempt went sour, resulting in the death of both gunmen, Tony DeRemer and Marco Delfina, a caretaker, Bill Monroe, and the senator's wife, Elizabeth Adams.

She heard a crash in the room and felt her heart jump out of her chest. Jake and Carly stood closer to the bathroom, and Chandler sat on the bed. All four turned in the direction of the sound. A purse that had sat on the window seat fell over and landed on the floor, spilling its contents.

"I didn't touch anything," Jake said.

"Me either," Carly affirmed. She walked over to the purse, grabbed the wallet that fell out, and flipped it open.

"Isn't the doc's name Stiller?" she asked.

"Yes," Lauren answered. "Mom's been seeing her for a few months now. Renee Stiller."

"Then why does this driver's license say Gina Delfina with the doc's picture?"

Lauren took two quick steps and stood next to Carly. The others joined them. Lauren snatched the wallet out of Carly's hand and stared at the picture and then the name. Realization hit her. She'd just seen that name. She lifted her head to the news clippings on the desk and pushed past Jake and Chandler. Grabbing the article in one hand and holding the wallet in the other she looked back and forth.

"Holy shit!" she exclaimed.

"What is it?" Jake and Carly asked in unison.

"Dr. Stiller isn't who she says she is. One of the guys that killed my grandmother has her same last name."

She handed both the wallet and news article to Jake. He moved back a foot and started to read it with Carly leaning over his shoulder.

Chandler looked up at Lauren. "What does this mean? Where's mom?"

Tears welled up in his eyes.

"I think we've been set up. Renee, Gina, whatever her name is...she's about mom's age. What if that guy was her father, and she's looking for revenge? We could all be in danger."

Jake looked up at her. "So what do we do?"

"They couldn't have left. All the cars are still out front. Our parents are here somewhere. We need to find them." Lauren thought for a moment. "I'm going to say the dumbest thing possible in a haunted house with a re-venge-oriented therapist around. We need to split up."

"Split up!" Chandler said. "Are you nuts?"

"She's right," Jake said. "We can cover more ground quicker."

"Chandler and I will take upstairs. We'll search every room. You two take the downstairs."

Lauren started for the door when Jake said, "Wait!"

"What's wrong?"

"She took our phones," he said. "They'll probably be in here somewhere. Let's find those first. Spread out."

Lauren's face extended into a smile for the first time that morning. She grabbed Jake's face between her hands and kissed him. "Brilliant," she said.

His face turned a deep red.

Lauren saw Carly go for the closet. Jake took a minute to recover before joining Chandler on the ground to look under the bed. Lauren went for the desk and rummaged through it.

She was opening the third drawer when she heard a loud knock against the wall in front of her. Her head sprang up. Turning to the others, she saw she wasn't the only one who heard it. They all stood silently for a moment. Suddenly, a series of thuds sounded against the wall, as if multiple fists pounded into it. The noise grew louder and louder.

"What is that?" Chandler yelled with his hands pressed firmly against his ears.

"I don't know," Lauren answered.

The volume grew, drowning out the sound of rain.

The four of them moved to the middle of the room.

The banging on the walls surrounded them, reaching a deafening volume, then stopped. Dead silence filled the room.

Lauren heard the sound of her heart beat in her ears. Their breathing filled the void.

"Oh fuck," Jake said and pointed to the bathroom.

A human-shaped shadow stood in the doorway, then stepped forward.

"Go," Lauren said. "Run!"

She sprinted out of the room and down the hallway. The other three were close behind her. She focused on the front door that they had left open, ignoring any figures in the pictures staring at her. She intended to run directly into the rain, but then the door slammed shut in front of her, stopping her, Jake, Carly, and Chandler in their tracks.

Standing in the foyer, Chandler, on the verge of tears, looked up at his big sister. "What do we do?"

"We *have* to find our parents. Jake, Carly, take the downstairs. Chandler and I will go up. Yell if you find anything."

PART FIVE

Symphony in Motion

ONE

"Where am I?" Ann asked as she opened her eyes. She tried to lift her head, but a sharp pain shot through her temple and radiated across her head. Her heartbeat pulsed behind her eyeballs. She'd had hangovers before, but this fucking hurt.

Her head dropped back onto the wet earth. The rain had slowed to a light mist. She was face down and freezing cold, her clothes soaking wet. The clouds overhead blanketed the sky, leaving Ann no way to tell if it was morning, afternoon, or night.

The more her senses came back, the more she became aware of her situation. Her arms stretched tight behind her, soreness ran across her shoulders. She tried to bring her arms forward but couldn't. Zip ties held them firmly in place. It felt like a weight was attached to the zip ties, making it impossible to move.

Struggling through the hangover migraine, she lifted her head. The tree line extended in front of her, and the pond swished behind her. Painfully, she twisted her neck to see what held her to the ground. Ann willed herself to stay conscious despite the white hot bolts of pain exploding in her head.

Kathryn lay next to her with her arms also zip tied behind her. Their ties were interlocked together, and Kathryn's head hung by Ann's shoes. She hadn't woken up yet.

Ann had no idea how they got there or why they were tied up. She remembered Kathryn going under hypnosis. Remembered hearing her retelling of what happened and those memories filling in puzzle pieces. But after that, the memories were foggy. Almost as a dream, she remembered Renee throwing newspaper clippings at her. Or was that actually a dream? There was a serious mindfuck going on somewhere.

None of that remotely explained why the fuck she and Kathryn were zip tied in the rain.

"Kat," Ann said in a whisper. Someone had hog tied them together. If they were close, Ann didn't want to draw their attention.

"Kat," she said with more intensity, but still a whisper. "Wake up."

Ann picked up her leg and nudged Kathryn's shoulder. What if Kat was dead? What if she was tied out here to a corpse?

When Kat gave a low moan, Ann breathed a sigh of relief. "Thank God, you're not dead," she whispered.

In a very groggy voice, Kathryn croaked out, "What?"

"Kat, wake up," Ann said.

She pushed a little harder with her shoe and felt Kat's whole weight shift. Ann ignored the throbbing pain still beating its rhythm in her head and rolled with Kat.

"What's going on?" Kat said muffled. Ann assumed Kat's face was pressed against the soaking wet grass and mud. "My head feels like I spent the night with the Jack Daniels and Jim Beam. Hell, all four of the horsemen. Where are we? And why can't I move my arms?"

"We're down by the pond, and we're tied together. As to what the hell is going on? I was hoping you could help me figure that out," Ann answered, maintaining her half whisper.

Ann felt her shoulders scream as Kathryn tested her restraints.

Kat let out a large sigh. "What's the last thing you remember?" she asked.

Ann told her what she could recall.

"You don't remember panicking and running out of the house?"

"Panicking?" Ann questioned. "No. What do you remember?"

"After Renee showed you the news clippings and berated you, you stormed out of the house. I followed you into the rain, but after that things go..."

"Foggy?" Ann finished.

"Yeah, foggy." Kat paused. "Holy shit!" she exclaimed.

"What? What happened?" Ann asked.

"That bitch fucking drugged us!"

"Who? Dr. Stiller? Why would she do that?"

"I don't know, but that's the only explanation. We both drank the water bottles she gave us, and we both have no idea how we got here. I'm assuming you also have a hangover from hell right now. She roofied us."

"Why would she do that?"

"I don't know," Kat said. "But the next time I see her, it's high on my list of questions."

Ann thought back to the interactions she'd had with Renee. The person she met with for the past few months. That she told secrets and fears to. Ann struggled to believe that Renee would do this to them, but memories and feelings continued to pour in. The vision of a snake in the grass waiting to strike. Ann was getting better and the clearer she became, the more she saw through whatever veil Renee displayed. Was she too lost in herself to see that before?

"Do you see her anywhere?" Ann asked. "I don't see anyone my direction."

"No. She must be back at the house."

Ann felt Kathryn tug a few more times at the zip ties.

"Hey Ann, this is going to get uncomfortable, but I need to reach my boot."

"Your boot?"

"Yes, my boot."

Ann felt her shoulders pull back and her back bow forward. Kathryn's leg pushed hard against Ann's spine as she slid her boot between the two of them. Screaming pain rushed through her joints again. Ann knew her arms were going to pop out of their sockets before Kat reached her boot. She tried unsuccessfully to hold back any grains.

"Almost. There." Kathryn said through a clinched jaw.

Finally, Ann felt the tension on her shoulders ease.

At the same time, Kathryn said, "Got it."

Ann heard the click of a knife's blade locking into place. She opened her eyes, not realizing she had squeezed them shut when her shoulders were trying to detach from the rest of her. She let out a sigh as the sharp, shooting pain eased into a throb.

She heard footsteps coming from the pond. Ann strained her neck and saw Renee a few dozen yards away, walking their direction.

"She's coming," Ann said.

TWO

C handler held close to his sister's side. In all his eight years, he'd never been as scared as he was walking up each step of the large wooden staircase. He wanted to be home in his room playing on his Xbox. Searching for his missing parents with a vindictive therapist on the loose while in a haunted house didn't chart on his list of favorite activities. His heart was trying to pound its way out of his chest.

Each stair groaned. They echoed in the dead silence. Although the house was empty, Cardinal Crest Estate felt crowded. That feeling combined with the silence made every hair on his neck stand straight up. Electricity filled the air.

Lauren reached the second floor.

"I'm guessing you don't want to split up?" she asked.

Chandler vigorously shook his head. There was no way he was exploring the house alone. Before he knew about the ghosts inhabiting the house, he hated walking to the end of the hallway. The pictures stared at him, and the crappy lighting caused dark spots and strange shadows.

"Good, me neither."

Knowing that Lauren didn't want to split up helped. Maybe she was just as scared as he was but better at putting on a brave front. Chandler and Lauren fought a lot, but when push came to shove, he looked up to his big sister.

With Lauren leading the way, Chandler turned down their side of the hallway. She opened their parents' room, softly saying "Mom? Dad?" as she did.

Chandler doubted they'd be there but still held out hope. Maybe everyone was using a different bathroom. Maybe Lauren really didn't see their grandmother's ghost. Maybe that ghost didn't really say their parents needed help. So many maybes and hopes cycled through Chandler's head. The same hope emerged with each room they checked. And then vanished just as quickly.

When they completed the left side of the hallway, Lauren turned to face the other direction. "What the hell?" she said.

Chandler turned and saw it too. A wooden ladder extended from the ceiling to the second floor. It wasn't there when they came up the staircase, but it was now.

Lauren hesitantly walked to the ladder.

Chandler stood in the middle of the hallway, determined not to get any closer.

"Lauren, what are you doing?" he asked.

"It leads to the attic," she said.

"That wasn't open just a few minutes ago. You don't find that at all suspicious?"

"Of course I do. But what if while we were looking in a room down there, someone came down from the attic. She could be holding mom and dad up there. We have to check."

"What if it wasn't the people holding mom and dad? What if the ghosts lowered it to trick us into going up there?" Chandler felt his argument made more sense. His eyes pleaded with Lauren.

"I'll take that chance in case they are up there."

Lauren grabbed the wooden ladder and climbed.

"Lauren." Chandler stood at the base and stared up at her. "Come on, Lauren."

"Chandler, get up here."

He sighed and begrudgingly gripped the ladder. After a few nimble movements, his head broached the ceiling. He placed his hands on the attic floor, hiked his leg up, and stood up. He used his shorts to knock the dust off his hands and coughed from the resulting cloud.

Turning his head from side to side, Chandler surveyed the large attic. Towers of brown cardboard boxes crowded the area. A tall mirror with a sheet over it stood in one corner. More sheets covered the furniture that had been haphazardly shoved around the attic. All the sheets were once white but had turned a dingy gray from age and dust.

Each wall had a small circular window embedded in it overlooking the farmland. Chandler thought back to the first day when he and Carly went to the pond and he saw the window from the hill. That also brought back the memory of the ghost girl he saw in the window, making Chandler immediately uneasy.

"Lauren, where are you?"

From behind one of the cardboard towers, she poked her head out.

"I'm over here."

"Don't wander off. Are they up here? It's hard to see anything."

"No, just us and the dust bunnies."

Chandler breathed a sigh of relief which brought on another cough. "Then let's get out of here. It's hard to breathe."

As he turned back to the hatch, he heard its springs make a piercing scream. The ladder folded up and the wooden door slammed shut. The light coming from the hallway vanished, leaving only a single light bulb for them to see by.

"No, no, no," Chandler said in a panic.

He dropped to his knees, kicking up a cloud of dust, and banged on the hatch. It didn't budge.

"We're locked in, Genius," Chandler said. "This was your stupid idea, and now we're stuck."

Lauren slid between the boxes and joined Chandler. She knelt and pushed on the door. It started to give but then slammed back in place.

"Shit," she said, dejected.

THREE

As Lauren and Chandler went up the staircase, Jake led Carly through the den and the living room. He knew that no one was down there, but he had to be sure. When he looked through the windows, he saw the rain had turned into a light mist. The cloud cover maintained its dark veil over the house and surrounding area.

As they left the den, Jake paused in the foyer and glared down the hallway leading to Renee's (or Gina's, whatever her name was) room. He felt the urge to go back there, to find their phones, and call for help. Their parents were missing. A psycho therapist on some kind of revenge kick was here somewhere.

He wondered about the two guys who worked at Cardinal Crest. Joe and Frank. Their absence became notably more apparent, raising his suspicion they were involved. It was possible the two of them had fallen victim to whatever scheme Renee(Gina) had planned, but his gut told him they worked together. Jake decided it was better to assume they were foe until proven otherwise.

"I'm not going back in that room," Carly said.

"Me neither. Or down that hallway," Jake added.

With haste, they turned the corner of the dining room and hurried into the kitchen. Jake stood just outside the cellar door when a loud boom broke the silence.

"What was that?" Carly asked.

Jake stood motionless in the kitchen.

"It sounded like a door slamming shut."

"Chandler! Lauren!" Carly shouted.

"Don't be so loud," Jake said. "We don't know who or what is waiting around the corner."

"What if they're in trouble?"

"It could've just been the air conditioning shutting a door left open."

"Shhh," she said and put her index finger up to her lips. She walked backward into the dining room. "Listen."

Jake didn't hear anything. He closed his eyes, hoping to heighten his sense of hearing, but still nothing. Just the drumming of his heartbeat and the sound of his own breathing. He opened his eyes, shrugged his shoulders, and shook his head. As he did, his eyes drifted towards the darkness of the cellar.

Something caught his eye.

"They need help," Carly said.

Before Jake could say anything, Carly ran out of the dining room. Her voice echoed as she hollered, "Chandler! Lauren! Where are you?"

Jake's attention didn't waiver. From his perspective, the door led down into a dark chasm. Except he saw something at the bottom. He placed his hand on the edge of the door frame and leaned his head in. He picked his foot up and placed it on the wooden step. It groaned under his weight. His hand gripped the railing, but he felt it wiggle under his grip. He took another step, followed by another. Using the railing as nothing more than a guide, he continued down.

Jake trained his eyes on the floor, hoping to see the movement that had caught his attention. Halfway down the rickety steps, his eyes adjusted to the darkness, and he saw it.

A shoe.

His dad's shoe.

He rushed the last few steps quicker. As he reached the bottom, he heard a low moan.

His dad and Jim were tied to a pole in the middle of the room, both beaten and bloodied. His dad looked really bad. Somehow Jim looked worse.

"Dad," Jake said and hurried over to him.

FOUR

"Ladies, wake up," Renee shouted.

Kathryn tucked the knife under her.

"We're awake," she yelled back. "Confused as shit, though."

"Renee, what kind of fucked up immersion therapy is this?" Ann screamed.

"First, stop calling me Renee. It's Gina. Renee Stiller was a lonely, old geezer who spent way too much time with her work and cats."

Gina walked closer to them.

Kathryn turned her head, fighting against the searing pain shooting directly behind her eyeballs. When she finally saw Gina, the psychologist with all the screws loose stood a few feet away, looking directly at Ann.

"I'd stand up to greet you, Gina, but I'm a little tied up at the moment," Kathryn said.

"Cliché, Kat. Cliché." Gina squatted down, putting herself eye level with her captives.

"Can we address my question then? What the hell is going on?" Ann said. Frustration blasted from her voice.

"Where should I start?" Gina asked rhetorically. "Oh, I know. How about I fill in some of the details left off Kat's story? The two guys who came there that night, Tony and Marco, were Tony DeRemer and Marco Delfina. Marco was my father. He and Uncle Tony were hired to talk some sense into your crooked father. Salvatore and your dad had a good thing until he suddenly grew a fucking conscience. Salvatore gave him *everything*. Gave *you* everything." As Gina talked, she pointed a finger at Ann as if blaming her for what happened. "If not for Salvie, your dad would've never been a senator. He made your father, and how did your dad repay him? By not living up to his end of their bargain."

Gina stood up and paced. She continued to talk, but she did so to herself more than to Ann.

"Daddy just wanted to scare him. That was all he was hired to do. Scare him so that things stayed the same. Daddy would stay in good with Salvie. The senator would stay good. Salvie keeps doing what he does. Everyone's happy." Gina turned her attention back to Ann and Kathryn. "But no. Instead, my dad comes home in a body bag. Daddy and Uncle Tony."

Gina sloshed through the mud and moved closer to Kathryn. The hot lead weight behind Kathryn's eyes made it difficult to follow Gina's movements, but she fought through the pain. She wasn't going to let this crazy bitch out of her sight.

"Kat, I appreciate you filling in some of the blanks for me. I knew your family had a lot to do with their deaths. Whenever I visited that bodyguard...what was his name? Brian? Just before I slit his throat, he told me a pretty close recount of what happened. Your version was so much more vivid, though."

"You killed Mr. Hayes?" Ann asked.

"Of course," Gina said. She circled back to Ann. "I killed him. I killed your dad, too." Gina chuckled. "If you could see the look on your face right now. Kat, I almost want to cut your ties so you can see this. Price of admission right here."

Kathryn felt her arms jerk as Ann struggled against the restraints.

"You fucking bitch," Ann said, thrashing around.

Kathryn heard the tears in her voice.

"Poison is a great thing," Gina continued. "At his age, the heart attack looked just like a heart attack. I stalked you next. I planned to break into your house and slit your family's throat while you all slept. Then I saw you acting strange, isolated, panicked. I thought you knew. I thought you knew I was there. Guess I felt a little paranoid myself.

"While learning your routines, I stood behind you in line one morning, and I overheard you set up that first initial appointment with the actual Dr. Stiller. That's when my plans changed. Why kill them in their sleep? She already thinks she's going crazy. Let's make her actually go crazy. With the right combination of antipsychotics, depressants, and a few other things, not only were you telling me your life story, but I pushed you to the brink of lunacy. It's fun for the cat to bat the mouse around."

Kathryn turned her head again. "So, you grew up without a dad," Kathryn said. "How about instead of killing a therapist, you just went to one? Mommy not around either?"

"She was a useless, drug addicted whore. She didn't deserve my dad. I went to a few therapists, but all I learned from them was the lingo. That was during the rare occasions that I lived in a foster home that didn't want me as a toy, or for the money, or for the dad's sick pleasure.

"You see, you and her," Gina said to Ann as she bent down closer to Kathryn's face. "You got to live a normal life. Hell, her daddy retired a fucking hero. The crook and his daughter."

Gina turned and paced again. She walked further away, bringing herself to the edge of the pond.

Kathryn seized on the opportunity to wiggle around while Gina was turned. She grasped the knife between her fingers and worked the blade back and forth against the zip ties.

After hearing that not only had Ann's father been murdered but that she'd been driven to the brink of insanity by this vindicative bitch, Kat couldn't imagine what fresh Hell was going through Ann's head. But considering the heaving sobs beside her, Ann must be revisiting grief all over again.

Sure, it wasn't Gina's fault that her dad died. If she really wanted to place blame, it was her dad's fault. He put her in that position, based on his own bad decisions. Yet, she blamed them. Blamed the survivors.

Kat figured if she survives this, maybe she'd get therapy. She suppressed a chuckle. Go see a therapist? After what this crack pot was doing? Fuck that!

As the knife continued up and down the ties, she concentrated on Gina. When Gina turned back to them, she stashed the blade back underneath her. From this angle, she saw Gina held something in her hand, but Kathryn couldn't see what it was in the dark.

"I'd planned to have the two of you watch as I kill your perfect little families, but I didn't think you would make it this far down the property before dropping. If I ever do this again, I need to make sure to add more sedatives to the water bottles."

"Told you," Kathryn said to Ann.

Gina walked closer to them.

"Instead of dragging you all the way back to the house, I guess I'll just give you another dose here and throw you in the pond. Let you drown. Then I'll deal with everyone you love."

Kathryn saw what she held in her hand. Gina flipped the syringe back and forth. The plunger stretched all the way out. If whatever was in there was the same thing she put in the water, Kathryn feared she and Ann would be out in minutes and dead not long after.

Even though Gina advanced towards them with a malicious smile stretched across her face, Kathryn grabbed the knife and continued to slice at her bindings.

FIVE

Not exactly to plan, but close enough.

Gina had no intention of her masterpiece being ruined just because she didn't want to drag these two kicking and screaming back to the house. A little improvisation wasn't bad. She'd drugged them enough that death wasn't far off, then let the pond do the rest. They would drown in the murky water, and then she would tell Frank and Joe to dispose of everyone else. None of that would change the story. Ann killed her family and Kathryn's. Kathryn chased her to the pond where they both drowned. Easy enough.

"If you two fight, this will hurt so much worse. Just relax." Gina smiled. She tried to sound like a caring nurse. "You'll feel a little stick, then it'll all be over."

She stepped closer and closer, the syringe bouncing in her hand. Gina relished the look in their eyes. Fear. Fear and hatred. They hated her, and she loved it. Their hate invigorated her.

"Ann," Kathryn said. "Ann, try pulling. See if we can break through these things."

The two thrashed on the ground, pulling at the ties that bound them together.

Gina's smile grew wider. If she could freeze her face, she wondered if she looked like the Joker. Her cheeks hurt from the joy she felt. So much planning. So much patience. So much waiting. Decades of it for the revenge, the payback on their families for killing her father. They had mere moments of their lives left. She was the Grim Reaper. She was Death, the Destroyer of Their World.

In the wind, a voice floated in, and she paused her forward advancement. "Gigi, Sweetie," the whisper said.

Gina's breath caught in her throat. She wavered in place for a moment, her grip on the syringe loosening to the point it teetered in her hand. In her head, she was five. Her dad had taken her to the zoo. She stood in front of the monkey cage and watched them swing back and forth from the bars and the trapeze. Behind her, her dad said her name, and she turned around. He snapped her picture with the monkeys.

Gina shook her head and came back to the present. Her grip on the syringe restored. All the stress of getting to this point must've been weighing on her more than she realized. No need to worry, though. A few seconds more and it would all be over. Salvie would love her. She'd have proven her genius to everyone.

"Gigi," the wind whispered again.

"Which one of you said that?" Gina said, suddenly furious with Ann and Kathryn.

She stood in place, brandishing the syringe like a knife.

"Said what?" Ann asked.

"How the fuck do you know that name?" Gina shouted.

She bolted forward and dropped on the ground, the needle inches from Ann's face. Gina knew how easy it would be to shove the metal point directly into Ann's eye. Bury the needle and depress the plunger. The entirety of the venomous liquid would explode into her eyeball. The goo would drip down her cheek.

Ann stared, transfixed on the sharp tip. Her eyes wide and unblinking. Her breathing came in quick short bursts.

Ann's fear calmed Gina. She smiled again, and the thought of the name drifted from her head. She stood up, dusted off her knees, and took a step backwards.

"Which one of you would like to take the long nap first? The bitch whose daddy didn't know how to follow directions? Or the bitch whose daddy and uncle drove my daddy's head into a fireplace?" Gina danced the syringe back and forth, pointing it at Ann then Kathryn then back to Ann again.

"Eeny, meeny, miny, moe," Gina sang. "Catch a tiger by its toe."

"Stop, Gigi," the whisper on the wind came.

Gina stopped singing and on impulse said, "Daddy?"

It was his voice. She knew his voice like she knew the intro to her favorite song. For years she dreamed of his voice telling her she could come home. When she was being abused or neglected in some pisshole foster home, she had prayed he'd ride in to rescue her.

Without realizing it, the syringe dropped from her hand. "Where are you, Daddy?"

"I'm here, Gigi."

The voice encircled her. It came from every direction and nowhere at the same time. Like the wind, the voice appeared and then vanished. She needed to find him. After so many years of being separated, she needed to see him again. She felt as if he had stood inches from her all weekend. Now, she didn't just feel his presence but heard his voice. His voice beckoned her.

"Where are you?" she said, child-like. She was suddenly five years old again, being whisked away into her father's arms.

"The water, Gigi. Come to the water."

She stumbled past Kathryn and Ann and headed to the edge of the water. Carried along by legs no longer connected to her brain, Gina followed the sound of water lapping. With the deluge of rainfall, the pond spilled over its border. Solid ground turned to mush and swamp. Before she knew it, she had walked far enough out to be knee-deep.

"Daddy?" she called. "Please don't leave me! Daddy!"

"I'll never leave you again," the voice said. It danced from one shoulder to another.

Gina laughed as it tickled her ear, scrunching her head into her shoulder.

She looked over the pond. A shadow stood on the far side. It walked onto the water and glided across the top. The closer the shadow drew to Gina, the more the features showed. She saw his slicked back hair with the touch of gray on the side. His blue eyes and smiling mouth materialized. It was him. Really him.

She couldn't control her jubilation and trudged through the thick water to meet him. The further into the water she traveled, the more difficult each step became, as if testing her resolve and determination. But she had come this far, she was not going to be stopped. The water rose to her waist. Her feet sank into the soft mud bottom. By the fourth step, her shoes were buried deep in the muck. A few more steps and everything below her chest was submerged.

The more she sank, the more her thoughts were consumed by her father. Closer and closer he came to her. She felt tugging at her clothes and branches brushing across her legs.

Hands reached out of the pond and dragged her under.

SIX

A nn watched as Gina dropped the syringe. As she began to call out to her father, Ann knew Gina was cracking. The look in Gina's eyes confirmed it for Ann. Gina's eyes stared blankly, searching for nothing, clouded over by a haze of lunacy. Ann knew the look. She'd seen the look in her own eyes while staring in a mirror.

Kathryn carved away at their binds as fast as she could. Ann felt the pressure against her skin and prayed Kat wouldn't slip and bury the knife into her wrist. It'd be some kind of great irony to finally find out she wasn't crazy only to then have her wrists sliced open while trying to escape her tormentor. She forced her shoulders to power through the pain, pulling on the binds as hard as she could, and weakening the spot where Kathryn sliced.

Ann heard Gina's footfalls slosh through the wet ground. Was she going for a swim now?

Ann laid as still as she could, trying not to have her wrist sliced open. A breeze blew past her that contained a whisper. Her mother's voice spoke gently in her ear. The sound of it sent her back to that first night at Cardinal Crest.

After being pressed against the railing, she heard her mother's voice tell her to go to bed. Now, she heard the same sweet voice again. A voice she hadn't heard in nearly thirty years. She soaked in the sound of her voice, the timbre, the cadence of the words.

Although the sound of her mother's voice was nectar to her soul, the message she delivered was anything but.

"Everyone's in danger. Get to the house."

Her family needed her. Her children needed her. For the first time in months, she felt like herself. Her normal self. The Ann Walker that didn't back down from a fight. The Ann Walker who learned how to stand her ground and fight when she knew she was right. Skills she learned from her father.

Those few words from her mother set her in motion.

Ann closed her eyes and squeezed out a tear. "Love you, Mom," she whispered to the wind.

A warm gust blew across her face. Despite the many years, Ann never forgot the feel of her mother's warm embrace. Although the wind was silent this time, she knew the message it contained. "I love you, Annabelle."

Ann heard the zip tie snap.

"Got it," Kathryn said.

Suddenly, without Kathryn's weight holding her down, the tension in her arms let up.

"Cut through mine. We have to hurry!" Ann said.

She kept her arms spread wide as Kathryn spun around and sat the blade to work against Ann's binds. With a better grip on the knife and more leverage, Kathryn cut through them after a few well-placed strokes. The moment the binds snapped apart, Ann brought her hands in front of her. Red welts circled her wrists, but they didn't hurt nearly as bad as the dull aching in her upper arms and shoulders.

Both ladies jumped to their feet. A rush of blood left Ann dizzy. If not for Kathryn steadying her, she would've fallen back to the damp earth.

Unsure of what was happening with Gina but not wanting to draw the psychopath's attention, Ann quietly maneuvered past the water. She followed Kathryn's lead and both ducked low to the ground. They stepped through the tall grass, and Ann hoped the sound of shoes squishing through the mud didn't bring Gina out of her trance.

As Ann glanced that direction, she saw Gina advance further into the pond. Only the woman's torso remained above water. A shadow hovered above the pond. Hands stretched out of the water and reached for Gina. They gripped her clothes and her arms. They tugged on her, and although she tried to fight them off, Gina fought a losing battle. All the while, the shadow watched.

"What the hell!" Kathryn said.

"We need to get to the house. The others need us."

"How do you know that?"

"My mother told me," Ann said without missing a beat.

"At this point, after everything I've seen this weekend, that's the least craziest thing I've heard."

As Gina was being swallowed by the pond, Ann stood up from her crouched position. Kathryn followed suit. They picked up their paces and ran up the hill to Cardinal Crest Estate.

SEVEN

"Chandler? Lauren? Where are you?"

Carly sprinted from the dining room and started up the stairs. When she was halfway up, she realized Jake hadn't followed her.

Alone.

Her quick dash up the steps came to a sudden halt. How could he let her take off on her own? Didn't he hear the same thing?

She knew she distinctly heard banging after the sound of a door slamming shut stopped both in their tracks. Muffled cries for help accompanied the banging. She knew they were in trouble. Chandler and Lauren needed help.

Carly debated going back to get Jake but decided against it. If it was nothing but her imagination, he'd pick on her about it. At least this way, she would know for certain. If she couldn't help them on her own, she'd go back and get him to help.

She stood still and waited for the sound to repeat.

"Lauren?" she said again. "Chandler?"

The knocking sound started back, almost giving her a heart attack. She bolted up the rest of the stairs and stood on the second-floor landing. The knocking came from above her. She looked up and saw the attic door rattling on its hinges.

"Help," came the muffled cry from the other side.

Carly stared at the wooden hatch in the ceiling.

"You guys up there?"

"Carly, is that you?"

She recognized Lauren's voice.

"Yes, it's me," she said back.

"Pull down the attic door. We're stuck."

"I can't. There isn't a rope. Just a small handle and I can't reach it."

The hatch rattled on the hinges again.

"Is something blocking it or holding it shut?" Lauren asked.

"Not that I can..." Carly's words trailed off. She stared down the hallway containing their rooms.

The few lights responsible for lighting the massive hallway flickered. They dimmed and brightened beyond what they should before flickering again. The bedroom doors all opened at the same time and slammed shut. They opened again and slammed in unison. The lights continued to dim and flicker. The hallway began to resemble a beating heart.

"Carly, what's that sound? What's going on?" Lauren's muffled voice asked.

All she could do was stand still in the hallway with her eyes fixated on the doors. Her legs wouldn't move. As much as her brain begged them to run, they might as well have been glued to the floor and stacked with lead weights. Her breath became faster as she gasped for air.

I'm going to hyperventilate, she thought.

The hairs on her neck stood on end, and bursts of electrical impulses traversed her spine. She felt something standing just over her shoulder and behind her.

Do not turn around. Do. Not. Turn. Around.

"Carly?!" the muffled voice repeated.

In a huge flash, every light in the hallway exploded. The bulbs in the large chandelier hanging over the foyer exploded, raining down shards of glass over the entryway. The entirety of the house was thrown into darkness.

Carly Miller, no longer able to contain herself, screamed.

EIGHT

"Dad, can you hear me?" Jake asked.

His hands furiously searched for the binds holding them to the pole.

Zip ties! Shit! He thought. He had hoped for a knot that he could untie. Zip ties required cutting.

Aside from his own panicked breathing, he heard his dad and Jim's labored breaths. If not for that, he would have feared that they had been beaten to death. Jake knew Jim needed medical attention soon. Congealed blood stuck to his misshapen face. One side sunk in. Jake had never seen a broken cheek bone before, but if he had to guess what it'd look like, this would be it. What wasn't recessed from broken bone was swollen and bruised.

"Ja, Jake?" his dad forced out. Doug's eyes were still shut, but he lifted his chin from his chest and rested his head on the pole behind him.

"Dad? Thank God. What happened?"

Slowly, Doug opened his eyes. He winced with every move he made. He dropped his head and placed his chin back on his chest. After a few seconds, he raised his head again and moved it from side to side, working out any stiffness and pushing through the pain.

"Frank and Joe," he finally said. "They hit me and threw me down here. Where's Jim?"

"He's on the other side of you. You're both strapped to a pole. He's not in good shape, dad."

"I'm sure we can both use some medical attention."

Jake stood up. "I need to find something to cut you two free."

Jake moved around the edge of the cellar. The dirt floor squished under his feet from rain that had found its way into the cellar. Moving from one side to the other, Jake realized the cellar was empty except for the shelves of boxes. No tools anywhere.

He glanced back up the rickety stairs. There had to be a knife in the kitchen. He grabbed the flimsy, wooden handrail and put his foot on the first step. As voices drifted down from the kitchen, he paused. Frank's and Joe's voices grew louder. Frantically looking for a place to hide, Jake dropped to the side of the stairs and squeezed next to them. He knew they were about to join him in the cellar.

It'd be him, a scrawny fifteen-year-old, against two very full-grown men.

Jake's heart beat out of his chest as he made himself as small as possible in the dark crevasse next to the stairs.

Instead of coming down, Jake heard the cellar door make a high pitch squeal as they closed it. He exhaled a sweet sigh of relief. Thank God for small miracles.

He still needed a way to untie Jim and his dad, though.

Without making a sound, he pulled himself from the small hiding place and eased up the stairs. He took each step as cautiously as possible, letting his foot gently fall on each step and applying as little pressure as he could. He used the railing to counter his weight, praying that the wood was sturdier than it felt.

When he finally reached the door, he stopped and waited. He listened to the conversation on the other side. With the door muffling the voices, he couldn't tell who was who.

"She should be back by now."

"Give her time. When has the boss ever failed?"

"Yeah, but isn't this just a little over the top, even for her? Why not just take them out now? The two guys are downstairs, and the kids are in their rooms. Let her handle the ladies, and you and I finish the job inside. No witnesses. That's how Carlisi likes it."

"She has her plan. She wants those two to suffer. We can't kill the family until she brings them back here. If that changes, Ms. Delfina will let us know."

Jake placed his hand over his mouth. Listening to two people talk so nonchalantly about killing him and his family was not something he'd expected to have happen at fifteen. Or ever. Yet here he was. So much ran through his mind that he hadn't done. No driver's license yet. Never been on a date. Never made out with a girl. Well, with the exception of that one time Kristy McIvie French kissed him during a football game. Outside of that, he'd never done anything else. There was so much in his life he wanted to accomplish; he wanted Carly to accomplish.

"So, Ms. Delfina gets the ladies back here. We kill the family then them two. Then it all gets blamed on the crazy one, like she snapped and killed everyone before off'ing herself."

"That's the idea. Let's wait for her in the den. I want a drink."

From upstairs, Jake heard doors slamming shut.

"Kids running around?" he heard one of them ask.

"Maybe. Should we start gathering them up?"

"We can let them play as long as they stay upstairs."

Jake heard their footsteps grow quieter as they left the kitchen. Not hesitating, he threw open the door and ran for a drawer. He found a kitchen knife, grabbed it, and bounded down the cellar steps, nearly falling on the knife as he slid across the dirt and mud. He landed just in front of the pole they were bound to.

With a quick flick of the knife, Jake sliced the zip ties apart. At the same time, Jim started to wake up. Jake moved next to him.

Doug brought his hands in front of him and rubbed his sore wrists, followed by the back of his neck. He winced when his hand brushed the tender flesh.

"Come on, Mr. Walker," Jake said.

Jake hoisted Jim from the floor, grabbed his arm, and tossed it over Jake's shoulder.

"We need to get out of here," Doug said.

"They're in the house," Jake said. "But we can escape through the cellar's outside entryway."

Doug nodded. He walked over to Jake and took the brunt of Jim's weight on his shoulder. The three of them hobbled their way to the steps. By the time they reached them, Jim had started to support himself. Jake watched him place his hands on the steps and crawl out of the cellar on his hands and feet. Doug followed close behind. Jake took up the rear.

As soon as Jake reached the top, he saw Jim and his dad laying in the mud. The light mist washed part of the dried blood from their faces.

Suddenly, a large lightning bolt struck the only transformer feeding the house. The sound of the explosion echoed off the hills. Jake heard shattering glass inside the house. The bulbs in the porch light fixtures shattered.

There was a moment of silence before Jake heard a scream.

"Carly!" he said.

NINE

Kathryn tried not to look as a half dozen hands emerged from the water and clawed at Gina. The bodies the hands were attached to hid themselves within the murky water of the pond. Hands and forearms, green with moss and grime, bloated and waterlogged, reached for whatever they could grab. Pieces of her shirt tore. Scratches streaked down her arms. One came away with a chunk of her hair. Gina fought to release herself from their grip, but not to escape the waters. She kept moving into the deep.

Kathryn wanted to look away, begged her eyes to look away. Not until the hill hid the pond did she finally bring her head forward. By then, a new terror, Cardinal Crest Estate, stood on the hill in front of her.

Kathryn saw the downstairs lights on, but the upstairs windows remained dark.

Dark clouds hung over them as if they had more rain to give. Lightning lit up the sky, offering some brief relief from the darkness, before plunging them back into it.

Ann ran with a determination that Kathryn found hard to keep up with. A new vigor propelled her to the house. She paused at the final hill, though, stopping and staring at the damned house.

"Do you see them? In the windows?" she asked.

Kathryn focused her view, not on the house as a whole, but on the windows themselves. As the next lightning flashed, she saw what Ann saw. Faces. Faces which hung just behind the glass in the darkened upstairs windows, watching them approach. The quick flash disappeared, but the faces remained. They stood motionless.

"Who are they?" Kathryn asked.

"People who've died in the house. I remember a few of the faces from the boxes in the cellar. You were right about what Mr. Monroe told you. The house is a ghost trap. I'm not sure if it's because of the land that the house sits on or if whoever built it did something wicked to it. But the house doesn't let go." Ann spoke in a reverent tone as if saying a prayer.

"Why are they staring?" Kathryn asked.

"They're watching, waiting, to see who the next occupants will be."

As they took that moment to breathe, Kathryn found the question she'd meant to ask since Gina's revelation. "How are you, Ann?"

"Determined. Our families are in danger in that house with two trained killers. Again. Except we aren't kids this time. I don't plan on standing idle and watching my family be massacred. I doubt you do either."

Kathryn took in the woman in front of her. Ann's hair was caked in mud. Streaks of dirt ran down her face, and her clothes, still wet, stuck to her. Yet, in the moment, Kathryn realized Ann's frame wasn't the skinny, frail blonde she thought. The clothes accentuated her features, showing the muscle tone she possessed. With the current adrenaline and tension running through her body, Ann was fucking ripped.

Kathryn reached into her boot and pulled out the knife that had freed them from their zip ties.

"I'm ready to kick some fucking ass."

The faces still stared back at them. The eyes bothered Kathryn the most. Dead stares from empty eye sockets. Despite no eyes watching them, she felt every eye on her.

With one last scan of the windows, she saw movement in the small one at the top. In it, she didn't see dead stares, but the faces of Chandler and Lauren. They banged on the glass, stuck in the attic, trying to escape. Kathryn hoped they could see her.

Before she could point them out to Ann, the two faces moved away from the window and disappeared into the darkness behind them.

Ann and Kathryn jogged down the hill to the cursed house.

Just as they reached the gravel, a bolt of lightning struck the transformer on the power pole outside of the house. Sparks radiated to the ground followed by loud explosions. Kathryn heard shattering glass as the house went dark.

It felt as if the house died, but something about that thought scared her to her bones.

A moment of silence settled across the front of the house until it was ripped apart by an ear-piercing scream.

"Carly!" Ann screamed.

TEN

The moment the explosion happened and Carly screamed, the attic suddenly came alive. Lauren saw blankets shoot off the covered furniture. Boxes flew into the air as if tiny explosions blasted them from the ground. The papers stored within those boxes fluttered to the ground.

"Lauren, what's happening?"

"I don't know," she answered.

The boxes continued to explode into the air, emptying their contents as they spun. The air tasted thick of dust and mildew.

"The window," Lauren shouted. "Maybe mom will see us."

Lauren and Chandler ran to the window. It was the only source of light in the attic.

"I don't see them," Chandler said. "Lauren, I'm scared."

"They must be around the front of the house. They'll find us."

She pulled her younger brother in close to her, trying to offer some comfort while putting on a strong front. Inside, she was doing everything she could not to crumble. If Chandler hadn't been there, she probably would have.

With the next lightning strike, a reflection appeared in the mirror. A third face hovered in the air behind the two kids. Lauren screamed, grabbed Chandler's arm, and ran for the corner of the attic. She dropped behind a desk and brought Chandler down with her. The two took in short, quick bursts of oxygen, trying not to cough from the dust-filled air. Tears streamed down Chandler's face, and his lip quivered.

"I want to go home," he said.

Lauren curled him close to her chest.

He buried his face into her shirt. His muffle voice continued, "I want to go home."

"Don't cry," came a little girl's voice.

Lauren tried to suppress another scream. Her eyes darted around, searching for the source. In the corner next to her, a little girl in a blue dress sat with her knees pulled up to her chest. Her arms wrapped around them, and her hands were clasped together.

Kathryn's story from the first night popped into her head. This was the little girl who drowned in the pond. The one whose parents hung themselves in the house.

"Don't cry. It's ok," she said again.

Lauren took a deep breath and forced her vocal cords to work. "Are you Betsy?"

"You know me?" Betsy said with a smile.

Chandler stopped his mantra about going home and picked his head off Lauren's chest. He turned to Betsy. "I saw you in the window the other day," he said and pointed to the small circular window.

"I like it up here. It's away from daddy. He can get mean sometimes."

"Did you know our mother?" Chandler said. A snot bubble expanded from his nose, and he used his sleeve to wipe it away.

"We spun in circles out in the yard," Betsy said. "She was a lot younger then."

"Is there a way to get out of here?" Lauren asked.

"There's the door in the floor, but you can't go out that way. Others are holding it closed. You don't want to leave right now, anyway. Daddy's upset from all the noise. That's when he gets mean."

"Did you drown?" Chandler asked.

"Chandler, don't ask a ghost that. It's not nice, I think. I don't know. What's usual ghost etiquette?"

Betsy gave a small giggle. "You two are funny. I like you.

"But to answer your question, no, I didn't drown, but I heard people say that I did. I was playing here in the attic. There weren't as many things in here back then. Daddy's head hurt, and he was upset like he gets sometimes. Instead of taking my beating, I ran away. He reached for me, but I slipped and hit my head against this desk." She pointed to the one they were hiding behind.

"Daddy felt guilty and knew everyone would blame him. I watched him take my body to the pond and put me in it. I cried too when they cried. Then, when mommy and daddy couldn't take it anymore, they joined me.

"Most of the time, the house is empty, and everybody's happy. There's usually no reason to fear the dead. I can't say as much for the living, though. These past few days, the house has been filled angry people. Some of the ghosts, the not nice ones, they are feeding off of that anger."

In the far corner at the attic, a large cabinet fell over with a resounding crash.

Lauren had almost forgotten about the danger they were in while listening to Betsy tell her story. With the cabinet crash, reality flooded back. She eased herself up and looked over the top of the desk. Across the room, she saw the thin figure of a man. His neck sat to the side at an unnatural angle. She remembered Betsy's dad hung himself.

He turned his head, but each movement seemed robotic. The head moved quickly then stopped. Lauren figured it could only go so far before the bone needed to be adjusted.

She dropped back behind the desk.

"That's daddy. I told you he's not happy right now. He wants to punish whoever made the noises. He thinks it was you. I'll talk to him and give you time to get out."

"How do we get out of here if other ghosts are holding the hatch shut?" Lauren asked.

"Your parents will be able to open it. They'll be here soon. Tell Annabelle hi for me."

Betsy turned translucent before vanishing into thin air.

"Bye," Chandler said. He looked up at Lauren. "What do we do now?"

"Wait for her to distract him. When we move, don't look at him. It's not a pretty sight."

"I have enough nightmare fuel for a while. Don't worry." Chandler's smile warmed Lauren's heart.

"You're alright, sometimes, Fungus."

"Love you, too."

Another box, this one closer to Lauren and Chandler, exploded into the air and sent more papers drifting down around them. A fresh wave of dust particles filled the attic.

"Stop it, Daddy," Betsy shouted. "My friends didn't make it loud. Leave them alone."

Lauren nudged Chandler. She moved onto her hands and knees, staying low behind the antique furniture and storage boxes. Chandler followed as she led the way, crawling across the dusty floor. Her hands caked with dirt and her knees left two lines on the floor as she scooted to the hatch. She hoped Betsy was right and her parents would be there soon.

"I'm sorry, Daddy," Betsy said. Her initial confidence turned into the voice of a scared little girl. "I didn't mean to shout. I'll be quiet."

Lauren didn't want to look up. She kept her eyes glued to the floor and hoped Chandler did the same.

"Ouch, Daddy, you're hurting me. I'll be quiet. Promise."

As much as she didn't want to, Lauren couldn't help but listen. She heard Betsy plead with father. Lauren's heart broke for the little girl, and tears ran down her cheeks and onto the floor, leaving small dark droplets in the dust and dirt.

"The noisy ones are downstairs, I promise. I'll be quiet. Please, Daddy, stop hurting me."

Eleven

C arly had never yelled that loudly, but the tension she felt across her whole body had also never been so tight. A tidal wave of emotion rushed out of her in that one shriek.

With every ounce of oxygen gone from her lungs, she doubled over and dropped to her knees. Carly inhaled as fully as she could, expanding her emptied chest. A hot soreness rose in her throat. She rested on her knees for a minute, light-headed from the release. If she rose too quickly, she feared she'd tumble down the steps. That wouldn't be helpful at all. She needed to find help for Lauren and Chandler.

Lauren and Chandler!

She'd forgotten the whole reason she was up there.

"Chandler! Lauren!"

While still on her knees, she tried to scream their names but only a croak came out. Her vocal cords demanded rest and hot tea. She coughed into her fist, feeling the rough rasp in her throat.

"You!"

Carly's attention moved to the first floor. Silhouetted by the front windows, Frank Malone and Joe Jacobs stood at the base of the staircase.

"Come here, Little Bit," Frank said. "We found your dad. He wants to see you."

Everything about his tone screamed that was a lie. Carly crawled to the railing and used the balusters to pull herself to her feet. She heard the staircase moan under Frank and Joe's heavy footsteps.

With a glance down both sides of the pitch-dark hallway, she decided on hiding in her parents' room. She sprinted across the hall, threw open the door, and stepped into the room. A twist of the lock made her feel a little safer, but she knew it wouldn't hold for long.

She outstretched her arms, feeling around in the darkness. She'd been in the room before with her parents and just needed to remember the layout. Her hands brushed across the bed, the dresser. The bathroom door sat on the other side of the room.

"Over here, My Dear," a female voice said.

Carly froze in place. Fear and adrenaline rushed through her.

Her first thought was the therapist somehow beat her to the room and waited for her. But the voice didn't sound like her, though. This voice had a soft tone, motherly. It reminded Carly of her own mother's voice. Carly tried to pinpoint where the voice had come from but couldn't.

"It's ok," the motherly voice said. "Don't fear the dead. I won't let anything happen to you. After losing my Betsy to this house, I will not see another child hurt."

"Where should I hide?" Carly asked.

A glow appeared inside the bathroom, illuminating its doorway.

TWELVE

F rank walked with a determined step up the staircase.
He led the way.

As they reached the top, Joe slowed behind him.

"What's your problem, Joe?"

"I don't like this, man," he answered. "This all feels fucking bad. It's the middle of the day. Where's the goddamn sun?"

Both men stood just under the attic hatch.

"Stop being jumpy," Frank said. "Have you seen how much fucking rain dropped out there? By the look of it, there's more to come. Let's split up and find that little bitch."

Joe shook his head.

"What now?" Frank asked with apparent frustration in his voice.

"This place gives me the fucking creeps, Man. Since we've been here, I've seen some shit. Shadows that fucking moved on their own and shit. I think this place is haunted.

I say we stick together and look for her. She's just a kid, probably scared as well. Plus, the boss should be back any minute."

"You think this house is fucking haunted?" Frank leaned back and bellowed laughter. "That's some bullshit there." He started poking Joe in the chest, enunciating each word. "You, sir, are a chickenshit."

"I don't even care," Joe said.

Frank grabbed his cellphone and turned on the flashlight.

"That better? Now take out your own damn phone, turn on the light, and go down that hallway." Frank pointed down the Miller's side. "I'll take the other side. Start at the far room and work your way back. We might as well grab all the kids and send them downstairs. We need them to finish the job."

Joe turned on the his cellphone's light. He kept shaking his head. "This is a stupid fucking idea."

"Noted."

THIRTEEN

After Carly's scream pierced through the sound of misting rain and the house went dark, Ann started to run headlong into the house. Kathryn did the same.

"Kat! Ann!"

"Mom!"

Ann heard Doug and Jake call out their names. Hearing their voices stopped her from blindly sprinting into Cardinal Crest. Relief washed over her just knowing they were out of the house. For a moment, she knew they were gaining the upper hand.

Kathryn ran to Doug and Jake.

Ann saw Jim lagging behind and ran to him. The closer she got, the more his misshapen face came into view.

"Oh, Baby," she said and wrapped her arms around his side.

"Ow," Jim exclaimed, wincing in pain.

She begrudgingly eased her grip on him.

Jim placed an arm on her shoulder, using her for balance.

"What happened to you?" Kathryn and Doug asked simultaneously.

Ann shook her head. "We can talk about what happened later. What's going on now?"

"Oh shit, Carly," Kathryn said. She turned her body as if she meant to run into the house.

"Wait, Mom," Jake said. "Here's the situation. The therapist lady isn't who she said she is."

"We know," Ann said. "Her name was Gina. Our parents killed her dad, and she wanted revenge."

"Was? Wanted?" Doug asked. "You're speaking in past tense."

"Scary pond," Kathryn said. "All you need to know. I'm guessing Frank and Joe aren't good guys?"

"No," Jake said. "I overheard them talking. They planned to kill us when Gina brought you back. Going to blame it on Mrs. Walker."

Ann spoke up, "Probably hitmen working for Salvatore Carlisi. Just like he sent the two guys to convince my father, he sent those two as muscle for Gina's insane plan."

"What do we do?" Jim forced out. His swollen jaw prevented his mouth from opening very wide.

"First, we need to get the kids out of the house. Then, we get in the cars and drive out of here as quickly as possible."

"Do we have any idea where the kids are?" Doug asked.

"We saw Lauren and Chandler in the attic window," Ann said. "I'm not sure about Carly."

"She's a smart girl," Kathryn said. "She'll find a spot to hide."

"Carly said she heard something," Jake added. "I bet she heard Lauren and Chandler trying to get out of the attic."

Ann watched the front of the house for any movement. She hoped a curtain would flutter, maybe a ghost would point the way, something. Instead, the house sat still.

"One other thing," Ann said. "In case you haven't noticed, the house is haunted."

"No shit, Mrs. Walker," Jake responded. "Sorry, Mom. I just hope it's more Casper and less poltergeist."

Jim took his arm off Ann. "How do we get the kids out?"

Everyone stood silent for a moment. Finally, Kathryn spoke up.

"Ann, you and Jim go through the front," she said. "Doug and I will go through the back entrance by the kitchen."

"Sounds good," Jim said.

"What about me?" Jake asked.

"You stay on the front porch. I don't want you anywhere near the inside of that house again."

FOURTEEN

Kathryn and Doug jogged to the back of Cardinal Crest. A small set of stone steps led up to the modest back door. Kathryn found it funny how the front of the house showed off such elegance, but the back of the house resembled a standard late 1800's farmhouse.

Doug grabbed the handle to the white screen door and peered through the glass into the kitchen. He slowly turned the knob on the kitchen door and stepped back into the house he'd just escaped.

Doug and Kat tiptoed their way through the kitchen. As he passed the counters on his left and the cellar door on his right, she tapped him on his back, causing him to jump.

He stopped and turned around.

She opened a drawer and pulled out a large eight-inch chef knife. Reaching back in, she withdrew another and handed it to Doug.

"Do you still have the knife in your boot?" he whispered.

"Of course," she whispered back. "That's for emergencies, though."

"If they're armed, we're bringing knives to a gunfight."

"Better than nothing."

"True," he said.

With the knife in his hand, Doug continued the cautious walk through the kitchen and into the dining room. Kat walked a few paces behind him holding the handle of her knife directly in front of her.

FIFTEEN

J im's mouth radiated a dull ache through his face. Every beat of his heart sent throbbing pain through his cheeks. Each time he took a breath, sharp stabs shot through his chest and sides. The metallic taste of blood still coated his tongue and throat. He tried to keep up with Ann as best as he could, but he was in bad shape. Jim knew he needed medical attention, but he also felt a burning desire to save his family. He still maintained that longing feeling that he could've done more to help Ann, to protect her as she struggled with her fears and anxiety. Damned if he was going to let his whole family be destroyed because of some vindictive grudge.

With those thoughts in his head, he pushed through the pain. Certain he was doing more damage to his insides than good, he increased his stride and caught up with Ann as she climbed the steps onto the front porch.

Ann quietly turned the doorknob and eased open the front door just enough to poke her head inside. She left just enough space to squeeze her body through the opening and into the foyer.

Jim followed suit, not wanting to open the door anymore than necessary. He didn't want strain on the hinges announcing their presence.

Once inside the dark house, silence enveloped them. The sound of the misting rain vanished. If not for Jim hearing his own labored breathing, he'd have thought his hearing had failed. He looked into the den on his left, but he couldn't see much. The windows cast shadows from what little light escaped the cloud cover. Jim tried to ignore the movement of the shadows. He needed to find his children and get his family to safety. He didn't need to worry about ghosts.

As Jim paused to look in the den, Ann started up the wooden staircase. She stepped down gently, not wanting to draw attention. Her hand delicately brushed the smooth, polished railing as she ascended.

Just as Jim stepped onto the staircase, a door slammed shut from the left side of the hallway. Both he and Ann stood completely still, hoping the darkness would mask them. A few seconds later, another door slammed from the right side. Jim knew that both Frank and Joe were about to walk across the second floor and see them standing on the staircase. There was no doubt in his mind that he and Ann would lose any fight.

He started to turn around when he heard a door open on each side of the hallway and shut. The moment the doors closed, Ann sprinted up the steps. She jumped and grabbed the rope to the attic hatch. Using all her weight, she tugged on the door.

Jim joined her and saw her face turning red from pulling on the rope. He feared she'd pass out if she didn't take a breath, then suddenly the door gave way, and Ann collapsed to the ground.

"Kids," Jim said in a forced whisper.

"Dad?" two voices asked in unison.

Jim saw the heads of both Lauren and Chandler appear in the hole in the ceiling.

"Oh, thank God you two are ok," Ann said rising to her feet. "Get down as quickly as possible."

Jim glanced down the staircase and saw Doug and Kathryn at the bottom. He saw a brief glimmer of light reflect from their hands and realized they each carried a knife. Smart thinking.

"Did you find them?" Doug whispered.

"Yes," Jim answered.

Chandler swung his legs into the opening, placed his feet on the ladder, and scaled down as quickly as he could.

As soon as his feet hit the wooden flooring, Lauren dangled her feet over the edge and nearly jumped out of the attic. Both gave Ann a huge hug then looked at Jim.

"Dad, your face," Lauren said.

"Oh, trust me," he said. "It feels a lot worse than it looks." He had to stifle a laugh. The thought of laughing sent phantom pains through his chest.

From the left side of the hallway, Jim heard another door slam.

"What the fuck!" Frank said. His eyes danced between the four of them standing in the hallway. "You're supposed to be in the basement, and you're supposed to be with the boss." Frank reached behind his back and pulled out a gun. "Where's the boss?"

"She changed her mind," Ann said.

Frank, with the gun held out in front of him, walked closer to them. "That's a lie. I'm going to ask one more time, then I'm going to start shooting. Where the fuck is Gina?" He danced the gun between Jim, Ann, Lauren, and Chandler.

Jim saw Doug and Kathryn move to the left side of the staircase. He hoped they didn't draw Frank's attention. If they managed not to, then maybe they could get the jump on him before Frank followed through on his words.

"She's not here. That's all I know. Please don't shoot us," Ann pleaded.

Frank stomped over to the four of them. He grabbed Lauren by the hair and tugged her against him.

"Oh my God, please no," Lauren screamed as Frank pressed the gun against her temple.

Ann trembled, and Chandler dropped to the ground in tears.

Jim's mind went into overdrive. He was not about to stand there and watch as Frank threatened his family. He had to do something before Frank followed through.

Frank spoke very slowly and deliberately while pressing the barrel firmly against Lauren's head. "I'm going to be *very* generous and give you one more chance to *ANSWER MY FUCKING QUESTION!*"

Lauren held her eyes tightly shut. A line of tears streamed down from both.

All Jim could think about was Frank plastering his daughter's brain all over the flooring.

"The pond!" Ann screamed. "Something happened to her at the pond."

"What do you mean, 'something happened to her at the pond'? What the fuck does that mean?" Frank moved the gun off Lauren and back to Ann.

Jim knew this might be his only chance. The moment the gun wasn't pressed into Lauren's skull, he had to act. He searched for whatever carnal protective instinct he had inside of him to come out. From his periphery, he saw Doug inching closer to the second floor, just out of Frank's view.

Jim took a deep, painful breath and lunged at Frank, one hand reaching for the gun and the other grasping for Frank's neck. He didn't know if he would just push his head back or try to rip his throat out, but he was fine with whatever worked. As long as his family was safe.

A loud clap echoed down the hallway when Jim collided with Frank. Frank fell backwards into the wall as Jim's momentum helped to pin Frank there. As Frank stumbled, his grip on Lauren's hair released, and she ran to her mom. Jim continued to press Frank into the wall, keeping his left hand firmly buried in Frank's throat. Jim's right hand pushed the gun's barrel away. He couldn't get a good angle to disarm Frank, but he wasn't going to let him get a good shot either.

A moment later, Doug ran headlong to help. He forced Jim out of the way and drove all eight inches of the chef's knife directly into the dead center of Frank's chest. Only the handle remained visible.

Frank's eyes rolled back in his head. He gasped for air but to no avail. The gun dropped to the floor, and Frank slowly slid down the wall, leaving a blood trail behind him. Doug had thrust the knife so deep into Frank that the tip of the blade protruded from his back, leaving a small groove in the wall as he collapsed to the ground.

Jim spun around and saw Lauren and Chandler cradled in Ann's arms. Adrenaline leaving his body, he tried to take a deep breath, but new waves of pain shot from through his stomach. Jim touched his side and winced at the new pain.

"Get your family downstairs," Doug told Jim. "We'll find Carly."

Doug gave Jim a pat on the shoulder as he walked past the attic ladder and down the dark hallway.

"Kids, Jake is just outside. Join up with him." Jim faltered on his feet for a minute and braced himself against the attic ladder. "Ann, I'll need your help getting down."

Chandler and Lauren pulled away from Ann and hurried down the stairs. They couldn't get out of the house fast enough. None of them could.

With the kids not at her side, Ann walked over to help Jim. She grabbed his arm to put it over her shoulder, and red-hot flashes of pain shot up his side. She looked down, and a deep red color spread across his chest and down his side.

Ann turned her face up to his. Jim saw tears wanting to form.

"Don't," he said. "Get me downstairs. Find the cellphones. Once an ambulance gets here, I'll be fine."

"We need to stop the bleeding," she said.

She grabbed his shirt and ripped it off his body, sending fresh waves of searing pain soaring through him. With his shirt off, they both saw the deep black bullet hole in his side and the crimson blood flowing from it. Ann pressed the shirt firmly against his side, ignoring the deep gasp of air caused by the pain.

Ann forced the shirt into his side as they slowly made their way down the stairs. The further down they went, the more of his weight she had to support.

When they reached the foyer, Jim said, "I saved her."

"I know. You saved us all, James Walker." Her eyes begged him to let her cry, but she held them back.

"I did, didn't I." He smiled as they stepped out of the house and onto the porch.

Ann led him to the steps. He sat down hard and leaned against the porch railing.

"Stay here," she told him. "I'm going to find the car keys and the cellphones."

SIXTEEN

C arly hid in the dark bathroom trying to not make a single noise. She stared through the vent in the wall and watched Joe's light illuminate the bed. He shifted to the closet and poked his head inside. Eventually, he'd reach the bathroom and find her. She had nowhere else to hide. Why did the ghost get her trapped in here?

Distant voices bled from the hallway into the room, but she couldn't make out what they were saying. Then suddenly, she heard Frank's voice from the hallway.

"What the fuck?"

Carly heard Ann's voice and then Lauren scream. She wanted to help, but with Joe in front of her, she was trapped. She placed her fist in her mouth to muffle any cries. When Frank shouted, Joe's light swiveled to the bedroom door, and he rushed over to it. He turned the doorknob and tugged, but the door stayed firmly shut. Joe fumbled with the lock on the door, clicking it back and forth. He pulled again, but it still wouldn't budge. After straining through a few more attempts, he slowly ambled backwards. He brought his hands up to his face and wiped away sweat.

Then came the gunshot.

Carly bit down hard enough on her fist that she tasted blood. It was the only thing that kept her from screaming. She knew her parents didn't bring a gun with them and doubted that the Walkers did. The only person who'd have one would be Frank.

Her mind tormented her with images of her dad lying in a pool of his own blood. She tried to push those away. She kept her knuckles pressed firmly against her teeth and watched Joe through the vent. She remembered back to her mother's words as she learned to fire a shotgun. "Calm your breathing and focus." Slow and controlled. Deep breath in, then deep breath out.

Watching Joe, Carly knew he didn't have the same kind of role models that she did. When the shot rang out, he ran against the door and threw his shoulder into it. He backed up and tried again, but the door didn't budge.

"Frank!" he shouted. "Can anyone hear me?"

He raised his arms behind his head, interlacing his fingers against his neck.

"Shit, shit, shit. Frank!" he screamed.

Carly heard Joe's screams, but something seemed off about them. In the band hall at her school, she once went into a solo practice room. She pulled the door closed behind her and immediately experienced a new sensation. Normal sounds that she heard, the air conditioning, her shoes brushing against the carpet, rustling of papers, disappeared. Sound fell dead against the walls instead of echoing. The feeling of isolation grew almost to the point of claustrophobia, as if the room shrank around her.

She felt that same feeling now. Somehow, the room had deadened. Joe could yell and scream all he wanted, but the gunshot from the hallway would be the last sound from beyond the door he'd hear. Carly didn't know how she knew that, but the protective ghosts had isolated the room from the rest of the world. They had barricaded the door and soundproofed it.

Carly watched through the vent as Joe gripped the cellphone against the back of his neck. The phone's flashlight illuminated the room behind him.

"Frank, I need help." His voice came out in a whimper.

A dark figure shaped like a person crawled across the wall to Joe's left like a spider. As it hung directly across from Carly, it picked up its head and brought its finger to its mouth. Carly read the signal loud and clear. Be quiet.

Joe must've seen something. He quickly spun to his left. He brought his hand in front of him and shined the light against the wall. But the dark figure wasn't there anymore. Joe's hand dropped behind his back and pulled a handgun from his waist. The gun shook as he held it in front of him.

Carly heard a noise by the window, and Joe spun that direction. As the light illuminated the corner of the room, Carly saw more apparitions standing behind him. If not for the ambient light of Joe's cellphone, she wouldn't have been able to see them at all. A handful appeared as just shadows standing in the middle of the room, semi-translucent. Others had more form and color. Some looked green and bloated. A few thin and emaciated. She tried to count how many there were, but each time Joe turned, they'd disappear in front of him and a new group appeared behind him. With each spin, the circle of spirits around him constricted. They moved closer and closer to him. He was being swallowed up by them and couldn't even see it.

He rushed to the door and pounded. It was no use, though. The banging sounded dull and hollow in this isolation chamber.

Carly couldn't tell if he saw the ghosts. Based on the frantic pounding, he at least felt their presence. He cried out in terror, a cry that had no echo, hoping the door would release him. The swarm of supernatural beings drew closer to him. It reminded her of zombie movies she'd seen.

As the first ones fell upon him, Betsy's mother whispered in her ear. "Don't look, Little One."

Carly briefly contemplated watching but rolled away from the vent. Sitting against the wall with her knees pulled tightly to her chest, she took her bleeding hand from her mouth and firmly covered both ears. She prayed for the bathroom to be sound proofed as well.

Joe fired his gun wildly, sending off muffled reports with each shot. As he started screaming, Carly wished those were muffled, but she wasn't that fortunate. They pierced through the sound vacuum and echoed inside of her skull.

After a few minutes of sitting in the utter darkness of the bathroom, knees pulled tightly to her chest, eyes squeezed shut, and hands pressed against her ears, Carly felt something touch her shoulder. She unfurled her body, kicking her legs out and swinging her arms to fight off whatever was there before opening her eyes. For the second time, she let out a blood-curdling scream.

Opening her eyes, she saw Kathryn and Doug kneeling beside her. Carly stopped flailing her arms and legs, jumped off the ground, and ran into their collective arms, hugging them tight.

"Carly, are you ok?" Kathryn asked. "What happened in here?"

Carly just shook her head. She didn't have the words to describe what had happened, and she doubted she'd ever find the right ones.

"Come on," Doug said. "Let's get out of this house."

Doug and Kathryn stood up. Carly stayed close to Kathryn as Doug led them out of the bathroom. As they passed the bed, Carly saw a faint glow from a light. Joe's cellphone lay on the ground with the flashlight facing the floor. She bent down and picked it up. The screen was smashed. The light illuminated part of the bedroom as she stood up with the phone.

"Oh God," Kathryn exclaimed.

Carly looked around the room. Bullet holes riddled the ceiling. On the floor, a large swath of blood ran from the door in a wide sweeping arc and continued under the bed. She didn't want to know what happened, and her parents didn't ask.

Doug bent down and reached for the bedsheets. Carly was afraid he would look under the bed.

"Dad, please don't," Carly begged.

"I agree, Doug. Let's get out of here."

He stood up, and the three of them headed out of the house.

PART SIX

NEW RESIDENTS OF CARDINAL CREST

ONE

"Jake!" Kathryn yelled as they stepped onto the front porch.

Kathryn saw Jim leaning against the railing, his blood-soaked shirt still pressed against his side. Lauren and Chandler stood by their car, waiting for it to be unlocked.

"Where's Jake?" she asked. "And Ann?"

"I haven't seen Jake," Lauren said. "Mom went to find the keys and phones."

Doug dropped down next to Jim. "Holy shit, man. How are you holding up?"

Jim tried to move and winced.

"Don't move," Doug told him. He took his own shirt off and tied it around Jim's side, holding the dark red shirt in place. "This is going to hurt." He pulled his shirt tight, and Jim inhaled sharply.

"Doug," Kathryn said, "they don't know where Jake is."

Panic flooded Kathryn's mind. After everything that'd happened so far, why would he just wander off? He should be on the porch where she'd told him to stay. Before tonight, she could see Carly being adventurous, but that wasn't Jake.

"We'll find him," Doug said.

"I got them," Ann said as she jogged out of the house. "Cell phones. Keys." She laid all but her phone and keys on the porch railing.

Ann clicked the button to their car, but nothing happened. She walked closer to the car and depressed the button a few more times, but nothing happened.

Doug scooped their key off the ground and clicked the unlock button. Nothing happened on their car as well.

"Fuck," he said.

He jogged over to their SUV, removed the key from the key fob, and manually unlocked the door. Doug leaned behind the driver's seat and popped the hood release. He walked to the front of the car and opened the hood, using the bar to prop it up.

"Sonofabitch," he shouted.

Kathryn quickly jogged over to him. "What's wrong?"

"They ripped stuff apart. The battery cables are disconnected, the spark plug cables. Looks like another hose may be missing."

"Can you fix it?"

"I can try to put some of this back together and see what gripes at me."

"You do that and stay here with Jim. He needs medical attention fast. I'm going to find Jake."

Kathryn ran back to the porch and grabbed her cell phone. Lauren was already dialing.

"I'm calling 911," she told Kathryn.

"Good, your dad needs help." Kathryn looked over at Ann staring into the engine of her car. "Ann," she yelled. "Please help me find Jake."

Ann picked up her head from under the hood of her car and turned to Kathryn. Frustration covered her face. As Ann walked with her head down to Kathryn, the slight mist of rain intensified once more into hard rain drops. The drops pelted the two ladies in the gravel driveway.

"Please, help me find Jake," she said again.

"Of course," Ann responded. Her lip quivered as she talked. "I thought we were out of this. That we could get in the cars and drive for help. That bitch is still fucking winning. Jim's dying on the porch steps. Jake's missing. They destroyed the cars. We are still trapped in her...her nightmare vendetta."

Kathryn wrapped her arms around Ann.

"Lauren's on the phone with 911 right now. We'll get Jim help. She's not going to win."

"I need them to hurry. Let's go find Jake."

Two

Ann and Kathryn trudged thought the mud and gravel, leaving Doug to fix the Miller's vehicle and the kids to call emergency services.

"Why would he have run off?" Ann asked.

"He wouldn't have."

"Fuck!" Ann said. Jake was fifteen and had been through enough this weekend to not want to wander off. Thinking about what happened to Gina at the pond, she remembered Jake's incident. Doubt rose up in her head that he had been stuck on a branch.

For now, though, she needed to focus. The increase in rain made it hard to distinguish anything other than vague shapes. What she wouldn't give for the sun to be out and the rain to stop.

When Ann glanced at Kat's face, she saw a look of stoned determination. Down the side of the house, they approached the opening to the cellar. Ann hesitated at the door and tried to work up the courage to go back down there.

"The barn door is open," Kathryn said.

"Could the storm have opened it?"

Ann doubted it as soon as she asked the question.

"I'm going to check."

They jogged over to the open barn door. Ann brushed a mixture of sweat and water from her face. Her shoes sloshed in the mud, and her clothes hung wet to her body. A cold chilled her to the bone. She'd not stepped into the barn the whole time she was there and had no idea what sat just beyond the open door.

The large door swung back and forth on its hinges. Even over the wind and the rain, Ann heard them groan from the strain of the wooden door. Kathryn gripped the side of the door and slung it completely open. The groan of the hinges became a scream piercing the air around them.

"Jake," she screamed. "Jake, are you in here?"

Ann and Kat stepped into the two-story barn and out of the rain. The pouring rain sounded like gravel pellets against the roof. Ann shot her eyes from one side to the other. The smell of hay, dirt, mold, and mildew filled the air. A single tractor sat in the middle of the barn with a thick layer of dust covering it. Various old rusty farm instruments hung against the back wall. Tractor attachments lay disorganized next to the tractor. It reminded Ann of every horror movie she'd ever seen. She waited for Leatherface to jump out wielding his chainsaw.

"Jake!" Kathryn yelled into the cavernous barn.

"That's close enough," came the answer.

Every hair on the back of Ann's neck stood up.

Gina emerged from the darkness. She held Jake firmly in front of her. One arm gripped under his arm and around his chest. The other held a knife against his side. Cuts and abrasions covered her face. Claw marks extended down her arms and legs. Her clothes hung in tatters. If Gina had said she'd been attacked by a bear, Ann would've believed her.

"Gina," Ann said. "It's over. It's just us. Let Jake go."

Gina's eyes reminded her of those nature documentaries where the host would come across a trapped and in pain wild animal and work to set it free. Even though it was dark, her pupils were contracted to the point where she could barely make them out in their vast fields of white.

"Just us?" she questioned, and then followed it with a deranged chuckle. "Just us? It's not just us here. There are many, many more."

"Let him go, Gina. This is between us," Ann said.

She shot a quick glance to Kat. Every muscle in Kat's body was taut. She looked ready to pounce on Gina, but with ten yards separating them, she'd never make it before

Gina gutted Jake. Ann stepped closer to Kat, placed a gentle hand on her, and moved in between the two women.

"My father called for me. Did you hear him call for me? He called, and it was really him. He said 'Gigi'. That was his name for me. He called, and I went to him. But then the ones in the pond...they wanted me." Her arm flexed and tightened around Jake's chest. The knife dimpled his shirt and a drop of red formed.

He inhaled sharply.

"This place. This land. It's sick. It needs to be fed, and it hasn't been. The land is dying. The ones in the pond told me. Did they tell you that? No, they didn't. They wanted me and told me their secrets." She smiled as if she'd been picked first for a team. "This place needs the living. Needs the energy, the blood, the life to feed. The land slowly drains life away."

"Gina," Ann said. "Listen to yourself. How many times did we sit down together? How many times did you tell me to hear myself? To hear if what I was saying was true?"

"I hear myself just fine. Those in the pond wanted me. They tried to pull me under and take me, but they couldn't. I told them I'd feed them. I can bring new life here. I'm the new caretaker. I need to feed them. I need to feed this place."

Ann took a few steps closer.

"Gina, listen to yourself."

A few more steps closer.

"No, you listen," Gina said. "This is my symphony. My masterpiece. And now I'm part of theirs, too. And it starts now with his blood."

She plunged the knife into Jake's side.

"No," Kat screamed and ran through Ann, pushing her out of the way.

Blood poured from Jake's side.

Gina ripped the knife out of his side and tossed the boy to the ground. As Kat ran to Jake, Gina sliced at her. Kat dodged out of the way. Gina ran forward and swung the knife in a large arc at Ann, cutting across Ann's right arm just under her shoulder. Instead of stopping, Gina bolted out of the barn and into the rain.

Kat fell to the ground next to Jake. She stripped off her shirt and pressed it against his side.

Ann yelled to Kat.

"Stay with Jake. That bitch is mine."

With blood trailing down her arm and her own burning desire for revenge and closure, Ann ran after Gina determined to finish this.

THREE

Ann sprinted out of the barn door. Unexpectedly, she found Gina standing on the gravel driveway waiting for her. She stood there in the pouring rain, blood from the gashes and claw marks washing off her. The marks gave her the look of red striped tiger. She held her arms out wide, beckoning Ann to come for her. Her right hand gripped the hilt of the knife.

Ann knew it was time for this to be over. Gina's attempts at vindictive murder ended now. When she saw Gina, she sped up. Gina wanted her. It was time for Gina to have her. Ann dug her shoes into the ground, exploding forward with each step. Just before she reached Gina, she lowered her shoulder and bent low into her stance. Her thighs flexed and every muscle in her leg built up potential energy.

With one last step, Ann unleashed the entirety of the stored tension within her muscles. Her shoulder collided with Gina's stomach in a colossal impact. Gina's body bent in two as Ann continued to pump her legs and drive through Gina. Ann drove Gina to the ground where both women slid through the mud.

Surprisingly, Gina held onto the knife, and she tried to bury it into Ann's side.

Ann caught her arm just before she connected, holding it millimeters from her skin. So close that Ann felt the metal hovering just above her. Gina bared down harder but Ann somehow managed to keep her attempts at bay.

Gina thrusted her hips and twisted her shoulders, catching Ann off guard. The next thing Ann knew the back of her head was sinking into the mud, and Gina sat on top of her. She held the knife in both hands and brought it down.

As fast as she could, Ann reached up with both of her hands, catching Gina's arms at the wrists. Ann felt her arms struggle to hold off the knife. Gina used the weight of her body, pushing down into the knife. The silver blade descended closer and closer to her head. Ann saw drops of Jake's blood still clinging to it. Her arms shook with failing effort. The tip of the blade pierced Ann's left cheek, and she knew Gina meant to drive it straight through her eye and into her brain.

With one last effort, she did the only thing she could think to do. Ann moved her head quickly to the right. The side of her face erupted in searing pain as the knife sliced its way across the left side of her face. Ann released the tension in her arms, and Gina fell forward. The knife punctured her shoulder. Ann felt it grind past the bone. Her left arm immediately became numb and laid uselessly in the dirt.

She kicked and sent Gina tumbling off her. Ann stood up with the knife still sticking out of her shoulder. A trail of red flowed down her arm. She ran forward before Gina could get up and kicked her in the stomach.

Gina tried to raise up but couldn't. Each time Ann kicked, Gina rolled and tried to stand up again. With each roll, she moved closer and closer to the house.

Ann remained relentless. Since her arm was out of commission, she didn't stop kicking. Ann landed one on Gina's head, followed by a kick to the stomach, and then another to the stomach. With each kick, she drove Gina towards the house. Ann hoped to pin her against Cardinal Crest Estate and keep kicking until she stopped moving or help arrived. She preferred the former.

Almost at the house, Gina made it up to her hands and knees. She tried to bear crawl away from Ann's constant barrage, but Ann connected just as she started to move. Gina rolled, but this time she moved in front of the cellar door. Gina raised her head and rolled before Ann's kick landed. She fell into the cellar and down the steps.

"No!" Ann cried out, realizing that her plan to pin her against the house wouldn't work now.

She ran to the cellar and saw Gina lying in the mud at the base of the steps. Gina held her side, and blood ran from her nose and mouth. Ann heard laughter from the cellar.

"Are you laughing?" she screamed down.

Ann Walker took a step back from the dark cellar and a wave of dizziness hit her. She fell onto her butt and glanced at her shoulder. Blood still poured from the knife buried there. She thought of pulling it out, but that thought came with a wave of nausea and more dizziness. She feared removing it would make her pass out. Passing out was the last thing she needed to do. With Gina working her way out of the cellar, if she passed out, she'd never wake up again.

Crawling on her knees and arm, she pulled herself over to the cellar. Just before she reached it, she saw Gina's hand grip the frame of the cellar door. An instant later, the other hand grabbed it. Gina lifted her head above the frame and stared into Ann's eyes. Ann saw only insanity behind those eyes. Nothing existed of the therapist she once knew.

Gina's expression changed to one of surprise, and her head dropped below the frame. She tried to pull it up again, but Ann saw pitch black hands and arms pulling at her. Shadows encircled her head and tugged her backwards. Gina gripped the frame of the cellar door as hard as she could, digging her fingernails into the wood.

Ann heard cries from the cellar. Screams from multiple voices streamed from the underground abyss. The wails of those trapped inside the house echoed inside of Ann's head. She heard them call out for Gina in a death yell. Ann wanted to close her ears but couldn't block out the howls. The shrieks permeated her soul. She felt them tug at her.

The shadows pulled down on Gina until her fingers gave way from the frame. Ann saw chunks of fingernails still in the wood, ripped off from their source. She watched the spirits consume Gina. The shadows passed over her, pulled at her. The floor became so dark with them that Ann only saw bits of Gina's body as an arm or a leg would flail upwards. Finally, she saw the woman's head lift from the ground. Eyes that no longer held onto reality, rolled white. She let out a final yell before the spirits ushered her beyond view.

Ann fell back into the mud as the doors of the cellar slammed shut on their own.

Four

"You did it, honey," Jim calmly said, standing over her. "It's over."

"We both did," she responded.

"Everything's going to be ok."

She lay on the ground, the cold rain refreshing, despite the knife still protruding from her shoulder. "Glad you think so. I still have a knife in my shoulder, and you shouldn't be up walking around."

"Help's on the way."

His tone sounded flat like this was an everyday occurrence.

"Why aren't you more excited?" she said. "Not every day we survive two mob hitmen and a psycho therapist. Oh, by the way, I think I'm cured so maybe she wasn't that bad of a therapist after all."

Ann laughed at herself.

She breathed deeply, dreading how bad standing up was going to hurt. She rolled onto her right arm, placed her legs in front of her, and slowly lifted. Her head immediately spun in circles, but she managed to find her balance. She reached for Jim to wrap her arms around him, and then realized he was no longer there.

"No," she said. "No!"

Tears welled up in her eyes. "Please God no," she begged.

She stumbled from the side of the house around to the front. Just as the porch steps came into view, she saw Lauren and Chandler crying. Ann fell to her knees in the gravel as tears streamed uncontrollably down her cheeks. She let go of everything she had inside of her and screamed. Pain and suffering forced their way out of her through the release. After everything they'd been through. After everything she'd put them through. Why? Why?

As Ann breathed in, she saw Doug stand next to Jim and gently close Jim's eyes. Lauren and Chandler ran to her and wrapped their arms around her neck. The three of them stood in the rain in sorrow.

From somewhere that seemed far, far away, Ann heard the faint sound of police and ambulance sirens.

FIVE

Sergeant Jack Rogers drove his squad car down the gravel road leading up to Cardinal Crest Estate. He'd lived in the area all his life, as had his parents and grandparents. His grandmother used to tell him stories about the house and the strange things that happened there. Now, he had to respond to the frantic 9-1-1 call from a teenage girl about mob guys and therapists who weren't really therapists.

I really hate this house.

As Jack pulled up to the house, he almost hit a little girl who was trying to flag him down. The squad car and ambulance behind him almost rear ended him. As his car screeched to a stop, sliding in the gravel, he couldn't believe his eyes. A guy that Jack thought was probably dead leaned against the porch railing. Another guy and a lady held towels soaked in blood against a teenage boy's side. A second lady knelt in the mud with her arms wrapped around two kids.

The girl ran up to his window.

Jack unbuckled his seatbelt and opened the car door.

"Thank God, you're here. We need lots of help," she said the moment the door cracked open. Her words came out in a blur. "My brother's been stabbed. Mom and dad are trying to stop the bleeding. Also, Mrs. Walker has a knife in her shoulder, and we think Mr. Walker is dead."

Jack hopped out of his car. Behind him, the other officers and emergency service workers also emerged. He hollered back at them.

"Two possible stab wounds. Possible homicide. Radio in. We are going to need more than one ambulance."

The EMT's ran to the boy on the ground. When they knelt to take over the situation, the two adults stood up. Jack walked over.

"Afternoon. I'm Officer..." His eyes danced around the scene. "Can any of you tell me what happened here?"

"I guess I will. My name's Doug Miller."

Doug relayed as much as he could regarding the events of the weekend. As Jack listened, he noticed a few elements that Doug hesitated over. Almost as if what the man wanted to say and what he finally said weren't the same thing. That could be all sorted out later, though.

"The bodies of Frank and Joe are on the second floor. Frank is just as you come up the stairs, and Joe is in the first bedroom on the left. It was dark, so I'm not sure where."

Two more ambulances and police cars arrived, along with the sheriff.

As Jack watched the house, he saw flashlight beams shining different directions inside the dark estate. Finally, a sheet covered gurney came out of the house with Frank Malone on it.

After a long wait, another officer walked over to Jack and whispered in his ear. Jack turned to Doug.

"We checked all the bedrooms. We didn't find the body of the second gunman. Do you have any other idea where his body might be?"

"That's the last place my daughter saw him. Should we be concerned, Sergeant?"

"I'm sure he'll turn up. There's nowhere to go for miles. What about Gina Delfina? Do you know her last known whereabouts?"

Doug pointed to Ann. She sat inside one of the ambulances with a medic working on her.

He walked in her direction. As he did, the EMT's stabilized Jake, attached a fluid bag to him, and loaded him in the ambulance. Kathryn hopped in the back of the ambulance. The doors shut, and the ambulance tore off for the hospital.

Jack approached the back of the ambulance where Ann was being tended to. Her two children had refused to leave her side. Ann had a bandage across her face and arm. A sling stabilized the shoulder but the knife remained.

"Are you going to take it out here?" Ann asked.

"No, Ma'am," the technician said. "That'll be during surgery."

"I'm not going to be awake for that, am I?"

"Not at all."

"Thank God," she said, then quickly had second thoughts. "I can't do that. My kids."

"We'll be right there waiting for you," the daughter said with her arm around her brother.

Jack heard the pain and exhaustion in her voice.

"Ma'am, we are trying to locate Gina Delfina. Do you know her last whereabouts?"

"The cellar," she said. "But I doubt you'll find her there."

Jack didn't expect that last statement. "Why is that?"

"They took her?"

"Who?"

"The occupants of Cardinal Crest. I doubt you'll find her body."

Ann's eyes drifted away from Jack and over his shoulder.

Sergeant Rogers turned around.

Jim's body was loaded on the gurney. He didn't have to turn around to hear the Walkers begin to cry. Jack scanned the area. Carly stood by Doug and tears streamed down his face. Doug looked to be fighting back his own tears but eventually lost the battle. He pulled Carly in close and hugged her.

Jack walked to the side of the house. As he did, the rain finally turned back into a mist. He'd been dealing with calls of flooded roads, downed power lines, and broken tree branches all morning. He couldn't wait for the Sheriff or Chief to get here and take over for him. Of course, by the time they did, the sun would finally be out. The night seemed to have stretched way too far into the day. He removed his flashlight from his belt and shined the beam next to the side of the house. Up ahead, he saw the white doors of the cellar standing open.

Unsnapping the restraint on his revolver, he hesitantly walked to the opening. His hand rested on the gun's grip. He held the light on the opening as he approached. Each footstep crunched the gravel into the mud. The closer to the house, the more he saw into the dark hole. His flashlight pierced the darkness until he saw the dirt floor. Jack knelt and shined his light as far as it would go.

He thought about stepping onto the ladder and going into the earthen basement.

"Nope," he said to no one, shaking his head. "The crime scene guys can go down there."

The flashlight's beam dropped to his feet as he stood back up. The beam danced at the frame around the cellar door. A reflection bounced off something stuck in the wood and drew his attention. Jack bent over and gripped it between his thumb and forefinger. After a few difficult tugs, it finally came loose. He placed it in his hands and shined his flashlight on it.

"What the hell!" he said.

A fingernail with dried blood still caked to the inside of it sat on his hand. He resisted the urge to drop it. Instead, he reached into his back pocket and pulled out a small zip-loc bag. He dropped the fingernail in the bag and glanced into the cellar. A shadow moved down below.

"I need some rest."

Jack turned away from the cellar and returned to the growing number of law enforcement arriving at Cardinal Crest Estate.

PART SEVEN

EPILOGUE

ONE

"Are you sure this is the place, Mr. Carlisi?" Anthony asked.

"Yes," the eighty-year-old man answered. Salvatore gazed at the large house from the back window of his Lincoln Continental.

It'd been over a month since the events of that weekend, and Cardinal Crest Estate sat silent. A dark red gem surrounded by a rolling green sea of fields. The window shades were drawn, and the front door was closed. Sagging police tape stretched across the front porch. Across the door, the remnants of police tape that'd been cut flapped in the wind. Salvatore doubted anyone was in a hurry to open this place back up. If left unattended, it wouldn't be long before it became a local legend. Teenagers would eventually throw rocks through the windows and dare each other to walk inside or stay the night.

The police report and extensive media coverage stated Gina Delfina was presumed dead despite her body never being recovered. A fingernail ripped from the quick was the only thing that remained of her. Joe's body was also never found. The only thing found from him was a large blood trail on the floor of an upstairs bedroom. Certain websites speculated about the sordid history of Cardinal Crest Estate and posited theories about paranormal activity. Rumors of shadows or the ghost of a little girl playing in the field, as well as the reports of presumed dead but no bodies found made for wonderful bathroom reading.

Anthony jogged around to Carlisi's side of the car and opened his door. Salvatore swung his legs out, placed his feet on the gravel driveway, and lifted himself off the seat. He shook out his stiff legs. Many years ago, he could've made this drive without an issue. At eighty, though, the journey took a lot out of his frail body. With his declining health, he rarely left his home in Virginia Beach. But a week ago, he had a missed call. According to the caller ID, it was Gina. He knew how resilient the girl was. Her dad wasn't much more than a hot head, but she was strong and smart.

Salvatore had kept his eye on her as she grew up. He watched her go from foster home to foster home. He loved her as a daughter but wanted her to be raised tough. If he had taken her in, he'd have spoiled her, and she would've been as soft as his own kids. Hardship had made Gina.

She had left a voicemail for him. It was only two words long, but it was enough to bring him here.

"Find me."

Salvatore had filled in all the blanks himself. Gina needed help. She and Joe had escaped and been hiding off the grid ever since. Since the house was empty, once the cops left, it would be the perfect place to lay low. Smart girl.

With Anthony's help, Salvatore limped to the porch. Sweat dripped down his back after only a few steps. Maybe his dark suit pants and white short sleeve button shirt weren't the best choice, but it was his usual attire. Anthony ripped apart the police tape, then took the two steps up, turned, and assisted Carlisi. Anthony then ran to the door and opened it. He rushed back to help his boss across the porch and into the house.

"Gina, My Dear," Salvatore said as he crossed the threshold into the house.

The air conditioning blew across his face and sent a delightful chill over him. A smile rose across his face. If the AC was on, someone had to be home.

"Anthony, help me to the seat."

Salvatore pointed to his left at the couch in the den.

Without hesitation, Anthony took his boss's arm and led him over.

"Go sit down." Salvatore ordered and Anthony walked to the chair next to the couch and sat down.

Once seated, the aged mob boss leaned back and sat a leg on top of the coffee table in front of him.

"Oh, Salvie, get your foot off of my coffee table."

Carlisi twisted his head from one side to another. It was Gina's voice, but he couldn't tell where it came from. His face lit up with a smile.

"Gigi, where are you? I knew you were too smart to get yourself killed. I knew it."

Her voice echoed throughout the house. "And close the door when you come in."

A large blast of wind shot from the den and through the foyer. The front door slammed shut.

"I don't like it here," Anthony said. "Something's not right." He stirred in the chair and made to rise, but something stopped him. The muscles of his arms bulged, but he stayed glued to the chair. As hard as he tried, he remained pinned.

"Don't leave yet," Gina said.

"Gigi," Salvatore said. "Show yourself. I'm here to take you home."

"Mr. Carlisi, I can't move." Anthony began to gasp for air. "Something is... pressing down... can't... breathe..."

"Gigi, what's going on?" Salvatore commanded.

"Sir..."

Salvatore heard a cracking sound coming from Anthony. He watched as Anthony's chest collapsed into itself. Dark red blood shot from his mouth, nose, and eyes. Where his massive chest once existed was now a pile of crushed organs. Broken ribs pierced through the flesh and extended away from the destroyed sternum.

"Gigi?" His tone had lost its sense of command. It sounded like the soft whimper of a frail body.

He grasped his own chest, feeling his heart beat faster than it should.

Suddenly, Gina appeared next to him on the couch. She sat there with her eyes closed as if she'd been there the entire time. One ankle is draped on the knee of the other leg. Her back rested against the back of the couch.

Carlisi couldn't believe what he saw. She wasn't there, but then she was. He felt his heart miss a few beats and grasped his chest harder. His lungs tried to draw in air, but the room felt out of oxygen.

Gina leaned forward and brought her face close to Salvatore's. She opened her eyes, but instead of staring into the eyes he'd known for so many years, he stared into empty sockets. A death stare that tore through his soul. He meant to scream, but his body didn't possess the necessary air. His heart skipped another beat, then stuttered to a stop in his chest.

"Only daddy calls me Gigi," she told him as she felt the life slipping from his body. She maintained the death stare of her empty eye sockets. "And this is my home. And it's yours now, too."

ACKNOWLEDGEMENTS

Writing a book isn't easy. It starts with a simple idea, a scene, a particular thought or dream. From that, characters grow, situations evolve. You can outline and plot, but when you start typing, when the characters come to life, you aren't making up their story anymore. You are an observer writing what you see and hear.

You also have to be patient. It's too easy to start writing the first page and want to rush through each scene. Turn what should be six pages into a few paragraphs so you can get to the scene you really want to write. Or finally get to that last fight scene so you can write the magical words "THE END".

Since turning on the computer and starting to write, I learned how hard this process actually could be. Without help and support, the task is almost impossible.

With that, I'd like to thank those who, if not for them, this book would not exist.

First, I must thank my wonderful wife Terri. She has been and continues to be my rock while writing. She kept the kids out of the office while I played the Dark Academia playlist on Apple Music (great backing track while writing). She put up with me bouncing ideas off of her constantly. Terri also went through the pain and torture of reading and editing my first draft. Constant readers, you should thank her if you enjoyed this tale. She clears up all the errors after my brain vomits words onto the screen. She tells me what works and what doesn't make sense. *Fear Not The Dead* wouldn't be the same book without her. I love you, and thank you!!!

Also, huge thank you to Crystal Baynam and the team at Unveiling Nightmares for taking a chance to publish this little work of mine, as well as Christy Aldridge for the magnificent cover art.

Thank you to every English teacher who made me use my creative gift.

Thank you, Stephen King, Edgar Allan Poe, Dean Koontz, Bram Stoker, Mary Shelley, and every other great horror writer for dementing me.

And thank you, constant reader, for hanging out for a bit inside of my head. You were great company. I hope you enjoyed reading this as much as I enjoyed writing it.

Until next time.

About the Author

Brad is the author of "Fear Not The Dead" (Unveiling Nightmares, 2024) and "The Night Crew" (Crystal Lake Publishing, 2025). He has a short story published in "Body  Horror Anthology, bk 1" (Unveiling Nightmares, 2024).

Brad lives in Central Texas with his wife Terri. Together, they have 5 kids that keep them constantly busy. During the day, he is an Account Manager for an online software company. At night, he enjoys listening to the little voices in his head and jotting down the stories they tell him.

A lifelong fan of Horror, Brad pulls inspiration from everyone from Edgar Allan Poe to Stephen King.

You can find more information and sign up for his mailing list at his website:

https://BradRicks.com

You can also follow him on social media:

Https://www.facebook.com/BradRicksAuthor

And there's always email:

Brad@BradRicks.com

He'd love to hear from you.

EXCERPT FROM THE NIGHT CREW

S uddenly, someone pounded on the front door.

Half asleep on the couch, Brittany White jerked her nodding head up. She'd been laying with her legs stretched across the other seats. Her arm propped her up, and the living room television streamed some Netflix movie that she paid no attention to. Background noise.

Mike had called earlier and told her he would be working another late night. He always volunteered for overtime.

After the initial jolt awake, she sat quiet, questioning if she actually heard a knock or if she dreamed it.

Brittany's eyes became heavy as she listened. She caught her head nodding, and the jerk of her neck woke her back up. Just as she dozed off again, convinced the noise was a dream, the door rattled from another thunderous hit. The deep tone reverberated through the small house.

Not expecting company at this late hour, she assumed it could only be Mike at the front door. Finally, he's home, she thought.

She walked to the door. "Got off early? Lose your key?" she said to the door, still half-asleep, rubbing her contacts into place.

She unlocked the deadbolt, turning the thumb-latch. The click jolted her out of the autopilot routine of unlocking the door, and she grew more awake. It was strange that Mike hadn't called on his way home. She glanced at the clock with her fingers, hesitating on the doorknob latch.

A prickle ran up her spine, but she told herself she was being silly. Mike was always telling her to be careful late at night, but she was so relieved that he came home earlier than expected that she unlocked the doorknob. As she did, she realized that Mike never responded from outside the door.

Before she could twist the small golden latch on the doorknob back to its locked position, the doorknob turned, disengaging the latch bolt from the door. Brittany pressed her shoulder against the door, bracing it. "Mike, is that you?" she hollered as the pressure on her shoulder increased. "Michael White, if that is you, you better answer me!" she demanded.

An immediate force on the door threw her back onto the floor, and a figure rushed in. She tried to scream, but a hand tipped with razor sharp nails grabbed her around the throat, catching the scream before it could escape. It tossed her into the middle of the living room. She felt an instance of weightlessness before her back collided with the floor on the other side of the couch. The thing pounced on top of her, ripping at her flesh with its long fingernails, burying them into her side and chest.

Her arms flailing, Brittany tried to fight. She felt her fingernails drag across the face and neck of her attacker, but they left no marks. She stared into its burning red eyes, captured by them. She felt searing pain as her blood spilled from her body. Her eyes grew heavy, but this time not from sleep. Darkness began to swallow her. As her vision blurred, she recognized the feel of lips against her neck followed by a sharp sting.

The darkness grew. Somewhere, deep in the abyss, she heard Michael's voice call out to her. She tried to call for him, ask him why this happened, but nothing came out. Blood coated her throat and flooded her lungs.

Join 'The Night Crew' Feb 2025

Made in the USA
Columbia, SC
25 June 2024

37530366R00233